No Exit

Sometimes glimpsing
the future can be
deadly

JULIE HARRIS

Chapter 1

MATERIAL THINGS, SHE'D ALWAYS SAID, meant nothing if there was no love, for the basis of life itself was Love. God was Love and man's inhumanity to man should not be blamed on God. Until recently, she'd believed her own words.

What had happened in the recent past was like the contents of a novel. If she told a soul what had really happened, she'd not be believed.

I saved the life of the future President of the USA.

All by yourself?

Well, a team of black ops commandos helped.

Really?

Yes, really.

A likely story...

Life was normal now. Of course, normal is only what a body becomes accustomed to. Ask any hostage, battered wife, anybody stuck in the rut of nine to five and mortgage repayments. Rebecca didn't pay any bills. She took few calls, because few knew her these days to phone. Now that she was somebody else. Now that she was normal.

Her gold MasterCard and driver's license held a name and nationality she was not born with. 'Rebecca Miller' was the name chosen by her parents after nine feuding months and another three weeks of indecision. They'd taken so long at choosing a first name that a second was out of the question. Perhaps that's what happened when both parents were teachers.

Ben and Jenny Miller were practical people and neither were

especially gifted, so what profound twist of fate delivered unto them a child who knew far too much of pasts, presents and futures? A child to whom the notion of God was not mysterious but rather a natural part of life? A healer? A child who was, well, a freak of nature?

"See, Mummy? The rose feels better now. Can I put it in my room with Nanny's freesias?"

Jenny Miller looked down at the red rose clasped in her daughter's tiny hand. It was one of twelve Ben had given her for Valentine's Day, two weeks before. Jenny had been too busy to throw the dead ones out, although each time she passed by the vase on the hall stand, she swore she would. The only red rose Jenny knew of grew in the next door neighbor's front garden.

"Where did you get that?"

"From the vase."

"You stop this nonsense and tell me where you got that rose."

"I got it from the vase, Mummy. I touched it and stopped it dying. Manwell said I should try. He did. He said if I held it and told it to re... regen... to come back to life, it would. See? He was right. He was right about Nanny, too. Can I fix the other roses, Mummy, just like I fixed Nanny?"

A thousand hairy caterpillars crawled up and down Jenny Miller's spine. "Stop this, Rebecca. Stop it now! Don't do this again. You have to stop. It's not natural."

Rebecca never fully understood why she wasn't allowed to make things better. After all, she was only trying to help.

"Things die when they're supposed to die. You must stop doing this. You must."

"Can I have a pretty bottle for my rose, Mummy?"

Jenny was frightened to look her daughter in the eye for fear of what she may see there. As she found a vase for her daughter's resurrected red rose, Jenny thought of her mother in law, the freesias, and most of all, the first miracle.

Ben and Jenny had taken the little girl to see her grandmother for the final time, and during the drive to the hospital, they had tried to explain imminent death to a child who already had unseen angel friends. The notion of life and death was beyond her understanding, or so Ben and Jenny thought.

Ben's mother had suffered a series of strokes. Hilda's condition was critical, and she was on life support. "Now don't be afraid of what you see, Becky. There'll be machines and all sorts of tubes and things. Nanny won't be like you remember."

Exactly how did she remember her grandmother? Magical things appeared from Nanny Hilda's refrigerator all the time, but mostly, Rebecca Miller followed her grandmother about, asking ceaseless questions and getting lots of cuddles. That was what she liked the most—cuddles.

The little girl gripped her pink elephant tight and followed her parents into the hospital room. There was Nanny Hilda, lying on a bed. Machines beeped constantly. "What's that for?" Rebecca asked.

"She can't eat so these tubes help keep Nanny alive," her father said with a shaking voice. The decision would soon be his and it was a decision Ben could not face. If he saved moths from drowning in the bathtub, how could he be expected to end his own mother's life by turning off the machine that kept her body alive?

"Don't be sad, Daddy. Nanny and me, we'll plant freesias in her garden. She'll give them to me and I'll put them in the ground, and she'll cover them up and she'll let me water them and when they turn into flowers she'll let me have a bunch for my room. You wait and see."

"Oh, Becky, no. Your Nanny will never get better. Not now. The doctors say she's going to die soon."

But the child shook her head and folded her arms, defiantly. "No, Daddy. Nanny's coming home with us next week. Pop's not waiting for her. Pop says it's not her time yet."

The child could see her grandfather, who'd passed away six months previously, but he wasn't waiting for his wife. He was with his son. His son didn't know. And 'Manwell' was there, too, telling her to get on the bed and touch her grandmother, and talk to her, and the angels would do the rest.

Ben and Jenny looked at each other sadly while the little girl climbed up onto the bed and touched her grandmother's face. "See my new elephant, Nanny? See it? I like elephants, do you? I used to ride on an elephant once. He was my friend when we lived in India. We had to move trees so I could have money for my kids. I had six kids when I lived in India. See my elephant, Nanny? Nanny? See? His name's Maya. It means…"

Ben's mother opened her eyes to a stuffed pink elephant centimeters from her nose. The ventilation tube choked her. People were soon rushing around in frenzies, talking about miracles.

The doctors had no explanation, but the child could explain it simply enough. On the way home, her father couldn't stop crying, so her mother had to drive and he never liked it when her mother drove, but today he didn't say a thing. They didn't even have one fight today. "How did you do that?" her father kept asking.

"Love did it, Daddy. Manwell says it is always enough."

"There's something wrong with this kid, Jen. There's something wrong with her."

Five weeks later, Rebecca Miller helped her grandmother plant freesias around a weeping cherry tree in Hilda's front garden. Hilda handed the bulbs to the child, the child put them into the small holes in the ground. Hilda then covered the bulbs, handed the garden hose to the little girl and tried to answer ten thousand questions as best she could. Rebecca could tell her grandmother anything. Mostly, the old woman simply nodded and agreed.

Ben and Jenny watched from the living room. "I only wanted a normal kid. Just one normal kid. Is that too much to ask for?"

"She's special, Ben. We can't ignore it any longer."

"There's something wrong with her. Can't you see that? She's not… she's not human. It's wrong."

By the time she was ten years old, Rebecca Miller lived with her mother and only saw her father twice a year for two one-hourly visits. She never understood why her father was frightened of her.

But he wasn't the first and would never be the last.

Most children rid themselves of their inner need for imaginary friends and a series of child psychologists assured Jenny that Rebecca would grow out of it, too. She never did. Rebecca would describe Emmanuel as her friend who told her all kinds of things. She no longer called him Manwell. By the time she was thirteen, he was a hippie who wore cool clothes and sandals made of reeds. By twenty, he was her guardian, her healer, her guide, her teacher of the ancient wisdom, but most of all, her path to notoriety.

Nothing electrical or electronic would function normally in her presence. She couldn't get a job after she dropped out halfway through a nursing degree. She couldn't use a computer because her presence caused immediate hard drive failures. Light bulbs proclaiming 'a thousand extra hours' lasted but a week. She couldn't use a cash register. Ticket machines at the railway station failed when she walked by. There was only one thing left: one thing she could do well. She was able to tell complete strangers of all significant events in their lives, what had been, what was now, what was to come, and a touch from Rebecca could heal. People queued in the living room for consultations and healings, and the sessions were always recorded, providing she set the microphone close and kept the recorder itself a safe distance away.

By the time she was twenty three, Rebecca Miller was on the road, assuring people of the existence of life despite the human notion of death. She had an international psychic telephone line; trod the boards in theaters packed with people desperate for a message from beyond; had a weekly column in five syndicated magazines, two television documentaries, and thousands of true believers treading a steady path to her door.

Occasionally she was asked to consult with police on missing persons and cold (unsolved) murder cases, and twice she'd worked with FBI profilers, and once, she suspected, the US Secret Service, too.

By the age of 25, Rebecca Miller was taken seriously by hard-nosed skeptics.

At age 28, life offered a well-worn, smooth path on which she confidently tread. It changed direction in a Sydney hotel room one rainy Thursday morning.

Her nine thirty appointment hadn't called to cancel. People rarely did: perhaps they thought that if she was indeed a psychic, she'd already know. By nine fifty, Rebecca needed a strong espresso and a place where she could sit without being bothered. She'd not had a moment to herself for weeks. She told her assistant, Annie, that she was taking a break.

"Don't forget there's an American lady coming at ten thirty."

Rebecca took the stairs down to the coffee shop, ordered, and sat outside under the sails. At a table close by sat an American couple. There seemed to be an awful lot of men in dark suits, too, just standing around. Security? What was going on here? She smiled at one of them. No reaction. She scanned the coffee shop for VIPs. Her attention was taken by the American couple again, although at the time she didn't know they were American.

She took little notice of the middle-aged man. The woman, who had the wild, untamed hair of her African ancestors, caught Rebecca's gaze and smiled politely. That's my ten thirty, Rebecca thought, and movement from peripheral caught her eye.

She hadn't seen Emmanuel for years. The long, fair hair parted in the middle and reaching his shoulders was glistening. His eyes were brighter than a summer sky's. His clothing hadn't changed. He still looked like a hippie in his long, loose robe and sandals made of grass. He smiled at her. No one else in the coffee shop could see him. Why now, after all these years...

I've never been away.

The answer came before the question had formed in her mind. He was reading her, just as she read others. She saw and felt the question forming high in the aura moments before the person had a sense of what to ask, and it was because of this that, at the end of a consultation, her question of: 'Any questions?' was always met with, 'No. You've told me all I needed to know. And more.'

Your life is about to change.

And then he was gone.

The waiter brought her coffee and assured her that if there was anything he could do to make her stay more pleasurable... He must have mistaken her for a tourist.

As she sat there, wondering how her life could change because the only thing missing was a tall, dark, handsome male, or even a short, fair unattractive one, the same waiter delivered coffee and pastries to the Americans' table. Their conversation continued, and Rebecca didn't want to eavesdrop, so she pretended to be studying her cell phone:

"But it's not the right time."

"There'll never be a right time. Someone's got to do it, hon. May as well be me."

"But I hate to think that this might be our last vacation together. Just you and me. John, baby, I don't know if I can cope with all this."

"You'll be fine."

Curiosity rising, Rebecca turned for a better view and at that moment, the African American man turned as well. Their gazes met.

Gone the dark skin.

A white man was smiling at her.

John F. Kennedy.

He nodded and disappeared.

Rebecca was used to seeing spirits in and around people, it was never a surprise. But this time her heart leapt to her ears and every hair on her body prickled to attention.

Why? She was staring at the next American President.

Holy crap, she thought, and wished she had a cigarette because she'd given up a month ago.

As if reading her mind, the man smiled at her and resumed his conversation with his wife.

After a glance at her watch, she quickly finished the coffee and walked off, past the Americans' table. Rebecca felt the gaze as she walked by, and heard, "But I was only looking, hon. Man's gotta look now and then."

Please God, she silently prayed. Let it not be him walking through my door at ten thirty.

Chapter 2

PETE HAMILL GLANCED AT HIS second in command. "What do you think?"

"It doesn't matter what I think."

"I'd appreciate some input here."

Kelly Nolan sighed. "So play it again."

The blond air force colonel replayed the mp3. The recording had been digitally enhanced so that all dialogue between the American and the Australian was clean, clear and precise.

No, you're not going crazy. Your husband will be the next President. But, Elizabeth, I don't know how else to say this. If your husband goes to England before the election, his life will be in danger.

His plane's gonna crash…

"This was recorded two years ago when John was on vacation in Sydney?"

Pete nodded.

No, nothing like that. It's like a stop over in England. He's going to visit troops in the Middle East.

England?

Lake? Water? No, that's not it… Heathlake? Lakeheath? I'm told you know it. Do you?

Lakenheath? It's an Air Force base in Suffolk. John was stationed there during the war. But he swore he'd never go back. Oh, Rebecca. What am I going to do?

You'll help your husband make a difference. Have faith, Elizabeth. Because we've been shown a glimpse of the future doesn't mean it's set in concrete. We've been shown the outcome as it stands now, but a year or two down the track it could be completely different... At this airbase I see a lot of blokes in uniforms. But they don't feel like ordinary soldiers.

Special Operations? Maybe it's a special ops security detail?

Whoever they are, you have to trust these people know what they're doing. The unit, squad, whatever it is, it's named after a bird. A hawk? Black, dark, night, some kind of hawk. Your husband's known the guys in charge for many years.

The blue eyed Air Force Colonel and the part Cherokee Navy Commander stared at each other across the desk but neither saw the other's face as they listened to the female conversation. Pete sipped his coffee from his black "Nighthawks" mug. Coincidence, surely?

When you said his life's in danger, do you mean someone's gonna shoot him?

Elizabeth...

I need to know. Please, Rebecca. You have to tell me!

I see your husband standing on the stairs of a Lear jet and

Pete Hamill hit pause again.

Kelly scratched his head. "And now we're expected to baby sit some new age space cadet who isn't even American?"

"Aha."

"Based on a forty minute recording of a psychic reading two years ago?"

"Based on a lot more than that." Pete Hamill passed over a thick file. In a plastic cover on top sat a DVD. "This Aussie girl works miracles. Apparently."

Kelly sighed. Psychics. Here we go again. Will it ever end? He'd honestly believed this crap was gone from his life for ever. He didn't like being wrong. The hair on the back of Kelly's neck prickled to attention when he glanced at the photograph clipped to the file marked REBECCA MILLER—just a young, attractive woman walking along a beach, a sarong covering her body, one hand on a hat, keeping it down. A young woman who had no idea her photograph was being taken by a surveillance team. Her life was going to change, big time. Something about the look on her face—this photo told him far too much, way too soon.

"You're to be at Heathrow, 1300 hours Thursday. Take Macpherson with you. The Bobsy Twins will meet you there."

Another sigh. Kelly reluctantly picked up the file and opened the door to his office.

"Yes, we drew the short straw."

Kelly glanced at Pete and knew the 'we' was simply a word. Kelly had drawn the short straw. He closed the door, put the Miller file on his desk, and glanced at the painting on his wall.

"Fuck," was all he said.

At the zero-eight-hundred-hours assembly Nighthawks gymnasium was filled with personnel and Kelly had no idea what he would say. "Keep it down. I said, keep it down! Come fifteen hundred Thursday we'll have a VIP on deck, duration unknown, reason for presence on a needs-know basis only. Are you assholes listening to me?"

There was an immediate, encompassing silence.

"This person is a civilian…" He had to stop talking because of the moaning. "Yes, that's right. Civilian. Therefore you will treat her with respect and politeness at all times, is this clear?"

"Did you say her, Commander?" came a voice from the assembly.

"That is correct. The civilian is female."

"How old, sir?"

Kelly chose to ignore it. They'd find out soon enough. "Dismissed."

Rebecca woke with a start, amazed she'd actually managed to fall asleep, however briefly. She'd felt uneasy from the moment she'd boarded the plane in Brisbane, and a five hour wait in Kuala Lumpur hadn't helped, either. By the time they were in the air again, she was enduring seventeen of the longest hours of her life, being force fed airline food when all she wanted was toast and Vegemite and a real cup of tea.

Another hour until her feet touched ground. Passengers were already lining up for the only place to wash, brush teeth and tidy up after the hellish flight from the other side of the planet. So she waited.

Rebecca closed her eyes again and was jostled from a half-doze in which she dreamed she was walking with a tall, dark-haired man. He looked half Indian. Native American. They were arguing. And then it was gone. It had been a vision, a flash forward, much like the quick, clear images she presented to the multitudes who sat with her, holding her hand as she told them all about what had been, what was now and what would come. But she never had any visions about herself. Maybe it's jet lag, she thought.

She shook the image away and got to her feet to stretch. She'd planned to change from the white tee shirt and jeans into the green velvet dress in her cabin bag but the line for the toilet was lengthening. No, she thought. No, I can't be bothered. I'll hang on till the airport.

Rebecca was traveling to the United Kingdom for both a well-deserved holiday and to attend a metaphysical symposium in London where she was a featured speaker on the final day. She still had no idea what she was supposed to be relating to her peers, but she'd discovered from experience it was best to give a short introduction and hand over to the audience. People learnt more from questions and answers than they did from listening to long, interminable speeches. Mostly, it was mediumship that kept them all satisfied.

She'd spoken, three times, to the organizer, a polite American who insisted she call him Leon. He said he'd try to meet her at the airport if he could make it. She'd said there was no need, she'd meet him at the venue. Yes, she was looking forward to it, too. He sounded nice on the phone.

The little airplane on the personal video screen was wobbling its way closer to London now and at any moment, if she looked from the window she'd see the coastline of England. Excitement grew and pounded her heart in little waves. In half an hour, she'd be back in her ancestral homeland. After the conference, she planned to rent a car and drive. Wherever the road took her for two and a half carefree weeks, so be it, as long as she included Edinburgh and Dublin in her travels because Annie, her best and only friend, had left a shopping list as long as Rebecca's arm.

The US Navy Commander, dressed in Nighthawks desert cams, waited patiently in the arrivals hall, Daniel Macpherson, also in uniform, by his side.

An hour passed. Two aircraft arriving three minutes apart had disgorged their contents and the subsequent queues at Immigration were lengthening. But she was here. He knew it.

A hundred people passed by before his attention was taken, perhaps captured, by a woman, jet lagged, tired. She was, maybe, thirty or thirty-two max. She had wild, dark hair caught in a ponytail, and large eyes he assumed were blue from a distance. She wasn't very tall, carried a few more pounds than she should.

Rebecca Miller. He'd imagined a new-age hippie type, wearing a dress, maybe one of those dark velvet witchy things, sandals, and enough rose quartz beads to strangle her guru. The exhausted female he was watching wore a sleeveless white shirt, jeans, and had trainers on her feet. And she was looking for someone—trying to recognize her name on a placard perhaps. Then her gaze caught his.

She propped, as if hit by a static charge. But so did Kelly because as soon as gazes locked, he knew who she was—the same girl he'd been painting since his tour on the Eisenhower. Kelly's heart lodged in his throat. He glanced behind. Macpherson was looking bored and there was still no sign of either Leon Carter or Gene Samperi—the CIA's

Bobsy twins had not appeared to encourage and or enforce cooperation.

Rebecca, lost in a traveler's fog, scanned the sea of faces. There was nobody holding a sign displaying her name and there should have been. Oh farking yay, she moaned. Now I have to get a taxi. After another glance around, this time her attention was taken by a soldier. Holy crap, she thought. Now that's one hell of a man-in-uniform. And he smiled. Rebecca turned to see who he was smiling at and when next she looked he was standing directly in her path. She tried to sidestep. But so did he. Another step to the side. Again and again she was blocked. She looked up into his face, ready to say, ok, your move. Her knees were immediately weakened by some kind of electrical charge and her heart thudded so hard it almost hurt. The only time she'd felt something akin to this was when an extremely famous and drop-dead gorgeous rock star walked into her living room, sat down with a sigh and said, 'Can you help me, honey?' That day, her sense of professionalism soon over-rode the shock. But nothing came to over-ride this. I know this man, she thought. I know him.

He was tall, about forty. Not bad for an older guy. He had dark, dark eyes. He looked part Indian. Cherokee? she wondered.

"Rebecca Miller?"

Again, she looked behind, her one thought being, is he really talking to me?

"You are Rebecca Miller?"

She nodded.

"Would you please come with me." It wasn't even a question.

"Is something wrong?"

"Your questions will be answered in due course. Come with me."

Before she had a chance to realize how softly lilting his accent was:

"I'll take that for you." Another soldier, wearing the same kind of uniform, took control of her suitcase. He was about her age, and he had a shaved head. So the tall one was American, the short one was Irish, and next she knew, Rebecca was being jostled towards an exit. The two soldiers stood very close to her even though the crush of humanity was stifling. Every time Rebecca dared a glance, the tall-dark-handsome was watching her. At that moment in time, Rebecca did not know what she should be feeling but a voice inside told her she must remain calm.

"This way," the tall-dark-handsome said and reached for her arm.

"No. Stop. Just stop for a second."

Kelly knew this would occur, but he did not want it occurring in the middle of a crowded airport arrivals hall. Samperi and Carter were supposed to be here, to explain the situation, encourage cooperation and then she was to be transferred to the asylum. Easy. He didn't need to be psychic to know this was not going to be easy. He had hoped jet lag would work in his favor.

"What's going on?" she asked.

"Not here, Ma'am."

"Ma'am?" Do I look old enough to be called ma'am? "One, I need a pee and two, I need a coffee, but before I take one more step in any direction, who are you and what is going on here?"

"Your questions will be answered in due course."

Rebecca tried to read those dark eyes. Impossible. "Sorry. My questions will be answered now or I start screaming. Your choice."

She heard a long, bored sigh. "You are currently in the protective custody of the United States government. You want to cause a scene, go for it. Personally, I don't advise that course of action."

"Look, whatever your name is..." He had a name, embroidered in capital letters on the pocket of his uniform shirt. NOLAN.

"Commander Kelly Nolan. This is Staff Sergeant Daniel Macpherson."

15

Mac gave her a shy smile.

"You've got the wrong person. I'm an Australian, on holiday in England. I've also got a conference to go to, so if you don't mind…" Rebecca's voice trailed off as realization finally hit, and it hit with the force of a cannon. "This has something to do with the elections in the states. This has something to do with that man I saw in the coffee shop of that Sydney hotel…" When was that? Two years ago? She'd seen his face on the news recently. She remembered his wife walking into the hotel room. Discovering somebody was going to kill the poor bugger.

Emmanuel's words echoed back. Your life is about to change. But that had been two years ago and she'd waited patiently while nothing changed at all.

Rebecca looked up into Kelly Nolan's eyes. All her anger and confusion had dissipated. "You guys are serious?"

Kelly tried very hard not to smile. Mac, standing behind Rebecca, couldn't help himself. "That would be correct. I have orders to bring you to Wiltshire with me, Miss Miller, and we're already fifteen minutes behind schedule."

"Look… what's your name again?"

"Nolan. Commander Nolan."

"Kelly. Girl's name."

Kelly's face remained expressionless, except for a flicker of something indescribable crossing his dark eyes. Amusement or anger, Rebecca couldn't decide. The last thing she wanted to show was fear. "Alrightey, then. Listen carefully. I only have the energy to say this once, okay? I've been traveling for the equivalent of two days and I'm jet lagged, sleep deprived, and I wouldn't be surprised if I'm temporarily insane, too. I'm trying to be calm but I want a pee, a cup of coffee and a bed, and if you don't get out of my way I cannot be held responsible for what might happen."

A flicker of amusement crossed the Navy SEAL's eyes.

"I mean it. On your bike. Go harass somebody else. I'm getting a cab to London. I've got a conference to go to in two days' time. I do not want to be in anybody's protective custody. I have rights. Good-bye."

But a sudden grip on her wrist halted any further movement. Kelly didn't have to say a word. As Rebecca looked up into his face a feeling of déjà vu flooded her every pore. And she didn't have to be psychic to know what was coming next: There is no conference.

"There is no conference, Miss Miller. We need you here, you're here, you're coming with us. It's a matter of National Security." He said it as quietly as he could.

"Whose National Security?" she asked, a little too loud. "I'm not American. I'm Australian and this, unless the pilot got it completely wrong, is supposed to be England."

"If you want to make a scene, be my guest." He put his arm around her and drew her close but there was no affection in it. He whispered into her ear: "I can have you unconscious in point one five of a second and the thirteen people staring at us right now will assume you fainted, so what's it to be?" And he wouldn't let her go. He had two fingers digging into her elbow and she was squirming. Her entire arm was on fire, and people walked on by, taking no notice of what they assumed was a soldier, greeting his girlfriend.

Had she been half sane, she probably would have made a scene and screamed for security, but one glance into this man's face and she decided, no. Because it had taken just one glance into his dark eyes and she'd seen what he was: dressed in black, armed to the teeth, swinging down from a black helicopter's rope. She'd seen things like that at the movies. At the movies, you could walk out when you wanted to, or there was always the stop button on the remote control.

"What are you going to do." It wasn't a question and he applied a little more pressure.

"All right, all right, you big wally. Let me go."

He let go, and she rubbed at her elbow. Her fingers were tingling. She had to shake her arm awake. She quickly looked for an escape but there was none. "I can understand your confusion, Miss Miller, but trust me, everything will be made clear very soon. We are not the enemy. We're the good guys here."

"Give the propaganda bullshit a rest. I need to pee."

"Half an hour and you got it."

She looked up into his eyes and did not know what she saw there. After that polite little hug of a moment ago, she wasn't too willing to discover any more. "I can't hold it for another half an hour."

"Yes, you can."

"No. I can't. These are not tears in my eyes."

And so the US Navy Commander and the British army sergeant waited outside the ladies. She was taking forever in there. "She's nice," Mac said. "Fiery. I like that."

"Don't even think about it."

"She doesn't look like a psychic. But I suppose you don't either."

Kelly ignored that one. "She has sixty seconds, and we're going in."

Rebecca reappeared on Kelly's mental count to twenty-two. She was calmer. "I've decided to pretend this will be an adventure, and not just for me." She sighed. "Lead on, Captain."

"I'm not a captain. I'm a commander."

"So there's a difference?" Her eyes were incredibly blue and that smile, Kelly knew, would haunt him for the rest of his days.

Mac drove to the airfield and Kelly sat with Rebecca in the back seat.

There was silence for a little while as she fumbled in her bag. "This has something to do with Senator Glover who's running for the presidency, yeah?" she asked.

"I can't comment."

"You're… in the Navy." And she sang it, Village People style.

Kelly didn't respond.

"You're part Cherokee Indian."

"Yes."

"I've seen you before."

"I seriously doubt that."

"No. I have. I don't forget faces. I've seen you before."

And I, you, Kelly thought. Every day of my life for nearly fifteen years.

And Mac glanced in the rear view mirror now and then, wondering how the commander did it. After a few minutes he had her full co-operation. She was nice. He liked her. She was pretty in an offbeat kind of way and even Mac wondered if he'd met her somewhere before.

Not a lot was said during the thirty-five minute drive to the airfield where a large black helicopter was waiting. At sight of the vehicle approaching, the rotor blades fired to life.

Rebecca's blood turned to ice. "No, no. No fucking way. Forty lashes, not that."

"Out of the car."

"Not that. Please. Not that. Can't we drive? Walk? Hitch-hike?"

Kelly got out. Her door opened. That bright blue gaze cored him momentarily.

"If I go near that thing I'll die."

"Get out of the car, now."

While they argued, Mac took the suitcase to the chopper where the territory was safer and there was less chance of being caught and wounded in any crossfire between impatience and ego.

Rebecca stood for a moment, swaying on her feet. "Please don't make me do this."

"Move." Kelly pushed her forwards.

From a vehicle parked in a woodland a safe distance away, the sniper had full view, a perfect view. One hundred and fifty yards from the car to the chopper, more than enough time to make the shot and make it count. Macpherson, throwing the bags into the Iroquois, Nolan coaxing the female towards it. Even through the scope the scene was amusing. He raised the sight a fraction—no, too much of a struggle for a head shot. He brought the sight down, and Nolan got in the way. The shooter was tempted, but waited his chance. Nolan moved. He took her arm. He looked like he was walking a puppy on a leash for the first time.

"If I go near that thing I'll die!"

"For Christ's sakes it's safer in the air than walking across the goddamned street! You either get into the chopper or I throw you in. Three seconds. One."

"No."

"Two."

"I'll take a bus."

"Three."

Her hand wrenched out of Kelly's grip and she crumpled. For half a heartbeat he had not a thought in his head except for pure disbelief. She lay sprawled at his feet, a bullet through the heart. He looked up. Mac was running back, pointing to the woods. The disbelief faded. Auto pilot set in.

Is that me? she asked.

It is you.

Did I really look like that? I always thought I was … ugly.

It is all perspective, my love.

Why's Kelly so upset?

It was his duty to protect you.

Emmanuel, why is he even trying?

For a moment of ceaseless time they both gazed upon the Navy SEAL who was still trying to breathe and press life back into a lifeless body.

Perhaps he knows what it was you would have done?

It was important, wasn't it.

Yes. It was important.

I can't go back now, can I.

Could it be that you want to?

I haven't finished what I came here to do. But look at that body. It's of no use to me now.

She looked back at the two soldiers who were heaving what had once been her body into the back of the helicopter. The door closed. The chopper took off.

There is always room for a miracle, Rebecca.

I want to go with them.

No sooner had she thought it she was with Kelly, observing from inner space as he tried desperately to bring her back to life when everybody, even the pilot and the crewman, knew it was futile.

There wasn't much blood. Far worse was Kelly's anguish. His pain. His panic. He was thinking, I've waited all my life for you, and I got forty fucking minutes. Why? Why? His thoughts were screaming but his mouth did not move.

She could hear what was being said, thought and felt, and the intensity of it was overwhelming.

Come with me for now, my love. You can return later. There is much we must discuss. Time is nothing here, but there it is everything, so best we not dally.

But I can't use that body again.

Always there is room for a miracle.

Emmanuel took her hand and they walked away into the light.

"It's no use."

But still, Kelly tried until Mac grabbed his shoulder and held it tight. "Leave it. She's gone. She was dead before she hit the tarmac and you know it. Here." Mac gave his friend a clean handkerchief to wipe the blood from his hands and looked the other way. He knew not to say another word. He knew who this girl was—the same girl the commander had been painting for as long as Mac had known him.

A thousand shivers hit Mac's spine when Kelly sat on the floor of the chopper and held his head in his hands.

Harlem guided the chopper home.

Headquarters and barracks for the 32nd Special Operations Unit, Nighthawks, was situated on Salisbury Plain. Broadmeadows, otherwise known as The Asylum, was once a run-down mental institution over two hundred years old when first leased by the United States government in 1982. It covered one hundred acres, mostly heavily wooded—hidden in the woods were various SAS and Special Forces training grounds, shoot-houses and obstacle courses. The facility itself comprised four buildings of old, gray-green sandstone; administration, personnel quarters, infirmary and gymnasium, linked by rabbit warrens of corridors and underground mazes. In the 1970s, the facility was used as headquarters for UFO research until it was decided that terrorism was a more tangible battle to fight.

The helipad to the rear of the gymnasium was attended by a welcome party of three: the Medical Officer, Royal Navy Captain Mike McLaren, Mitch Stafford, chief medic on loan from Australian Army SAS, and the Commanding Officer, USAF Colonel, Pete

Hamill.

Had the VIP been alive, the red carpet would have been rolled out by half the company, most of them curious to know what she looked like.

Kelly closed his eyes when he saw the greeting party. At assembly that morning what had he said? You will make this female civilian welcome. You will not invade her privacy. You will comply with any request providing the primary objective of her presence here is kept as a priority at all times. You will not o-fend, you will de-fend—more will-nots than wills. Kelly wished that he could eat his words, go back eight hours and perhaps send someone else to collect her. Perhaps she'd still be alive if someone else had been sent.

He alighted and stood back while the medics stepped in and Rebecca Miller's body was lifted on to a gurney. Pete walked to it, pulled the blanket back. One glance was enough. She wouldn't have felt a thing. He looked at Kelly. The face was expressionless. Macpherson walked past without a word to anybody.

"Washington's been informed. You've got half an hour."

Kelly walked quietly to his quarters, inquisitive men not voicing a thing as he passed. Kelly closed the door to his room and rested his head against it tiredly for a little while. Home. Photographs amid the Eastern junk. A few books he never had time to read. The red Persian rug he'd bought in Karachi. The cushions from Turkey. His great grandfather's tomahawk. A collection of sabers and one 600 year old scimitar he'd found in the desert in Iraq.

Home, he thought. A junk shop. Most of it Marianne refused to allow in any of their houses. Not that it mattered now, if indeed it ever had.

He rubbed at his face and realized blood was still on his hands.

Kelly stripped, showered and changed into his blacks, back into a sense of normality. He fished his portfolio from under the bed and searched quickly for a drawing he'd done five, maybe six years ago. A girl on a beach. Sarong. Hand on hat. The same pose as the surveillance photo of Rebecca.

I never saw this coming, he thought.

But she did.

I didn't listen.

And it was over before it began.

Kelly reported to the CO's office even though his old friend had given him a half hour's grace.

Mike, the Scottish Medical Officer, had five daughters of his own, and this lass was perhaps as old as Bessie. Someone's daughter, he thought as he studied the body, knowing that death had been instant. Mike shook his head and said, "Deal with it, Mitch."

Mitch Stafford waited for the MO's office door to close before he delegated the body duty to Faraday, who, in an hour's time, was supposed to be meeting a blind date at The Lazy Cow in Salisbury.

Jamie mumbled to himself and wheeled the gurney into the small cold room otherwise known as the morgue. He figured it wouldn't take long, photographing, washing, itemizing personal belongings, body bagging and finally, the cooler. Then he was off to Salisbury to meet the mysterious Linda. Jamie Faraday could not wait.

Jamie uncovered the body completely. He didn't know why the commander had bothered with CPR. Looked like a .338 to him. It wasn't a spectacular entry but he knew the stretch cavity was ferocious.

He took photographs before undressing the half naked body. He started at the trainers. Reeboks. Levis. Easier to scissor the underwear.

While he was itemizing the personal effects—sapphire ring, gold band worn on right hand, gold cross on chain, the lights in the morgue dimmed, flickered. Stafford was playing another practical joke.

"Mitch? Knock it off. And don't lock me in here again."

No reply. Not a sound except for a buzzing noise, like an upturned hive of angry bees. It was weird. And there was a smell, too. Sulfur and roses. The lights fizzed, crackled, and dimmed again before flickering back to full strength and then some, until it became so bright that Jamie thought his eyes would explode if he didn't shield his face. The hell was going on here? Jamie squinted at the body, and what he saw next remained indescribable for the rest of his life.

Rebecca Miller's body was alive with light—pure, bright, white-gold light. He may have had his hands shielding his eyes, but he saw the bullet wound closing. From the inside. The light was inside her body as much as it was outside. The entire room was alive with it. No, the light was alive in the room. How long the phenomena lasted he hadn't a clue. Thirty seconds or half an hour, time had no meaning. And then it was gone. Jamie closed his eyes and opened them again.

The wound was healed. Light scarring there now. Jamie backed away until he could move no further. He tried to call for help but he had no voice. The girl, the woman, the VIP, whatever she was supposed to be, started breathing. She moved. She made a sound—a whimper, as if she was waking from a deep sleep.

Had Jamie Faraday been able to climb the stone wall against his back, he would have.

"Mitch? Captain? Captain?" he called, each successive call louder than the previous. The female opened her eyes. She blinked. Frowned. Tried to raise her hand. She made whimpering noises again. She had physical reactions to the cold. Her skin was forming goose bumps. Jamie wanted to move. He wanted to say something. But he could only stand there, the wall against his back, staring. She tried to sit up and couldn't. She tried again, successfully. She looked about, trying to focus. She looked down at her body and then directly at Jamie. She had the biggest blue eyes he'd ever seen but they weren't as big as his at that moment. Then she screamed, and so did he.

"Who else knew, Pete?"

"In this country? Carter and Samperi. They were supposed to meet you at the airport, talk to her there."

"They never showed. Samperi's where I start."

Kelly's beeper activated. He looked at the message. He looked at Pete.

"What?" Pete asked.

"She's alive," Kelly said. He looked at the message again.

"No," Pete said. "She can't be."

And then the call came over the PA: *Commander Nolan, report to the infirmary.*

From the CO's office to the infirmary was normally a ten minute walk, cutting through two adjoining buildings. Kelly made it in three minutes, kicking open the double doors and sliding to a stop on the tiles. But what he saw, he, too, could not at first comprehend.

Faraday was sitting on the floor, his face white, hands shaking. His eyes were the size of saucers. Mike, the fifty-three year old company doctor, was on his knees under a table, endeavoring to coax Rebecca out. She was huddled, blanket pulled tight, confused, disorientated and most of all, terrified. "Lassie, pet, you've got to come away now. Let me look at you, hen."

"Captain?" came Kelly's voice from the door.

"Here he is, now. He's here."

Kelly, heart in mouth, crouched and dared to look. "Thank you, Captain. I'll take it from here. I'll call if I need you."

Mike took the hint and silently ordered Jamie Faraday out of the room.

Terrified blue eyes stared at Kelly. He wasn't sure if she knew him or not. How much brain damage has there been? he wondered. "It's ok. They've gone. Just you and me now… Do you know who I am?"

After a moment, she said softly, "Girl's name… Kelly?" Hesitantly, she reached out and touched his arm. It was solid. Instantly she was hit with some powerful images, sudden, shocking. She withdrew quickly as if burnt. "You're real."

"And you are?"

"Rebecca. You forgot me already?"

"No. Hell no, I… that's… good. That's… what's the last thing you recall?"

"Seeing a chopper. I had to get away. But something hit me and I couldn't breathe and then there was… What happened?"

"You were shot." Kelly touched his chest.

"Me?"

He nodded and watched as she opened the blanket and peered down.

"But… that's where my heart is."

"Aha."

"But… I should be dead."

"You were. You were… gone… for an hour and a half."

She knew he wasn't lying. Images floated in from peripheral, glimpses of Emmanuel, of a beautiful beach. The Light. Home. That's what it felt like. Home. She'd been there before, many times. She'd always wanted to stay. But not this time. She had to come back. But now that she was back, she couldn't understand why the need to return had been so powerful. "But why would someone shoot me?"

"Maybe you were considered a credible threat. Maybe you know too much."

"Me?" she squeaked, dumbfounded.

Again, Kelly nodded.

"But I don't believe in violence," she said softly. "You do. You shoot people."

"Sorry?"

"I saw you in a desert. You were camouflaged and you had this big rifle thing on a stand and… But you're a sailor. What were you doing in a desert?"

"I was a Navy SEAL and I've been to the Middle East a few times, and that's all I can say."

Rebecca stared at him. "Navy SEAL?" What the hell is that, she wondered.

"Come on outa there now. No one's gonna hurt you here. Let the doc look you over."

"Can I please go home?"

Kelly had to look away. "I know you want to go home and if I could, I'd take you there myself, but that's not possible right now. Come on out. Please, Rebecca." Kelly put his arm around her shoulders and eased her out from her hiding place.

"But you don't understand. Awful things are going to happen unless I get away from here. I have to get away from here. Please let me go home? Please, Kelly?"

Crying now. She tried to stand but her knees refused to lock and Kelly took her weight before she fell.

Half an hour later he was watching her sleep beyond the glass in the isolation room, the MO by his side. Both men were quietly thoughtful.

"What have we got here, Mike? A .338 in the chest and two hours later she's telling me I was a sniper in Iraq?"

Mike said nothing for a moment. "If you'd be wanting answers you'll be needing a higher authority. Is a miracle we've got here, Kelly. A miracle. I'm keeping her in for observation, but I suggest you not be too far away. Tis only you the lassie wants."

"I'm familiar. There's no other reason."

But Mike shook his head and almost laughed. "Oh, aye. Familiar. She's not the lassie on your wall then? How many years you been painting her? Ten? Twelve?" Mike walked off, still shaking his head.

Fifteen, Kelly replied silently. I've been painting her for fifteen years.

Back in his office, the CO twice lifted the phone to call Washington. Twice he hung up. Third attempt successful... It would not be the last time that any kind of logical explanation concerning Rebecca Miller would elude him entirely.

Jamie Faraday cancelled his blind date and sought the company of valium and his bed, while the first of his digital photographs was circulated around the base via email. The VIP who came in DOA was now alive and well. It was a miracle. Nobody knew what else to call it.

The first face she saw when she woke was Kelly's and for a moment neither of them spoke.

"What else do you remember?" he asked.

She remembered begging him to let her go home. He probably thought she was a brainless twat. Why couldn't she 'read' him?

"What else do I remember... I saw you," she said. "I saw you doing CPR. I heard what you were thinking."

It was easier to study the wall or his fingernails than look into her intense blue eyes.

"I was watching you. You were thinking, I waited all my life and all I got was forty fucking minutes." Still he said nothing, but, she noted, he swallowed because his Adam's Apple moved.

Rebecca gazed out into a middle distance only she could determine the depth of, and she returned her gaze to his. Her expression burnt a hole into his soul. "You and... Mac? Is that his name? The Irish guy? He kept telling you to stop but you weren't listening. 'She was dead before she hit the tarmac.'" That's what he said. And you stopped and you sat there on the floor of the chopper and… I went somewhere, then. But all the while I knew I had to come back. There was something undone, something I had to finish." She frowned, as if trying to remember what it was. "Then I woke up and I was cold and there was this English guy screaming for help and trying to climb the wall to get away from me. I didn't mean to scare him. And then there was this Scottish guy. And you." She paused for awhile. "That's what I remember."

Kelly sat by the bed, his hands clasped between his knees, wanting desperately to touch her and not able to. Nothing on this earth could dispel his outward composure except for the haunting expression in this young woman's beautiful, intense eyes.

"I do not know what to say to you, Miss Miller."

A smile of sorts creased her face. "I wouldn't know what to say to me, either. Look, you don't have to be here if you don't want to be. Really. You've had a day you'd rather forget, so go eat and sleep it off."

"Are you sure?"

"Positive. You go and eat. You're hungry. You're tired. Go on. Bugger off. I've seen enough uniforms for one day."

"I'll see you tomorrow." Kelly walked to the door and came to a standstill when he heard:

"Check the ropes."

"Excuse me?"

"The ropes. Somebody's coming down from a chopper onto the roof of an old, burnt-out building. Check the ropes are intact because there's a sharp edge somewhere. Will you do that? Will you look?"

"Yeah. Sure." And he was gone, up to his office first, and then to the mess to eat and fend off a hundred questions for which he had no logical answers. Yes, she was dead. Yes, she's now alive. I walk out the door and she's warning me of an accident during a chopper insertion exercise set for tomorrow morning and she doesn't know what a chopper insertion is.

Pete's arms were folded as he looked at the images on his screen. "It's all here in front of me, in full color and I still can't believe what I'm seeing."

Kelly said nothing.

"What does she remember?"

"Everything."

"This is extraordinary."

Understatement, Kelly thought.

"Have you seen Faraday's report?"

"Not yet."

Pete poured another whisky for them both. "There has to be a logical explanation for what happened. Light. Noise. What's he been smoking? That's what I want to know."

The silence was thick. It was a pitiful attempt at a joke and the commanding officer knew it. Kelly wiped a trace of dust from the bronze eagle that stood on the CO's rosewood desk. "By the time I got to the infirmary there was still some kind of static charge in the air. Plus I don't doubt a word Faraday has to say. I don't think any of us should. Who called first, Pete? Gene or Leon?" Kelly asked as he took a swig of whiskey.

"Gene. I know what you're thinking but we don't have proof."

"I don't need it. What's his ETA?"

"Tomorrow, time unknown."

"You're allowing access to the female already?"

"I have no choice. She's fit. I've got the MO's report here if you want to read it."

"It's a mistake. She needs time to readjust."

"And I said I do not have a choice. This cannot be deferred indefinitely. There's too much at stake."

Mike McLaren was in his office, studying the assortment of photographs on his computer screen. A bottle of Glenfiddich was close by. And by God he needed it. He shook his head and refocused his eyes for a moment on the photo on his desk, taken last Christmas up at the loch. It was hellishly cold that day and there weren't any tourists about, and all the girls were happy their da had come home on leave. Jeanie, young Mary, Agnes, Bessie and ten year old Kate in his arms, clinging tight. "Don't go back, Da. Stay home." If she said it twenty times... A distance between Mike and his Mary though. A distance that was by far greater than the miles between Wiltshire and Inverness. Two more years, he thought. Two more years and I'll be home to stay.

"Excuse me?"

Rebecca, wrapped in a blanket, stood in the doorway of the doctor's office.

"You shouldn't be out of bed, hen."

"I can't sleep," she said. "I want to but I can't."

"I've just the thing for us both." Mike reached for another glass. "Sit yourself down here by the radiator. Damn place sucks the heat from your bones." Mike quickly hit the power switch on the monitor. When he poured her a whiskey his hand shook a little.

"Can I see the before-and-after photographs? The ones you were just looking at?"

"Oh, hen..."

"Please? I need to know it's real. I might be able to deal with it if I know it's real."

Mike turned his screen on again.

If she got too close, the PC would fail... but it hadn't made any weird noises yet. So she angled closer and studied the pictures, one by one. It was her body, there was no mistaking it. And yes, she was dead. No wonder Kelly's face was pale. No wonder that English guy screamed to get away. Then she looked into the doctor's eyes. "Everybody's seen these already, haven't they. The men here." Mike didn't say a word. He didn't have to. "They think I'm some kind of freak."

"No, lass. No one's thinking that."

"I'm thinking that. I don't need this. People never see past what I do anyway and now I've got resurrection to add to the repertoire. Fark." She picked up the whiskey. It was gone in one. Mike poured her another shot. He still wasn't sure what to say. She reached for the desk photo of his family. He didn't say no. He watched. He was trying to figure this out, too. Rebecca studied the framed photograph even though her head was swimming and weariness descending. "You're a lucky man," she said quietly.

"I've a nice family, aye."

"Five beautiful girls. I bet you feel outnumbered when you go home."

"Ach, no. And you, pet? What about you?"

"Family? No. Not any more. There's no one."

"Not a man in your life?"

"Me? Hell, no. That happy ever after stuff's for other people." She finished the drink, and went back to Mike's photo. "Your girls are all beautiful. It must come from their mother."

"Cheeky shite, aren't you."

Good, she thought. He has humor. He's going to need it. "This was taken last Christmas, wasn't it. The first Christmas you'd had at home in three years."

"Aye. How'd you know that?"

"The little one. Katie? Is that her name? She was crying when you had to come back here. I don't know who's the luckiest. Your daughters or you. I never really knew my dad."

He poured another shot and Mike shared his scotch with no one. "So you've got the gift then."

"Only people who don't have it call it a gift. I don't know what I've got, if you want the truth. I know I'm caught between two worlds. I pass on information, I see what has been and what will be but I have the gift of healing more than anything. Maybe I can be of some use to you here? I'm sorry, but I still don't know what to call you. Doctor? Captain?"

"Mike'll do fine, lass."

"Can I?"

"Can you what, pet?"

"Help you here?"

"Oh, I don't know. That's up to the CO."

"Who is he?"

"You'll find out soon enough who he is, but you watch him. He's an eye for a pretty lass. Be warned."

"Ach, I love a wee challenge."

"I'd not call the colonel a wee challenge, pet."

He was trying to change the subject.

"I am a healer, Mike. It's what I prefer to do. It's what I do best."

"Aye, I'll keep it in mind." It was a good-natured dismissal from yet another medical practitioner. She'd been expecting it. Rebecca put the whiskey down, entwined her fingers and she studied the doctor from the top of his head to his toes. "What are you lookin' at me like that for?" he asked.

"You know the whiskey isn't helping your ulcer or your arthritis."

"Ulcer and arthritis, is it?"

"Duodenal and rheumatoid respectively. Except for a trace of osteo in your left knee. That developed… let's see, about a year after the fracture." Rebecca didn't say she had seen the accident occur: he'd been drunk at the time and had tripped on the stairs. "Your bad cholesterol's too high and the good is too low, and you've been ignoring the occasional chest pain, too. It's a different pain to the ulcer, isn't it. You, Captain Mike, should know better."

There was a moment's silence. "I tell you what we'll do, hen. If we're to be friends, you'll keep your opinions to yourself."

And then she smiled and when she smiled, Mike thought the sun had risen again. "You're an old softie."

"I'd not be that bloody old."

Again, that smile and he returned it.

"Thanks for the drink. I think I'll be able to sleep now. Goodnight, Captain Mike." She held out her hand and it was taken, but it wasn't a handshake. No, it was more of a friendly squeeze, but it was all Rebecca needed even if she hung on for a few seconds. She had an overpowering urge to hug him, and she trusted her instincts.

He needed a hug as much as she did, and for a moment, they both basked in the moment.

"Goodnight, hen. Sleep tight."

"My name's Rebecca. So far you've called me lassie, pet and hen."

"Oh aye, hen. I know your name."

She finally let go and walked away and Mike watched until the door to the isolation room closed.

A moment or two of bemused silence passed before he realized that the reflux pain he'd endured for the past seven years, despite medication, had diminished. His knee did not object, nor did he feel the crunch of bone upon bone in his hip. He splayed his fingers. No stiffness. No pain.

"I'll be damned," he whispered. The medical officer, completely pain free, walked the length of the ward, past the solitary, sleeping occupant whose appendix he'd removed but yesterday. Mike opened the door to the isolation room, mouth open to ask what in hell she'd done and how she'd done it, but Rebecca Miller was fast asleep.

For a moment he watched, making sure she was breathing, which she was. Then he drew the covers high over her shoulders, touched her hair and thought, she's a miracle all right.

Everybody, once in their lifetime, needed a miracle.

The captain let her rest in peace, for tomorrow, he knew that peace she'd not have much of.

She woke in the early hours and for a moment wasn't sure where she was. Then reality reared. Alone, but not really alone. It was an isolation room, a tiny room with its own bathroom. The walls were a stark white but nothing could mask the darkness that had once reigned there.

This place used to be an asylum for the criminally insane. Rebecca sank lower into the bed. The poor tormented souls who had died horribly in this place were still here amid their memories of that life: the filth, the deprivation, the chains, the tortuous living hell. And they could see her as clearly as she could see them. Rebecca pulled the covers over her head and willed them away but they would not go. As in life, so in death.

Then came footsteps and Captain Mike's Scottish voice again. "Ach, you can't hide, lass." That voice belonged on the other side of reality where the walls were white.

Rebecca drew the covers back and looked up at the bearded face. She liked this man. He had kind green eyes and Rebecca thought he looked a little like Billy Connolly. She wondered if he was as entertaining. Somehow she didn't think so. "I feel all right," she said softly.

"Aye, I see that, lass." He put the stethoscope into his ears and warmed it on his hand first. He can't look at me, she thought. He wants to ask me a thousand questions but he can't find one word.

"Don't look at me like that."

"Like what, pet?"

"Like I'm some alien life form that just oozed in under the door."

"Ah, the things you say."

"Peanut?"

The doctor propped.

"Why do you call your eldest daughter 'Peanut'?"

"Oh lass, you don't have to prove a thing to me. I don't need convincing."

"Your grandson is three weeks old and you haven't seen him yet and Peanut's been…"

"You'll stop telling me my business now." He gave her his displeased father expression, to which she was immune. She'd only recognized fear in her own father's eyes. "That's the end of it, hen. Aye?"

"It sure will be unless you call her. I'll keep nagging until you do."

Mike sighed and made some notes on her chart. "Jamie will be bringing breakfast in soon. After that, I suggest you shower and dress. The colonel wants a wee chat with you, hen."

Chapter 3

"COMPLIMENTS OF FRANK, THE FITTER and turner."

Rebecca looked at the meal tray questioningly. "Fitter and turner?"

"Fits food into a pot and turns it into shit." This one was from Liverpool. There was no mistaking that accent.

"Oh. Sounds like me in a kitchen. What time is it?"

"Early." He had a nice smile and he was almost familiar. Rebecca suddenly realized who he was. He'd been the one screaming for help and trying to climb the wall to get away from her yesterday. Today he seemed fine. She wondered if he'd had counseling.

Jamie Faraday had very short brown hair and brown eyes that could not hide the vast well of compassion and intelligence dwelling within. Rebecca also wondered if his queue of girlfriends stretched to infinity.

"Obs, then you can eat. CO's gracing us with his presence."

Jamie put a thermometer into her mouth and picked up her wrist. At the touch, Rebecca was flooded with images, all of which she kept to herself. At a distance, she was able to block herself off from unwanted information, but a touch she could do little about. When the thermometer was extracted, she said quietly, "I didn't mean to scare you yesterday."

"You're back with us, that's all that matters."

"What's your name?"

He pointed to the FARADAY sewn into the pocket of his uniform shirt.

"No. Your other name."

"You can call me Jamie if you want to get personal, but I have to get personal first." He slipped the stethoscope down the hospital gown, listened to her heart and lungs, and Rebecca noted, refused to look into her eyes, probably for fear of what he might see there. Because he was afraid. Very afraid and trying valiantly not to let it show. When she touched his hand, he literally jerked away, realized his error and scratched his forehead. "Look luv, you're dead, you're alive. It takes time, yeah? Just give me some time."

Jamie lifted the lid on the meal tray and exposed a small red rosebud in a very tiny vase. Bacon, eggs, tomato, mushrooms. Toast. A little pack of Vegemite... "Are there more Australians here?" she asked, hopefully.

"One, but I don't think he'll cure any homesickness."

They both heard the squeak of boots on tile. Jamie sighed, as if he knew who was coming. A moment later: "Thank you, Faraday. That will be all."

So this is the commanding officer, Rebecca thought as she sipped at her tea and used a paper napkin to wipe away the traces of Vegemite she knew were on her face. She watched the tall, blond uniformed male walk in. HAMILL was emblazoned on his shirt pocket. On his shoulder, some kind of eagle. He was carrying a heavy file. That's me, she thought. That file is all about me. "Good morning," she said for want of something else to say.

Pete Hamill looked up quickly and returned the greeting. He seemed surprised by it. Could it be that nobody ever said 'good morning' to this man? Confusion was alight in his eyes. Confusion he tried to hide under—Rebecca was soon to discover—an exterior of politically-correct ice. Rebecca doubted she'd seen eyes as deep a blue on a human being in her life. Surely he wore contacts? His hair was a shade of blond that hair designers couldn't achieve yet genetics had. He was broad at the shoulder and narrow of hip, not that she could distinguish much else, really, because she could not look away from his eyes. And he knew it.

The doctor's warning floated back in a soft haze. I've seen him before, she thought. She wondered, momentarily, if it was on the aircraft carrier that had stopped over in Brisbane for a week? What was it? The Eisenhower? Rebecca's mother had posed for a photograph with a pilot who looked a lot like this man. He'd wanted her phone number. He'd called, her mother had disappeared for three days and two nights and was in a daze for weeks, long after the ship was well out of Australian waters. Holy crap, she thought. This guy slept with my mother.

"Don't mind me. Carry on."

"No, I'm finished."

Pete Hamill put the file down, took a seat, adjusted the sleeves of his uniform—a man meaning business—and looked into her eyes. "I am at a loss for words here, Miss Miller, and I am never at a loss for words."

Rebecca tried not to imagine what she looked like. Her hair was achieving with ease the gorgon look she was faced with each morning upon awakening. She was bursting for the toilet, she hadn't brushed her teeth, she'd had one too many whiskeys with the doctor last night, and there the company commander sat, resembling a Hollywood superstar stumbling over scripted lines. This man slept with my mother, she kept thinking. This is a cosmic joke of immense proportions.

"Welcome to the 32nd Special Operations Unit otherwise known as the Nighthawks of which I am Commanding Officer."

Rebecca quietly considered what she'd just heard. "Say that again after a few Southern Comforts and see how it comes out." But the commanding officer regarded her blankly. "So what's Special Operations... whatever... mean in my language?"

"Nighthawks. We specialize in counter-terrorism operations that include certain offensive and defensive measures taken to prevent, deter, preempt, and respond to, acts of terrorism."

"Oh." What the hell am I doing here? she asked silently.

"Colonel Pete Hamill at your service, Miss Miller." He extended his hand and Rebecca took it. He gripped her hand hard and Rebecca was sucked down a tunnel so fast, so strong, that she had to pull back quickly to get out.

"Test pilot," she gasped.

"Excuse me?"

"You're a test pilot."

"I… was. Yes."

"You wanted to be an astronaut. You've been in one of those whirly round and round things at NASA."

The CO studied her closely. "Yes, I have been in a centrifuge on more than one occasion. How did you know that?"

"I was just in it with you."

"But…"

"When you touched me, you showed me."

"You got that from a two second handshake? Is that all you need? No crystal ball, cards, stuff like that?"

"I don't need focus tools."

"Now I am at a loss for words."

I can fix that, she thought. "How did you people find out about me?"

Pete considered the question carefully. "What do you mean by 'you people'? This outfit? The CIA? SS? NS? FBI, State Department? There are a lot of 'you people' here to choose from, Miss Miller. Where would you like to begin?"

"You can tell me why I was brought here under false pretenses."

"It was made clear you were being taken into the protective custody of the United States government, wasn't it?"

Silence. There was something in this man's eyes that Rebecca could not read. Nor could she see his colors properly. But some people were like that. Some people built huge walls of defense so impenetrable that no one could get in. Why, she wondered. What's he hiding?

"Is that supposed to be some kind of waiver? Excuse? Sorry, I don't buy it. I fly halfway around the planet under the false impression I'm to talk at a conference in London. A Navy Commander meets me at the airport, tells me there is no conference, I'm in protective custody, I'm to come here instead, wherever here is. If it begins with lies, Colonel, how is it going to end?"

"It ends when the job's done. Not before."

"And the job is?"

"In a nutshell, keeping Senator John Glover alive when he visits Lakenheath air base."

"I don't see how I can help you. If you don't mind?" Rebecca climbed out of bed and closed the door to the private bathroom. The CO talked on. Rebecca wondered if he'd talk under wet cement. She didn't care if she was being rude.

"Two years ago you… read… is that the word? Senator Glover's wife, Elizabeth, in a hotel room in Sydney. The transcript is in this file if you'd like to refresh your memory."

"That recording was supposed to be for Elizabeth Glover and no one else. It was private and confidential," came the muffled words from the bathroom.

"Miss Miller, according to the OSIR there are only three other people in the world as good as you."

"And who do they work for now? The CIA? State Department?"

He ignored that. "We know more about you than you know about yourself."

Rebecca eventually emerged from the bathroom. "You could have simply asked me to assist and I would have. I could have done this from home."

"This was the preferred option."

"Who for? Whoever was waiting to shoot me?" Rebecca picked up her suitcase, heaved it on to the bed.

"Let me do that."

"I am not an invalid!" She found what she was looking for, a crushed blue dress, and went back to the bathroom. Again the door closed. "I still have not been asked yet. My co-operation is somehow assumed. This is not a good beginning."

When she emerged, the blue of the dress matched the blue of her eyes, dark and haunting. She swept her hair into a semblance of order, caught it and as she pulled it into a ponytail, the thin straps of the dress fell from her right shoulder. Bracelets jangled. Pete had seen this before, in Kelly's office. The hair on the back of his neck stood to attention. "Will you help us, Rebecca?"

"I'll do what I can but I ask only one thing of you. No more lies. It's either the truth or it's nothing. Is this agreed?"

"You have my word." And he also had something, twenty five pages long, that she had to sign as well. She'd need to consult a lawyer to make sense of it. This had come from the US Government. Five different pages for five different departments.

"If I don't sign?"

"Basically, we cannot guarantee your safety."

Fark, she thought. Am I supposed to be reassured by all this? She took the pen and signed. "This means I'm one of you guys for the duration. A Nighthawk."

"More or less," Pete said as he shuffled signed papers and slipped them into a folder.

"And?" she asked.

"Sorry?" he replied.

"Is there something else you want to tell me?"

"Yes. Two operatives from the Central Intelligence Agency will be here this afternoon to talk to you."

"And?"

"There's a team of paranormal investigators wanting to study you as well."

"The OSIR?"

"Well, yes, but…"

"For what reason do they want to 'study' me?"

"I'm told it's research."

"Are they coming to discover how useful I might be to whatever cause suits your government's fancy at any given time?"

The CO didn't reply.

"I thought you said there'd be no more lies?"

"That's what I was told, Rebecca. The study will be to gauge the percentage of risk we can or cannot afford to take."

"Basically, if I pass, you'll trust me. That's what you're saying."

"Yes, I suppose that is what I'm saying."

"If I fail?"

"You won't." Of that, Pete was certain. It had been a childhood dream of his to be an astronaut but he'd physically failed the centrifuge three times. Not even his wife knew about that.

Rebecca closed her suitcase, rested it by the door. "Can I please go to my room now? I don't like the atmosphere here. It used to be a dungeon. They used to lock up the criminally insane down here. It reeks of darkness."

Pete glanced around at the room. The walls were painted stark white. There was no darkness. And then he realized what she meant. He never liked coming down here himself and unless he was at death's door he wouldn't sleep down here either.

"I'll give you the economy tour. It might take some time to get used to the place. Also, you have to wear these at all times." Pete took a set of dog tags from a plastic packet and handed them to her. "Use them as pass keys. The chips will allow access to most, and I repeat, most areas of this facility. Do not lose them. I'll take your suitcase."

"Be my guest."

As he walked beside her, through the maze of corridors from the infirmary to the officers' quarters via the mess, Pete Hamill knew that there was a walking miracle amongst them, and he didn't believe in miracles.

"Kelly said he'd see me today. Where is he?"

"Commander Nolan," he said, emphasizing the correct title, "is on a dawn training session."

"Oh. Doing what? Jumping out of helicopters?"

"You should ask him that. Stafford."

"Sir. Miss."

Mitch Stafford was the first in the corridor, coming down the stairwell, going into the infirmary. He gave his fellow Australian a quick glance.

Rebecca could smell food which meant that the kitchen was close by. And then the thunder of booted feet was heard as the CO and the psychic rounded the first flight of stairs. Rebecca heard a few curses and all was quiet the moment she was seen. She hoped it was caused by the CO's presence and not hers. Eight uniformed soldiers nodded to her, and eight voices said, Miss or Ma'am, as they demurely went by. Then came a loud, resounding curse and a thud. Rebecca continued her journey up the stairs. Somebody had been watching her and not where he was going.

"Let me know if the behavior is, at any time, unacceptable."

"It's the 21st century, Colonel Pete. Aren't we all equals these days?"

Not in a place like this when you have to squat to piss, honey, he thought.

"You'd rather I was male, wouldn't you, Colonel. It'd be easier for everybody if I were."

Jesus H Christ, could she read minds, too?

She looked back at him and smiled. "Sometimes," she said, and his face went pale.

Rebecca was shown the mess. "Why isn't it called a dining room or a restaurant?"

"Because it's known as a mess. Always has been, always will be."

Rebecca looked in. There were only six people in the room, finishing breakfast. Rebecca wished she'd finished hers now because the smells were very inviting.

Across the hall from the mess, a pub area. Bar, stools, tables and chairs, a small stage and on the stage, a set of drums, two acoustic guitars and a Roland keyboard. There was also a huge Wurlitzer juke box. Cool, she thought.

The next room down the hall was a library. It felt as if the air hadn't been breathed here for years. There were two sitting rooms, another large room that she guessed was a small cinema, and another stairwell. An ancient cage elevator was nearby.

The staircase led to yet another three flights of stairs which opened on to a long corridor with dark, thick carpeting. There were close circuit cameras at either end and both cameras were lighted. Every door was the same. Pete put the suitcase down by a door at the far end of the quiet corridor. "You'll need your passkey."

Rebecca took the dog tags from around her neck. She slipped one in, the red light turned green. "I'm surprised it works. I usually annihilate electronics."

Pete walked in and put her case on a small stand by the narrow built-in wardrobe. "It's not what you're used to, but there's a hell of a view from here. We hope that will be a small consolation."

And it was. The view was magnificent. Beyond the decaying Victorian rose garden directly below was a clearing, and beyond the clearing, acres and acres of woodland, and beyond the woodland, hilly plains of farmland as far as she could see.

"Salisbury Plain has been used for military exercises and training for a very long time. It's not uncommon to see a tank driving across a plowed field, or through somebody's corn. There's also air traffic in and out of here at unusual times of the day and night. Do not be startled if, at any time, alarms are heard. When that happens, for God's sakes get out of the way of any man you see in a black uniform. I don't reside on base, I live with my wife and daughter in Salisbury. So when I am not here, if you need anything, anything at all, you talk to my 2IC, Commander Nolan. He's one door up the hall. This side. So for now, settle in and make yourself comfortable. Lunch is at noon. I suggest you get there five minutes early. Welcome aboard, Miss Miller."

"Thanks, Colonel Pete," she said.

Colonel Pete. God help us, he thought. "My pleasure."

The CO departed and Rebecca closed the door.

The room was actually bigger than some hotel rooms she'd stayed in. She had her own bathroom—loo, shower. There was a small hutch by the window, a perfect place to write, think, meditate. It'll do, she thought. A few crystals, a couple of plants…

In the distance she saw a chopper hovering over the woods. Was that gunfire she could hear? Was something on fire out there?

32nd Special Operations Unit. Nighthawks.

These men are like mercenaries. I'm now sharing their space. If it was some kind of cosmic joke, Rebecca was not laughing.

She unpacked her suitcase, put her clothes away and thanked God for giving her this second chance. She swore she would not let Him down.

She looked in the full length mirror adhered to the wall behind the door. She let the straps of her dress fall. All she could see was the raised, red scar over her heart. She turned around and looked over her shoulder at the reflection. A bigger scar on her back.

I wasn't sent back. I came back…

What do you want me to do? she asked silently.

Only what you must, Emmanuel's voice replied.

But I don't know what they want from me. I don't understand how I can help.

Time, was all Emmanuel said in reply. *Time*.

Chapter 4

Rebecca woke to the tap on her door. She had no sense of time. Her watch had stopped at twenty two past one and had refused to move since. It must have stopped the moment I was shot, she thought. Rebecca opened the door, expecting she knew not who.

Kelly. And again, her knees went jelly. He was dressed completely in black. There was some kind of microphone from his ear to his chin and, as she looked down, she saw a black balaclava tucked into his belt. Also tucked into the belt was a bloody big gun. Now she realized what the colonel had meant when he'd advised her to get out of the way of any man wearing a black uniform. Right now the only alarm was the quickened beat of her heart. She hoped nothing showed on her face. The commander's dark brown eyes were sparkling today. But did he ever speak? Why did he just stand there? Was he testing for telepathy?

"Kelly, what time was it when I d… when I got shot?"

He wasn't expecting the question. "Ah, approximately thirteen twenty-five. Why?"

She thought hard for awhile. She wasn't good with twenty-four hour timekeeping. "My watch stopped at twenty-two past one."

"Want another?" he asked.

She shook her head. No, she thought. It won't go beyond one twenty-two, either.

Why was he just standing there?

"What?" she asked.

"You want to eat? Follow me."

"Is it lunchtime already?"

He started walking down the corridor before she closed her door. She had to run to catch him. "What's that for?" she asked, pointing to the microphone.

"Communication."

He wouldn't look at her today.

"Is something wrong?"

He came to a standstill. "Is all your clothing like this?"

"Pardon?"

"Your dress might be ok for Surfers Paradise, but this is not Surfers Paradise."

"Yes, I know. It's Wiltshire. Are we close to Stonehenge?"

"What you are wearing is inappropriate, Miss Miller. I advise you to change into—"

"What? A hijab? Maybe a chador? If my breasts offend you, don't look."

Kelly studied her face for a little while. Again, that resigned sigh. He walked on and obediently, Rebecca followed, pulling faces now and then, almost running to keep up with his long, impatient strides.

He came to a sudden halt at the door to the mess. "Please reconsider. I'm only trying to avoid embarrassment here."

"Look, Captain Kelly. Nobody will notice me. I'm invisible. The only time I'm not invisible is when somebody wants to know something, so don't freak out about what I'm wearing. Guys don't see me that way."

"Excuse me?"

"Guys don't see me that way. I am invisible."

Kelly did not have to voice what was on his mind.

"Your concern is touching but it's unwarranted. I'm a big girl now, I can look after myself."

"Yeah?"

"Yeah."

"I won't say I told you so." Kelly held the door open.

Rebecca walked in under his arm. "Holy crap." She tried to turn and run but Kelly was barring the exit.

"Nobody notices. Guys don't see you that way."

The immediate hush, Rebecca was certain, could be felt globally.

Fuck me, she thought. It's raining men.

The room was overflowing with special ops soldiers who were all staring at her and worse, there was barely a spare seat.

Kelly whispered, "Follow me, Miss Invisible."

Heart pounding, face flushed, she followed Kelly's lead to the buffet, picked up a tray, a plate and cutlery, and chose from a wide variety of hot and cold foods. Her appetite had fled and so had her fake courage but she couldn't stand there like a stunned mullet indefinitely.

There was one spare table with two seats, and it was obviously Kelly's regular spot because there he sat, no doubt expecting her to join him.

Rebecca scanned the room and tried valiantly to ignore the stares. The only other spare seat was opposite someone who wasn't staring, but reading from a Kindle as he ate. Something about his face, perhaps it was his bald head, that was familiar. Without glancing at Kelly, she made her way forwards, into the depths of the inquisitive crowd of men in uniform.

Yes, Kelly was right. The dress wasn't a good choice. Too much cleavage. Not many of the men were looking at her face. Maybe it's the scar, she thought. Yes, it had to be. Rebecca focused on the spare seat.

Mac looked up in time to see the VIP coming towards him and, heart thudding, he cleared space immediately. She's going to sit with me. Me. Not the commander.

But before she was halfway to Mac's table, a thick, hairy tattooed arm stretched out, blocking her way. Rebecca looked into sparkling, amused and faintly misogynistic eyes. Mitch Stafford, chief medic on loan from the Australian SAS, asked, "If I said something, would you hold it against me?"

"What?"

"Breasts."

Mild amusement from the boys in uniform. This was a test and Rebecca knew it.

"Get your hand off it, you big jessie."

More amusement.

Rebecca glanced at Kelly. Even though his face was expressionless she could almost read his mind. It was now or never, that was all she knew. "Are there any questions?" she asked, loud, and caught almost everyone in her wide, sweeping gaze. Suddenly, the amusement evaporated. Nobody met her gaze, except Kelly, and his face was no longer expressionless. He was curious.

"Are you sure there are no questions? That's weird because yesterday I came in here, as dead as a friggin' doornail. Photos shot around this place faster than the speed of light, am I right?"

Silence was assured now.

"Let me tell you, every one of you right now, there is no such thing as death. It's not something soldiers want to hear, is it. I'll ask again. Any questions?"

Somebody coughed. That was the only sound.

"No? Can I eat now?"

Rebecca proceeded, through the low murmur, to the only spare seat available. Her face was hot and very pink, her eyes a deep sea blue. And, Mac noticed, her hands were shaking. "Well done."

She looked at Mac and caught his smile. "Thanks."

"Bark's worse and all that," Mac said quietly in a faintly-Irish lilt.

"but it's best not to provoke. All right?"

She nodded. "Point taken. You were at the airport." She saw his name, Macpherson, on his shirt. "What can I call you?"

"Mac."

"No, I mean, what's your real name?"

"Mac."

She glanced across the room at Kelly but he wasn't watching. Or maybe he was. It was hard to tell. "Pleased to meet you again, Mac. Derry or Belfast?"

"Belfast," he said, and went back to his Kindle, or at least, he pretended he was reading.

The food was good—she didn't understand why they called the cook a 'fitter and turner'. Mac said very little, but each time she looked up he was watching her, and when he smiled his aura turned a beautiful shade of pink. She'd only seen that around women, and it could only mean one thing when found exuding from a male. Mac was gay.

There was noise in the mess now: a lot of voices talking at once. She was still being watched, but at least she wasn't being stared at anymore.

Gradually the men dispersed. Mac excused himself, saying he had to get back to work.

Before long, the mess was empty but for two people. Rebecca turned to Kelly. He was reading a newspaper. "Do you know where my office is?" he asked without looking at her.

"No. The boss gave me what he called 'the economy tour'."

"When I'm done here, come with me. You're being interviewed in thirty minutes."

"Interviewed or interrogated?"

"Interviewed."

"You can say it you know."

"What?"

"I told you so."

"And I told you I wouldn't say it."

Silence.

"Do you have a problem with me?"

"Not yet," Kelly said and turned the page.

Rebecca finished her cup of tea, returned her dishes and tray to the buffet and waited in the corridor for Kelly. She knew he was deliberately making her wait.

When uniformed males went by each greeted her with a nod, a 'Miss' or a 'Ma'am'. She wondered if they were allowed to say her name. Each man had his surname embroidered on his uniform: Bennett, Mancuso, Brannagh, Rydell, McLaren…

"Hello, Captain Mike."

"Lass. Did you ask the colonel?"

"No. Not yet. I think I'll have to time it where he's concerned. You know, choose the moment."

"You'd be a fast learner, then, lass," he said and walked off, back to the infirmary.

Kelly finally appeared. "Follow me."

"Aye aye, captain."

"I'm not a captain. I'm a commander."

As Rebecca followed Kelly, she pulled a face.

"I saw that. And yes I have eyes in my ass."

Rebecca half ran to keep pace again. "You've had a personality transplant. Yesterday you were nice."

"Nice doesn't exist here. Get used to it."

"Fair enough. I enjoy a challenge."

Kelly stopped walking. "I have a question for you. If you're so psychic, why'd you get yourself into this mess?"

"You should know the answer to that."

"If I knew the answer, I wouldn't be asking the question."

"Have you ever known what's been ahead for you?"

"Sometimes."

"But it works better with other people, right?"

He remained safely non-committal.

"I don't know why they want me here when they've already got you."

He studied her carefully, almost smiled then thought better of it.

Rebecca followed him into the administration block. He used his passkey to gain entry but the moment Rebecca stepped inside, alarms screamed. Within seconds uniformed, armed men appeared from nowhere. Kelly held up his hand and the men dispersed. "Give me your tags," he yelled over the screaming alarm.

"What?"

"Tags!"

"What?"

Kelly pulled the tags over her head, slipped one into the slot, and punched a sequence of numbers into the access decoder by the door. The alarm stopped instantly. He pulled the tag out and handed it back. "With me," he said and this time, Rebecca had to run to keep pace with him.

"Rebecca, you're going to…" he realized she wasn't beside him. He looked back. She was stopped, for breath, at the top of the stairwell. "All you had to say was slow down."

"Slow … down," she managed.

He walked back. "You're unfit. We've got to do something about that."

"Oh, do we now. What's the hurry? Where's the friggin' fire? Do you live your life as fast as you walk?" The world was spinning, she balanced herself against the wall.

"Do you need a medic?" He took hold of her arm before she fainted. Rebecca was hit with a mountain of quick, successive flashes and none of them was pleasant. Especially not the image that remained as she shook his hand away. He was making love to a beautiful, elegant woman. She knew it was his wife.

"No. I don't need a medic and don't touch me. For God's sakes, don't touch me."

He stood back, hands raised.

"I don't like being touched."

He looked at her strangely.

"At a distance, I can block it; I've learnt how. But please don't touch me because I don't want to know. All right? I don't want to know."

"Know what?"

"You. Things about you."

"Is that how it works? By touch?" he asked quietly.

"Something like that, yes. Are we there yet?" she asked.

He walked on, slowly this time, towards his office on the top floor of the administration block. He used his passkey to get in and when Rebecca entered, no alarms sounded.

It was a large office and there was not much space left on the walls. Many photographs, too, of ships and choppers, submarines, aircraft carriers. Navy SEALs in strange-looking rubber boats. Kelly was obviously one of them. Commendations, awards, university degrees. A spare jacket hung on a hook behind the door. There were orderly piles of paper everywhere and a computer sat on a large desk. Every now and then it made a whooshing noise. Email coming in? she wondered.

On the window sill sat a tiny plant—God knew what it tried to be—a fern perhaps? Rebecca walked to it and touched the only frond that seemed half alive as she looked out at the view. "Where's Stonehenge?"

"It's not visible from here."

"Oh. Bugger," she said softly, almost disappointed. "Have you ever been there?"

"Too many tourists." He didn't want to say he'd taken Marianne there on his last leave—they'd also had two weeks traveling around Scotland. She'd tried to kill him on the Isle of Skye.

"I was going to be a tourist." Rebecca walked about the room. On top of a filing cabinet was a rigger in a glass bottle. "I was going to do the conference, then rent a car and...' Her chatter ceased.

On the wall, in a beautiful frame, was an oil painting of a woman. The subject in profile was well-endowed and barefoot. She had wild, long hair, her face into the wind. She wore a gold cross around her neck. It was identical to the one Nanny Hilda had given Rebecca when she turned thirteen... The one she wore at this very moment. Coincidence, she thought. But the dress this woman wore was very similar to the one Rebecca wore now, even to the shoestring strap which kept falling from the subject's right shoulder. This is me, she thought. This is me. Her mouth went dry as she slipped the loose strap back to her shoulder again.

"Rent a car and?" Kelly asked, noting her reaction.

"Drive. Is this your wife?" she asked.

"No, that's not my wife." He waited for a response but Rebecca dared not look at him.

"Well, whoever she is, she'd be proud of this painting. You're a very talented sailor."

"I'm not a sailor."

"I know. You're a commander and a Navy SEAL. And you're an artist and a musician and your grandfather was a shaman. What you do may have a label but who you are does not."

"And who are you, Rebecca Miller?"

Her heart lurched momentarily. Her brain went numb. Nobody had ever asked her that before. She had no answer.

"I thought so. I'll be present for this entire interview," Kelly said. "I suggest you hold nothing back."

"Well, that depends entirely upon what they want to know."

"You agreed to cooperate."

"I'm here, aren't I?"

"I'll give you some advice, Miss Miller. Do not fuck with these people."

"I don't, as you so politely put it, fuck with anybody. Tell me something, Commander Kelly. If there's white at point A and black at point Z, and most people live their lives in the grayness between, exactly where do you and I fit?"

Kelly glanced at her, and this time, he smiled. "Maybe around the N."

"Ah, yes. N for Nowhere. My thoughts exactly."

Corporal Sam Tighe led Leon Carter and Gene Samperi into the commander's office and, after a quick glance at Rebecca and the scar on her chest, and then the painting, he departed.

Rebecca studied the CIA operatives. She did not want to judge too soon, even if it was obvious that Kelly had little time for either of them. Or maybe he had better things to do, like jump out of helicopters, because he hadn't changed out of his black uniform yet.

Leon Carter, in his mid thirties, was dressed in jeans and a pale blue shirt and had Nike trainers on his feet. Rebecca liked him, instantly. The other one, Gene Samperi, was older, perhaps by five years but it was hard to tell. He wore expensive baggy trousers and a designer shirt that, she guessed, came from Paris.

She'd seen snakes with kinder eyes.

"Leon Carter. Happy to see you looking so good," Leon said and offered his hand.

Rebecca took the hand, registered absolutely nothing from his touch, smiled politely and said, "Don't you mean looking so alive?"

Kelly rolled his eyes, shook his head, but Rebecca ignored the silent warning and continued.

"So you're the mysterious Leon. I know your voice. I've spoken to you before. You called me to verify details about the conference. Times, venue… You guys went to a lot of trouble making me believe it was genuine. My congratulations to your graphic artist, by the way. Very professional indeed. And the airline tickets? Hotel room bookings? All for this? How can I ever thank you?"

Kelly rubbed the back of his neck.

"I never forget a voice, Leon and I don't forget lies, either."

Gene Samperi, who as yet had not introduced himself, stood quietly, trying not to express amusement at what he'd just heard. "For the falsification, we apologize. It was a means to an end."

Rebecca caught Samperi's amused gaze and refused to let go. "Good choice of words there."

"You can call me Gene." He extended his hand.

This time when Rebecca touched, Kelly was watching closely. Her face paled. He could see a pulse thudding in her throat. Her breathing pattern changed. What did you just see? he wondered. She covered well, sat on the sofa and crossed her legs. She also folded her arms so nobody could see her hands shaking or hear the bracelets rattling.

"What can I do for you, gentlemen?" Rebecca asked.

"Just a few questions for now."

"Fire at will. Poor Will." Rebecca's glance at Kelly was swift and frightened and he could do nothing except remain impassive. He was getting used to the strange things she said, but any attempt at humor was lost on Samperi. Or was it humor?

"Did you know who Elizabeth Glover was when she walked into your hotel room in Sydney almost two years ago?"

"No. I didn't know who she was. An American Senator's wife is not someone you expect to see on a daily basis. Until she walked in and the reading began, she was just an American lady coming for a reading."

"Fair enough," Leon said.

Gene wasn't as satisfied. "I've heard it's usual practice to ask names, get phone numbers and do some checking before the gullible party walks in with a handful of cash."

Here we go, Rebecca thought. "That's a crock and you know it. When I'm on the road, I read fifteen people a day, and give them an hour each, average, depending on circumstance. I'm on the road nine months of the year. You do the math. I hardly have the time to soak in a bathtub, why would I run background checks on complete strangers? I take phone numbers in case of cancellations because I have a bloody long waiting list."

But Gene Samperi didn't believe her. That much she knew. "So take us through what happened."

"I'm sorry, but what happened is between the client and myself. It's called confidentiality."

Gene turned to Kelly and implored his help. Kelly shrugged.

"You agreed to co-operate."

"Does Elizabeth Glover know about this?" she asked.

"Yes, of course she does. Where do you think we got the recording?"

"And the senator?"

Carter and Samperi looked at each other.

"I thought so. He still thinks it's crap. Mumbo-jumbo. Has he heard his wife's session?"

"Whether he has or not is irrelevant. The recording was passed on to the Secret Service. Who passed it on to… look, just tell us what happened in Sydney."

The 'interview' took one and a half hours. One and a half hours of the same questions, over and over. But the only true question was, who is going to kill the senator? One and a half hours of the same repetitive answer later—how many ways could she say she didn't know—the two from the CIA departed. One believed her, one did not. And the one who did not… She could not erase what she'd seen in her mind the moment hands touched. And people who weren't psychic thought it was a gift?

Kelly guided Rebecca back to her quarters, mostly in silence. This time he adjusted his pace to suit her shorter legs. She was very subdued. The interview, as far as he was concerned, had been relatively mild. Then again, he taught a vast array of interrogation techniques. And yes, she was holding back information, but whether it was relevant or not, he didn't know. News this morning came that Glover was now a viable candidate for the Presidency. Early polls were already in his favor.

"Are you going to talk to me?" he asked as he stood in her doorway, watching as she lay on the bed and rolled to her side.

"I've got nothing to say."

"Bullshit you've got nothing to say."

"Leave me alone."

Kelly closed the door and stood by the bed, arms folded and feet apart. He looked like a warrior chief. "What did you see when Samperi took your hand? I know you saw something."

"Go away, I'm tired."

"That wasn't a difficult interview. They were being polite. You are holding back information."

"And you'd know of course."

"Yes, I would know! What do you think I teach here? Grade school?" The force of the voice frightened her. She recoiled and he was glad that she did. Fear was a good sign. It proved she was human. "Do you want me to tell you what'd I have done if you'd fucked me about like you did those two idiots?"

"I didn't f…"

"Talk first. When talk fails, other methods are employed. Are you listening to me?"

She looked at him, she had to. She didn't know what he'd do if she did not acknowledge him in some way.

"There's a myriad of methods. There's deprivation for a start. There's mental and emotional blackmail, physical threat. I know fifty ways of dealing with a female and most times all it takes is a well placed knee between her thighs or a hand on her chest. This is what I do. It's what I'm good at. And you'd be easy, Rebecca Miller. Do not fuck with these people and don't you ever, ever fuck with me because there is more at stake here than one man's life or death. So you talk to me, and you talk to me now."

There was silence for a little while until she got off the bed and looked out of the window, seeing nothing. "I saw what he did," she said softly.

Kelly waited. Nothing else came. "Saw who doing what?"

"Samperi. The Armani man. It was him. The rifle was a dark color and it was on some kind of tripod thing on top of a four wheel drive… sorry SUV. There was a scope—like you see in the movies. What snipers in the movies look through. I saw what he saw. I saw him try for my head first but no, I was moving too much for that. So he aimed it at my chest. And then you got in the way and he pulled back until he had me again. And he… when the bullet lifted me off my feet he said, 'beautiful'. He enjoyed it, Kelly. He got a real buzz from it and I mean a real buzz. And I had to sit there for one and a half hours knowing that he'd shot me, and he'd enjoy doing it again. And what was he wanting to know? Did I see the face of the person who was going to kill the senator on the stairs of his aircraft. Look, I saw that two years ago and it lasted half a second. I do not know any more than that. How many times can you say you don't know until people like him will listen? If you'd seen what I'd seen: if you'd witnessed your own death through somebody else's eyes, how would you have reacted? You tell me that."

Kelly said nothing. He was inspecting his hands. He knew she hadn't finished yet.

"I am still trying to figure out why in God's name I had to come back and I tell you, watching yourself die is not the most pleasant thing to experience but when you feel that some guy who's never even met you damn near had an orgasm from it... I'm sorry if I've disappointed you but I am not you. The world I live in is not the world you live in. The sight of a uniform or a gun scares the shit out of me. It always has and it always will. And where am I now? Surrounded by soldiers. This is some kind of cosmic joke. It's got to be."

"Yeah, and we're both laughing. What did you get from Leon Carter?"

"Nothing."

"I don't believe that."

"He doesn't have a future."

"Excuse me?"

"Leon Carter doesn't have a future."

"How can you know that?"

"The same way you would know if you tried. Now leave me alone. Go on. Bugger off. Go do your soldier stuff. Go leap tall buildings with a single bound, just leave me the fuck alone." ·

But Kelly wasn't going anywhere. "I'm sorry," he said. "Truly. I'm sorry you had to be dragged into this. I'm sorry you got hurt."

"Hurt? Is that what you call it? Hurt?"

He wanted to touch her hair, her face. He wanted to offer some kind of comfort but he didn't know how, so he stayed where he was. "Rebecca?" When she turned to him, she had to wipe her eyes. "I only ask that you trust me. Can you do that?"

She studied his face for a long moment before turning back to the view. She didn't answer his question. "He didn't even know me, Kelly. How could he do that? How could he?"

It's easier when it's a stranger, Kelly thought. He walked to where she stood. "He's either acting alone and I doubt it, or he had orders. He knew when you were coming in. He knew where the chopper would be."

"Look at me. What kind of threat am I?"

"To some people you must be a major one. Believe me when I say you're safe here."

She wished she could believe him. "I never wanted to be like this. I'd give it all away if only I could be normal. Even for one day. Just one lousy day."

"But you're not like everybody else. You never will be."

She was staring out the window and seeing nothing. He wanted to touch her, badly, but he couldn't.

"Tell me this, Rebecca. Tell me that. Can you heal me. Help me make sense of my life. They walk out the door, happy, and I sit there, staring into inner space wondering why the hell I can't do the same for myself. Why did Elizabeth Glover choose me? Out of every psychic on earth, why did she walk through my door?"

"Why? You were recommended by the FBI."

Chapter 5

AFTER KELLY DEPARTED, SHE LAY back on her bed and tried to rest. Although she longed for proper sleep, she'd awoken agitated and the feeling had not departed. She had also lost all sense of time. Rebecca picked up the phone. No dial tone. No hint of instruction anywhere. Choose a number, any number. She hit 0 and waited. "Yes, Ma'am?" an American voice asked before she'd uttered a word.

"What's the time?"

"Fifteen-fifteen, Ma'am."

She closed her eyes. What was worse, twenty-four hour clocks or younger men calling her ma'am? "What's that in my language?"

"Three fifteen, Ma'am."

"When's tea?"

"Excuse me?"

"Dinner. Food O'clock. Eat. Starvin' Marvin."

"Oh, right. I got you. After eighteen thirty, sorry, six thirty until eight thirty, Ma'am."

"Who am I talking to?"

"Barrett, Ma'am."

"Do you have a first name?"

"Yes, Ma'am, I have a first name."

The pause was infinite.

"Don't call me Ma'am, Barrett. I'm not that bloody old." Rebecca hung up and stood by the window. She knew that unless she had something viable to do while she was here, she would go insane. For now, Rebecca thought she'd take a walk. The sun was shining and it had been too long since she'd felt it on her skin.

Rebecca changed into jeans, sneakers and a pullover, and went down two flights of stairs to the mess floor. There was a lack of exit signs marked by a running man. Just cameras. Most of them were on and one in particular was tracking her. So she turned to it, curtsied, and turned around again.

"She's right," Joel Barrett said from his seat in the communications room. "She's not that old."

Rebecca walked into the bar. Chairs were off tables, there was one person working the bar and two people sat on the better side. Stafford and Faraday. She didn't need to read pockets to know who these two were. Mitch did not acknowledge her presence and continued drinking his can of Australian beer. Jamie stood and greeted Rebecca warmly. "He was just leaving, weren't you, Sarge."

Mitch mumbled to himself and kept drinking. Rebecca sat between the two and Jamie bought her a Coke. She wanted nothing stronger.

"Where are you from, Mitch?" she asked.

"Perth," was all he said.

"Miss it?"

"No."

"Is there any chance that someone could show me around? I'd like to take a walk in the garden."

Mitch did not respond.

"I'll have to get permission," Jamie offered with more enthusiasm than was necessary.

"You need permission to take me for a walk?"

"Aha."

"It's too dangerous for the likes of you roaming around here unaccompanied," Mitch mumbled.

"And what exactly is the likes of me?"

"Civilian," Mitch said. "Female." And with that, Stafford threw his empty can into the bin by the door and he walked out.

For a moment, there was silence. Rebecca sipped the Coke and looked at the young man behind the bar. He would have been nice looking were it not for the scar from his left eye to his nose, and his shaved head, and his tattoos. He too, was watching her closely. This must be how scientists regard new life forms, she thought. "What's your name?" she asked because there was no hint—this one wore normal clothing of jeans and a tee shirt that advertised spark plugs.

"Greg," the barman said, digesting Rebecca with his amused gaze. He extended his hand. Rebecca reluctantly touched. She discovered he played the drums on the stage at the other end of the room. She also knew that he was a diver and attached explosives to objects: boats, buildings, doors... The only family he had was this one. It was the only kind of family he wanted.

She didn't want to touch him again.

"Want me to ask if I can show you about?" Jamie offered.

"I don't think the colonel's here."

"Christ, we ask him nowt." Jamie picked up the phone on the bar, dialed four numbers and waited. No reply. The call was intercepted by Sam, who told Jamie the commander was on training ground 17B. Communications patched Jamie through. "Sir? Our VIP wants a tour of the grounds." Silence for a little while. "I thought I would, sir, if that's all right."

Silence again except for a lot of noise in the background and Jamie's raised voice when he said: "Thanks, sir. Yes. Will do."

Jamie resumed his seat. "Thirty minutes max. Drink up."

Rebecca, this time, took more notice of where she was being led. One floor down and a left turn. Double doors opened into a grand entry, with wide sweeping staircases off to either side of the heavy, castle-like wooden doors. And even here, at these ancient doors, was an access decoder. A moment later, Rebecca stood on the front stairs, breathing in the chill, clean air and hoping some elusive afternoon sunshine might find strength enough to touch her face.

Flagstone stairs were worn down from the constant footfalls of humanity. These same stairs were in existence hundreds of years ago when circumstances of occupation had been less than ideal. Most people coming in here never came out again. Rebecca sensed it had sometimes applied to the staff, too. She hoped times had changed. "Talk to me, Jamie Faraday," Rebecca said.

"I can't offer you information, Miss, but maybe I can answer some questions."

"Basically you're saying that if you think I need to know anything about the whys are wherefores of this place, you'll tell me?"

"You must be psychic," he said.

"Is it always this cold?"

"Cold? Today's warm in comparison."

"In comparison to what?"

"If you're here long enough, you'll find out." Jamie pointed to the west. "Main car park. The black Ducati's mine."

"And the BMW?" she asked, although she already knew whose it was. Two door. Luxury Sports, latest model.

"The Commander's."

"I don't suppose you could take me for a spin on your bike?"

"That could be pushing it, Miss."

"Please call me Rebecca."

"Sorry, Miss. Against orders. There's a garden this way. If you can call it a garden." Rebecca walked beside him. She did not have to run. "Top level middle is the CO's office. I believe we're being watched."

Rebecca looked up from the circular rose garden with a Victorian fountain in the middle, long since inoperable, to the middle window of the top floor. There was a silhouette by the window.

"How did you know he was up there without looking up yourself?"

"I could tell you but then I'd…"

"Have to kill you, yeah, yeah. I've heard that one before."

A hundred yards from the rose garden was a twelve foot high fence with razor wire at the top, and beyond the fence, woodland. "Out there is where the training grounds are. Close quarters combat, firing ranges, kill houses, sickeners, post assaults, room entry drills, staircase clearings, that kind of thing."

She had no idea what he was talking about, she was simply enjoying the fresh air and trying to take the new information on board.

"Back here is the ration assassin's garden but never go in unless you've got permission. That's Frank's territory and he's very protective of it. Touch his basil and you die, slowly. In a lot of pain." Jamie had effectively steered her away from any questions about what lay out there in the woods. Things she'd rather not know, perhaps.

"Fitter and turner. Ration assassin. What other names does that poor man have?"

"Tucker fucker. I believe that's an Australian term."

She laughed. "Really?"

"Yep, but I didn't say that."

"I think I'll call him Frank."

"I think he'd like that."

An old ginger cat was asleep on the ancient garden wall. "That's Ceefor. C for cat. He doesn't like anybody." Oh really? He purred when Rebecca stroked his head, then he stretched out and yawned. She peered over the wall. A small greenhouse and herbs in a garden that was immaculately structured and ordered. Like the cook's life, she thought. Like everybody's life here, except mine.

Jamie led her onwards, the cat following at Rebecca's heels, past two industrial garbage bins, to what, she guessed, was the entrance to the kitchen, across a quadrangle.

"These buildings are linked underground, aren't they. Tunnels."

Jamie said nothing.

"What exactly goes on below the ground?"

Again silence.

"I'm only curious. Like you are."

"I'm not curious about this place."

"But you are curious about me."

"Who wouldn't be?" Jamie opened the door to the gym. The cat would not go in. He was restricted to outside areas. He'd been caught under too many booted feet and knew better.

The gym was filled with a variety of bodybuilding and fitness equipment. There were also thick rope nets hooked to two walls and on the third was a rock climbing construction, but how they got to the top, she had no idea. There were no ropes. There was nothing to gain foot or hand holds with. The long building was divided into two sections. The other half contained a swimming and diving pool. The fumes from chlorine brought tears to her eyes.

Jamie led her outside again and glanced at the time.

"I'd like to sit in the garden if that's all right."

"Sure. Five max."

Jamie followed her back to the rose garden where dormancy for the coming winter was just beginning. There were no blooms, so where did the cook find that red rosebud?

"You don't have to stay with me."

"Yes, I do."

"What can happen to me here?"

Again, Jamie said nothing.

"Why am I so important to you people?"

"I do what I'm told, Miss."

"Struth. I'd last five seconds as a soldier."

Jamie said nothing to that, but his face creased with a smile.

"What do you want to know, Jamie? For the past twenty minutes, you've been rehearsing fifty different questions."

"Actually, it's been one question fifty different ways." There was a pause until finally, it came. "What happened, you know, when you… when you… died?"

"I suppose my answer would depend a great deal upon your own personal beliefs. It's no use me telling you that death doesn't exist, that the part of you that thinks and feels, the part of you that IS, stays alive. I can't say that if you believe that once you're dead, all that greets you is a huge, big nothing. So tell me, Jamie Faraday, what do you believe?"

"I've seen death too many times to doubt the reality of it."

"And when a corpse sits up and starts screaming? I asked what you believed, not what you've seen. There's a huge difference. What does your heart say?"

"That I'll end up in hell no matter what I believe."

"Why? You're a medic. You help people."

"I'm also the third best sniper in this outfit, luv. With the right gear I can take out a target from a mile away."

That information silenced her and he knew he shouldn't have said it. Damn. He thought he was on a winner here, too.

"You use your intuition a lot."

"I suppose so. I get feelings, hunches about patients."

"And girls."

"Girls?" he asked with a grin. "That's easy. If I'm in a pub and I've had a few pints, I see the colors easier. I've learnt that green means go.

Literally." Now, why'd he say that?

"So what color am I today?" Rebecca asked.

"I've never seen anything like it before. It's …" He paused while he studied her. "Gold."

"Where does this ability to see auras come from, Jamie?"

"Don't know. I never questioned before."

"Perhaps you should. You might be surprised by the answers you get."

There was silence again for a little while. Rebecca studied the poor, unkempt roses and was silently placing a color to each bush while Jamie studied his fingernails.

"So what happened at the airfield?" he asked.

"One moment I was arguing with the commander. I was frightened about getting into the helicopter and the next moment, I'm watching some futile CPR from inner space."

"So you didn't feel anything? No pain? Nothing?"

"If you're asking did it hurt, no. If there was pain I wasn't aware of it. Only a vast lightness of being and this encompassing sense of freedom. I was still me but it was different being away from my body. How can I say this, Jamie? Visualize that your knowledge of everything imaginable is as big as an elephant. The Upstairs Management assigns you a body and all the knowledge that's the size of this elephant is suddenly crammed into something the size of a matchbox. That's what it's like being here, on earth, in a body. But being dead is having your freedom again. You know so much and there are no restraints. You can see all and feel all and it's not a burden. It's not more than you can cope with. It's nothing to be afraid of. But I was a bit angry and confused because it wasn't my time. That's the only way I can explain it."

"So this talk about spirit guides, they're the free ones. We're the prisoners."

"Something like that, yes. It's all a matter of degree."

"And some people have a connection to the other side and some people don't."

"Aha."

"Some pretend to have connections and bullshit their way through."

"Aha."

"You don't."

"I just tell it as I see it. They call it a gift. But it isn't. Not if you want a regular life. You put your own life on hold for others all the time. Who you are isn't important. What you can do for them is. That's how people see you, Jamie. Always. It's a bit like being a police officer. You're only wanted when something's wrong. I suppose I'm like you in some ways. Not all, mind. Maybe some."

"The captain was nearly crippled with arthritis in his knees and his hip. You touched him and he hasn't limped since. How did you do that?"

"Jamie, I think we're needed."

"Sorry?"

"In the hospital. We're needed. Come on."

"I haven't been paged."

"No, that'll go off when we're halfway down the stairs. Don't sit there gawking at me. Come on!"

Jamie had to run to catch her.

"I told him. I told him but no, no, why should I expect he'd listen?"

"What are you talking about?"

"Someone's been injured."

"How do you know?"

"I saw it happen. Damn it. I told Kelly. He said he'd check the ropes."

Halfway down the stairs, Jamie's pager activated.

When Daniel Macpherson was brought in, his left ankle was rotated 180 degrees and he had a compound fracture of the lower left leg. He was too high on morphine to acknowledge anything at all. Rebecca stood well out of the way, watching Mike, Jamie and Mitch working as a well-oiled machine. They had worked together as a team for so long that not one of them needed to speak. Rebecca's hands were on fire as she stood in the background, watching.

Also watching in the background, Kelly. Gazes met across the treatment room. No words were needed. He had not heeded her warning and worse, Mac was a good friend.

Mike decided the fractures needed setting under a general anesthetic by an orthopedic surgeon and was about to arrange a transfer to a fully-equipped military hospital when Rebecca stepped forward.

"Can I have some time with him, Captain?"

"Out of the way, pet. We've no time to waste."

"Please?"

Mike sighed.

"Please? There's time before the medevac comes. Please? Let me try."

Because Macpherson was stabilized and there was nothing to lose, Mike nodded and left the room to organize the transfer.

"Jamie. I'd like you to stay."

Mitch stood with Kelly and surveyed the situation. "This is crazy," was all he said. "You're all fucking mad." Mitch walked away.

"What happened, Commander?" Rebecca asked.

"Fifty foot free fall."

"It was the rope, wasn't it."

Kelly didn't comment. He had remembered her warning too late. Memory came as he watched Macpherson's plunge.

"You can stay if you want." She turned her attentions to the injured soldier. "Mac? Do you know who I am?" The most he could do was nod. Please God, let this work, Rebecca prayed. "I want you to open your eyes and look at me. Come on. Open your eyes and look at me."

Before she touched, she felt his agony. But he endured it quietly until she leaned over him and placed one hand flat on his forehead and the other over his heart. He jumped as if hit by an electrical charge.

Jamie, again, could not describe, nor fully comprehend, the magnitude of what he was experiencing.

It wasn't Rebecca Miller leaning over Macpherson.

It was an angel. He couldn't even see Macpherson. The light was too intense. The only thing he could hear was the beat of his own heart. And there was a smell, too, of roses. Roses and sulfur.

Meanwhile, Kelly witnessed phenomena of a different kind. Amid the rose-scented, gold-colored fog that had enveloped the room, another being—he had no other word for it—had transposed itself into the woman. It was male, that much he knew.

Mac felt nothing except a dull aching, replaced by fizzing sensations where a moment ago, agony had lived. He didn't concentrate on what his body told him because there was an angel touching him. She smelled of roses, her touch was hot. Her touch was Love. He never wanted it to end but end it did, and when it did, there was a total absence of pain.

Whoever, whatever, had taken over the woman's body retreated. Rebecca lifted her hands and stepped back. The room was dimming and she couldn't focus. Kelly saw it happening before it occurred and caught her as she fainted.

Macpherson sat up on the treatment table. Twenty minutes ago, there'd been a compound fracture six inches below his knee, and his ankle had snapped, leaving his foot rotated 180 degrees. There was nothing now to show that any injury whatsoever had occurred, except for some blood on the table and a scissored uniform on the floor, a bright red wrist and bruising across his chest.

And the three men were staring at the girl who was passed out in Kelly's arms.

"She fucking what?"

Kelly had to say it again, not that repetition made it easier to digest for either of them. "She healed Macpherson."

Silence.

"But… how can she do that?"

"NFI, Pete. Faraday was present. I don't know if what he experienced will correspond with what I witnessed."

"So what exactly did you see?"

Kelly's hands were still shaking somewhat when he scratched his head and replied with a shrug. But say it he did. Eventually. "An angel."

"An angel. Oh, for fuck's sake."

Kelly inspected his fingernails.

"You say Macpherson's fit now?" Pete asked.

"Fitter than before, I believe."

"How'd she do it?"

"I don't know," Kelly lied. Or was it a lie? Had the healing taken place by her or through her?

"Jesus H. Christ, news of this had better not leak. Get the three of them in here. Now."

Kelly turned away for his own office, where for a minute or two, he needed to sit and think, before he had Faraday, Macpherson and Miller paged to report to the commanding officer. But he couldn't think.

Someone knocked on his door. Normally there was a knock and the visitor entered. Again, a soft knock. "Enter."

Rebecca peered in. She was fine now. When she'd woken, all she'd wanted was a cup of tea and for everybody to stop fussing. It was no big deal. But Kelly had sensed it was a big deal, because even she couldn't believe it when Mac walked by without a trace of a limp.

"Your timing's impeccable. The colonel wants to see you."

"I thought he would." She came in and closed the door behind her. Kelly hit the intercom and told Sam to page Macpherson and Faraday. "Can I sit down?"

He shrugged, non committal. He can't look at me, she thought. He doesn't know what to say or do. Nobody does. I can't blame them.

"What did you see?" she asked.

"NFI." Her face was blank, so he explained. "No fucking idea."

"Rubbish."

"What do you want from me? You asked me a question, I answered."

"Kelly, when are you going to take me seriously?"

"How serious, exactly, do you wish to be taken? What are you, Rebecca? Some kind of freak?"

He'd have hurt her less had he driven a knife into her heart and twisted it half a dozen times. He saw that in her eyes, immediately. And he knew he shouldn't have said it but he did not know how to apologize for what was, indeed, the truth. She was some kind of freak.

She inhaled deeply and he saw tears forming in her eyes but they never fell. Instead, she said softly, "The boss is next door, isn't he." And without waiting for a response, Rebecca was gone.

When she walked into the CO's office, there were another two chairs as yet unoccupied. She knew who they were for. The adjoining door opened and Kelly came in, and he stood to the side of the blue-eyed colonel, hands behind his back.

The silence was very thick. "You wanted to see me?" she asked.

Pete Hamill nodded but said nothing further until both Macpherson and Faraday entered. Macpherson was not in uniform. Mac took the seat next to Rebecca, and she knew that all he wanted to do was touch her hand but he sat, as she did, and as Jamie did, like a trio of misbehaving school kids brought before the principal, awaiting some kind of punishment for what misdemeanor, exactly, nobody in the room knew.

"Faraday?"

"Sir?"

"What the... what the hell happened today?"

"You got me there, sir. I don't know."

"Macpherson?"

"Sir, all I remember is free-falling, hitting the building. That's all."

"Rebecca?"

"Sir?" Faraday offered. "I was showing Miss Miller around the grounds and we were talking when suddenly she said, we need to go to the infirmary. I said I hadn't been paged. She said, that'll happen halfway down the stairs. It did. What I'm saying, sir, is that Miss Miller knew someone had been hurt before we did. Anyway, sir, the MO allowed her some time with Mac while he arranged the medevac and all she did was put her hands on him."

"Why would he do that, Faraday? Why would the MO allow this woman time with Macpherson?"

"Probably because she cured his arthritis, sir."

"Jamie, I told you that wasn't me."

He elbowed her to be quiet.

"Is this true?" Pete asked. Rebecca had no reply except for a noncommittal shrug. "When did you do this?"

"The first night I was here. We had a couple of whiskeys. He didn't believe I was a healer. I was going to ask you if I could help out down there, but I was going to choose the moment. I don't suppose the moment is now, is it."

"She's good, sir. I only stayed in the treatment room because she wanted me there. And all she did was touch. Nothing else. Just touch. It was fucking amazing. Sorry, Miss."

Pete was ignoring virtually everything Jamie tried to say. "Is it true you saw this accident occur before it occurred?"

Rebecca looked at Kelly and their gazes met, momentarily. She looked away first. "Yes, it's true."

"Why wasn't I told?"

"I didn't think you'd want to be told."

"In future, you will tell me everything. Is that clear?"

"You might regret saying that."

Amusement crossed Kelly's eyes.

"I believe I already do, Miss Miller. So you do this all the time?"

"What?"

"This. This miracle stuff." He pointed to the water dispenser in the corner of his office. "Because if you do, you might want to turn that into wine while we're at it? A smooth, deep merlot would be good."

Kelly grimaced and looked the other way. Mac grabbed her hand, held tight and Rebecca squeezed, reassuringly. "I'll pretend I never heard you say that."

But there was no apology and there never would be.

She looked at Kelly. He'd called her a freak and he'd meant it. Now the other one was asking her to turn water into wine. She had two allies here: Jamie and Mac. "I heal when the need arises and only if I have permission of the injured or ill party."

"This true, Macpherson?"

"Sir? Yes, sir."

Jamie added, "She's good, sir. I'd have her working with me any day."

"Was I speaking to you, Faraday?"

Rebecca sighed. "Can we lighten up a little here? If you want the truth, I didn't think I could do much for Mac, what with the compound fracture and the foot all back to front, plus the ribs and the internal bleeding and the wrist. All I wanted to do was take away some of his pain so he wouldn't need any more morphine. That's all I was trying to do. I never expected that."

"But you did more than simply take away Macpherson's pain, didn't you."

"Am I in trouble for helping him? For saving you from being one man short?"

"I don't know, as yet, what you are, Rebecca. Faraday, I want an incident report. That will be all."

Jamie was excused. His next task was to write out what had occurred and not make it seem science fiction. He didn't know where to begin let alone what to say.

"Sergeant. Did you run a safety check on the equipment?"

"At a glance, it looked fine, sir."

"But you didn't run a full safety check."

"There wasn't exactly time, sir."

"And you feel?"

"Fine, sir. Fine. Better than I did when I woke up this morning if you want the truth."

Mac was also excused. There was no trace of any injury as he headed for the door. But before he left he smiled at Rebecca and she returned it.

"You will not do anything like this again, do you hear me?"

Rebecca tried to meet the CO's blue gaze. There was no politically correct ice today, only confusion. On his mind lay the questions on everyone's mind, including Rebecca's. How did she do it? She'd never healed like that before—not as quickly or completely. She was also seated relatively close to his computer and it hadn't caught fire yet. She hadn't blown any light bulbs. Had there been some kind of transformation during her re-birth to life?

"Did you hear what I said?" His voice was raised. Impatient. Confused.

"I heard what you said. I can't make promises I know I'll break."

"You will assure me that you will never do anything like that again."

Silence.

"I am waiting for a response."

"If you wait long enough you'll grow cobwebs, pal."

Kelly closed his eyes. Why does she have so little respect?

"Respect, Commander Nolan, is not a one way street. It's something that's earned. It's not a right. Notice, please, that I'm not wearing a uniform. I am a civilian and you have no right to tell me what it is I can or cannot do. Is that understood? Good. I'm outa here. Good bye." She rose, took half a step and heard:

"You will sit down! I haven't finished with you!"

She turned quickly. "Bullshit! You were finished with me before I left Australia. You hoped the plane would crash so you wouldn't have to deal with me. Well, guess what, Pete? Sit on it and spin, buddy! I take orders from no one. Is that clear?" Rebecca slammed the door so hard that his jacket fell off its hook.

Pete Hamill stared at his bronze eagle but saw nothing. "What happened to the new age love, light and laughter space cadet?"

"Want me to go after her?"

"No. No, no. Let her go. She'll apologize."

Kelly was not optimistic about an apology in the near or distant future. Truth known, he agreed with her sentiments. Firstly, he should never have told her she was a freak, and Pete should have refrained from asking her to turn his water into merlot. As for the order to refrain from healing ... that'd be like asking her to stop breathing voluntarily. "She warned me about the accident."

"When?"

"Her first night here. I thought she'd tell you but she didn't. So I'm telling you now. I was warned. This could have been avoided."

"Well, at least we know she has loyalty to someone around here."

"It's time we took her seriously."

"Are you emotionally involved already?"

"Me? Hardly."

"You expect me to believe this horse-shit? I know who she is. She's the same girl you've been painting since the Eisenhower. How many years is that?"

"It's coincidence."

"Coincidence, my ass."

"She also told me Leon Carter had no future."

"What's that mean in my language?"

"It means he'll die soon. And if he does, Samperi becomes of head of operations and that's been his goal for five years now. What I'm saying is when she gives us a warning, maybe it means the destined outcome can be altered if the necessary precautions are taken. It's almost as if her presence here is a warning in itself about John Glover's candidacy."

"You're serious?"

"I've been quietly observing. If the warnings are heeded, then maybe what is fated will occur i.e. we get ourselves another black President. If we ignore it, we get another white one. Sounds simplistic but it's the conclusion I've drawn."

"You believe this shit? She's nothing but a decoy."

"Is she? Think about it. How much proof do we need?" Kelly sighed and rose to his feet slowly. "Can I make a suggestion?"

"Please do. I don't know what the fuck to do with her."

"She's a woman, not 'a female civilian'. She's idealistic and spiritual. She doesn't know her ass from her elbow in a place like this, but she's trying. She's doing her job, we're doing ours so we've got to compromise somewhere. We need her co-operation."

"And?"

"Instead of treating her like a POW, we treat her like a human being."

"I'm pleased you never said treat her like a lady."

Kelly left the colonel's office, finished up some remaining paperwork—mainly his report on the accident that occurred on area 17B—and went in search of Rebecca. She wasn't in her room. She wasn't in the mess, or in the bar. She was, instead, sitting in the rose garden, coatless, shivering and alone except for the feline that ate kitchen scraps and kept rodents in check. Ceeforcat was sleeping on her lap, responding to caresses. No one could ever get close enough to touch him.

Kelly sat down beside her. The ancient bench seat creaked in protest and the cat took fright but a simple touch from Rebecca brought calm once again and he settled. "You're not supposed to be out here on your own."

"So smack me." Rebecca held out her hand. Kelly ignored the gesture. She knew he would. "If you're lucky I might get kidnapped and you guys could have your lives back."

Kelly wondered why she said that. "The CO and I have come to the conclusion that our attitude needs attention."

"Really? Shall we all have personality transplants?"

"Look, Rebecca…"

"Kelly, you don't have to say a thing. I didn't mean to explode. It just … happened. I don't deal with authority very well."

"No shit, Sherlock." Kelly peeled a layer off and put the padded shirt over her shoulders. "If you want the men to call you Rebecca, they can. You've got free run of the place, however, if you need to go outside of these grounds, you'll see me first."

"Does free run include a phone call? I need to call Annie. She'll be out of her mind by now."

"Who's Annie?"

"My assistant. She was going to come with me but she couldn't leave her little boy. He's still a baby and her ex is … yes, well. She's about the only friend I've got. A real one at least. I need to call her. I won't tell her where I am exactly, I just want her to know I'm ok. I can't lie very well, is all, so you'll have to help me come up with something believable."

"How about … you've met someone and you're going to stay longer than you anticipated? Something like that."

"Oh, that won't work."

"It happens all the time. Boy meets girl. Holiday romances."

"Come off it. Me? What planet are you from? Annie knows me."

"Are you gay?"

"No. Are you?"

Kelly rolled his eyes and for a moment the only sound was the Ceeforcat's loud purring.

"Guys don't like me, Commander. They're only interested in what I can do. Not in me. Not who I am. I have the sexual magnetism of a dying cockroach."

"Excuse me?"

"I have never got past a first date in my life."

"How come?"

"NFI. If I knew the answer I'd have half a dozen kids and be living in suburbia by now." She sighed. "Nah. I can't tell Annie I've met somebody. She'd know it was a lie."

"So tell her the truth."

"What? That I'm living with a mob of men in uniform who are all highly trained killers and lethal weapons? She'd wet her pants laughing. She'd never believe it. Who would?"

"Exactly. Want to call her now?"

"Annie?"

Over the speaker phone in Kelly's office, the other voice was set on auto pilot. Rebecca waited for a break in the traffic of excited and mostly angry words. "Yes, I know you've been worried. I know I should have called and yes I should have taken my mobile phone…"

Where the hell are you? I rang the hotel but they hadn't heard of you. I've been out of my mind! Where are you!

"I'm in Wiltshire, living with a unit of counter terrorist commandos until the US Presidential election is over."

There was a stunned silence.

You've met somebody haven't you. Is he nice? What's he do? Is he rich? Nice looking? How old is he?

Kelly was trying not to smile because Rebecca's friend was on a roll, firing questions and not waiting for responses.

I told you that you'd meet somebody but you wouldn't believe me… He's tall, dark and handsome, isn't he. And he's stinking rich, too. Dammit. Has he got a brother? A father? A clone? So is he any good in the sack? You finally got yourself a live one, huh! Fantastic! Have a good shag for me, willya? Now don't forget, I want a claddagh but it has to be from Ireland, and a royal Stewart tartan when you get to Edinburgh and…

On and on and on went Annie's shopping list.

"Annie! Annie, I've got to go. Give Michael a big hug and tell him I love him, will you? You too, Annie. I love you, too. Bye, Annie. Bye." Rebecca hung up and sighed aloud. "She could talk under wet cement."

"Who's Michael?"

"Annie's two year old son. I cut the cord when he was born. He's the light of my life and the closest I'll ever get to having a child of my own. Can we eat now? Starvin' Marvin."

But she wouldn't sit with him in the mess—she always went straight to Macpherson.

It took a week of observation before Kelly realized that what she'd said had been, basically, true. Nobody wanted to see past what she did. The men, he knew, because he was one himself, all regarded her with a sense of wonderment. Yes, she was attractive, and friendly, and she had the weirdest sense of humor he'd ever known, but 99% of questions she was asked pertained to what she did. Nobody, but nobody, asked about the woman.

So she sat with Macpherson at mealtimes and he was polite and told sick Irish jokes guaranteed to make her laugh, but even Mac's attitude had changed since his accident. Faraday had seen an angel. God knew what Mac had seen because he wasn't saying. Mac was in love and too scared to do anything about it.

It was as if she were something untouchable, unreachable. She immediately commanded respect. Rarely did anyone use her Christian name even though they could.

The men's reactions were not what Kelly had expected.

There had been a female presence on base only once before. Sandy, a nurse, had lasted barely a month before she transferred out. But with Miller it was different. There were no queues to dance with her. Not like there were with Sandy. Rebecca spent most of her rec time sitting on her own at the small table she now favored in the bar. It looked out onto the garden.

No one bought her a drink, or asked her to dance, or simply talked to her for the sake of conversation. Everybody had to have a reason before she was approached.

Sandy hadn't been able to cope with the attention. It had been a different kind of attention.

So, it took a week of observation before Kelly realized that what she'd said to him, about never getting past a first date, was indeed the truth. They're only interested in what I can do. Not who I am.

What had she said? How she'd give anything to be a normal person for just one, lousy day? How guys weren't attracted to her: not in a regular male-to-female way?

Kelly, from observation alone, knew that this, for her, was life. It was normal. It had always been this way and nothing would change it. He guessed she'd had a lonely childhood because she was different. The isolation would have been worse during her teenage years because she was different, and most people only tolerated such a difference while it was of use to them. That came from his own personal experience.

She liked the music most of all—not what came from the juke box, but the music the boys made for themselves. And Kelly knew, too, that she was only waiting to be asked. Would you like to help us out with a number? Hey Rebecca, get up here and sing, huh? That's okay, we can't sing either, what the hell?

It never happened.

She spent her life observing a world she wasn't welcome in.

The night she saw Leon Carter die was like any other. She ate, talked to a few men who needed an ear and some advice, she had a couple of wines in the bar, decided she couldn't sit through another Rambo ever again, and went up to bed. She hardly spoke to Kelly of late because there was nothing of importance to discuss. It was a quick hello, usually in passing. He could not approach her without good reason and damned if he could even imagine a reason.

But the night she 'saw' Leon Carter die, he sensed beforehand when she was retiring and departed earlier than usual. Maybe if she saw him on the stairs or in the corridor, she'd stop and talk. Or at least say hello, and not send him her shy smile that was over before it began.

She just walked quietly by, towards her room. Kelly was going into his. He looked over and smiled. "How you doin'?"

"I'm okay, Commander. You?" She looked up into his eyes and tried to smile, and she let herself into her room.

And the realization of what was wrong hit him like a brick between the eyes. "Rebecca?"

She peeked out.

"You sure you're all right?"

"Yep. Fine." For a moment there was an uncomfortable silence. "Did you want to talk to me?"

"I'd like that," he said.

"All you had to do was join the queue."

Kelly walked into her room and she closed the door. Sadness emanated from her in waves. There was a sea of it in there, enough to drown in. Why? he wondered. She's nice. She's pretty. Why's she always so damned sad? "You're settling in well. It hasn't taken long."

"Since the lads have loosened up it's been better. I try not to see the uniforms anymore. So what do you want to know? If it's about the Senator, I can't help yet, but if it's about your wife or something like that, maybe. So here's the deal. I either hold your hand or I hold your watch, or …" He didn't have a wedding ring on.

"I need to apologize for calling you a freak."

"Why? You were only saying what everybody else was thinking. I'm used to it. Really. I am."

"No," Kelly said. "It was a stupid, inconsiderate thing to say."

"And I just said I'm used to it."

"I don't believe that."

"Look, Commander, when I was five years old I touched my dying grandmother and miracle, she got better. After three strokes, Nan was a vegetable, but there they were, taking her off life support because she opened her eyes and asked for a cup of tea and a piece of fruit cake. Don't look at me like that. It's true. After that my father re-named me That Thing. I wasn't Velcro anymore."

"Velcro?"

"He'd call me that because he had to peel me off him. This five year old kid who was the light of his life, suddenly became this thing that lived in his house. He wouldn't come anywhere near me. If I walked into the room, he'd get up and leave. I wasn't even allowed to sit at the dining table with him. There was always fear in his eyes and the day he walked out, I heard him tell my mother that I wasn't human."

"And you believed that?"

"I was a kid. Of course I believed it. It made sense. Sometimes I wonder that maybe he was right. I've always been ostracized from the mainstream and I've learnt to live with it. But I've been called a lot worse than freak. All right? Never apologize for a truth. Are we clear on this now?"

"I haven't been purposely avoiding you."

And her blue eyes caught his lie and tossed it back immediately. "You've got your job and you had it long before I came here. It's just that you're the only person apart from Mac who never asks me for anything and that's refreshing. But yes, it did hurt when you called me that because I'd hoped you'd know better. I was wrong. It happens. But you want to ask me something now, so what is it?"

"I only wanted to touch base. Nothing more," he lied.

Rebecca sighed. "What's her name?" she asked quietly.

"Who?"

"Your wife."

"Marianne."

"Do you have any kids?"

"Alive? No. Our son was stillborn eight years ago, this spring."

"Paul?"

"Paul."

"I'm sorry," she said quietly.

"So am I," Kelly said. He wanted to linger a little more, but damned if he could think of anything to say, so he wished her goodnight and closed the door behind him. He wasn't sure what might have happened if he stayed.

Chapter 6

KELLY WOKE TO THE SOUND of quick tapping on his door. He looked at the time. It was three thirty. No alarms, no pagers. Dressed only in boxers and dog tags and half asleep, he opened the door.

Rebecca stood in the corridor, wearing a tee shirt that reached her thighs. She had nice legs. He looked up to her face. Was there anybody home there? Was she sleepwalking? And then she spoke. Her voice was expressionless. "Leon Carter's going to die."

"Say again?"

"Leon Carter. He's going to die. A car accident."

Kelly stepped aside and let her in. He turned the light on and Rebecca shied from it. "Did you dream this?" he asked.

"I'm not sure. I think so. It was raining. The road was slippery and he went under a truck. I was in the car with him. It happened in the day time. It was raining. Did I just say that?"

"You're referring to an event which is yet to occur but you're speaking in past tense. How can you be in the vehicle with him?"

"I don't know. But I was in the car. Some kind of a Ford I think. It's dark red. We were driving on a motorway, and we were both singing along to Bob Seger when it happened. Fire Lake." Rebecca said nothing more.

"Bob Seger?"

"Fire Lake. Do you know it?" She sang a few bars.

Yes, he knew it. Vaguely. "And you? Were you hurt?"

"I don't know. This only works for other people. I get squat about myself."

"You told me you'd die if you went near the chopper."

"And that was a one-off. I'll have to tell Pete about this. What time does he start work?"

"You leave it to me."

"Is that so we don't end up screaming at each other again?"

"One of the reasons, yes."

She had to look away from the sight of him half naked, hair tousled. He was well muscled, well proportioned, and very fit. She felt almost shy whenever he was close, so she looked at the room instead. It was like a junk shop, but at least it had character. Her attention was drawn to the tomahawk on the wall, an ornate thing, intricately carved. And then she saw who it once belonged to: one of Kelly's ancestors. The facial features were similar but the warrior's hair was to his waist. He smiled at Rebecca warmly and was gone. Kelly's a healer, she thought. He doesn't know it. "I should let you get back to sleep."

"There's no chance of that now." He was regarding her oddly. "Couldn't you have waited till morning?"

"Do you always wake up such a grumble bum?"

"Mid way through a damned good dream, yes I do."

Next thing he knew he was staring at a closed door.

"I want to know why I wasn't informed."

"You're informed now," Pete said, abruptly.

"I was under the impression that if they wanted access, they gained access on our terms."

"Look, Kelly. Carter's coming to pick her up this morning and he'll bring her back tomorrow night. They've set up some kind of paranormal testing facility in a safe house in north London. She'll be fine with Carter. She liked him."

"I'll take her."

"Carter will take her and Carter will bring her back."

"I got a visit at three thirty this morning. Miller informed me that Carter will die in an RTA and she is in the vehicle with him. So before we make another move, can you get on the phone and ask him what he will be driving today. Also ask him what music he plays. If he comes back at you with a dark red Ford and Bob Seger's Greatest Hits, I take her to London. Call him. Please." But Pete didn't lift the phone. "Indulge me."

"I don't have to. He drives a red Ford and he plays nothing but Bob Seger."

Rebecca packed a change of clothing, knowing that indeed, there was at least one person not willing to risk disbelief. And, better still, Kelly was defrosting. Or at least, that was what she thought until she met him in the foyer. He wasn't in uniform and she barely recognized him. Did he always dress in black even when he didn't have to? Be still oh beating heart, she thought. I do feel I've won him in a raffle. Twenty four hours. Him and me. Together. Alone. It was a wonderful daydream, until she heard, "Move your butt, we don't have all day."

"Yeah, yeah, keep your shirt on."

Kelly unlocked his dark blue BMW sports, threw her bag into the trunk. She climbed in and hardly had time to put on the seatbelt before he was reversing out and taking the tree-lined drive at lift-off speed. If it took two hours to get to London from here, he'd make it in one.

Nothing was said for quite some time. Once she became used to Kelly's two driving speeds, stop and fast, she almost started to relax. Almost.

"I never asked you to drive me. For all I know, what I saw this morning might have been just a mirror of my fears and that was only because when I shook hands with Leon Carter I got squat. I might be wrong. I might be wrong about everything. This might be the biggest waste of time…"

He changed the subject and pointed to a church spire in the distance. "Salisbury Cathedral. Heard of it?"

"Of course I've heard of it. I had planned to visit it. Where's Stonehenge?"

"Maybe, just maybe, we might go there on the way home. You can't get close. It's all hype and full of tourists. And no, I don't want your theories on a pile of old rocks and Druidism."

She stayed quiet for a little while. Now that they were able to talk freely, and it seemed like an entirely new person was beside her, driving the car, she couldn't think of much to say. If anything, she felt nervous and a little shy but why, she had no idea. He seemed brighter and more alive away from the base. This, she thought, must be the real Kelly.

Who was married. The M Word. All the semi-decent ones, courageous ones, possibly even breathing ones were already accounted for. Best to simply get on with it, get the job done and go home. She had to keep this in perspective. There was no other choice. She glanced at him. He smelled good, too. Fark, he's gorgeous, she thought, but I wish he'd take those sunglasses off.

Kelly took his sunglasses off and threw them on the dash.

Rebecca's heart almost stood still. Say something intelligent, her mind screamed. Now's your chance. Nothing intelligent would come yet she couldn't tolerate the silence. Rebecca moved in the leather seat and a noise, rather akin to a loud fart, reverberated around the interior. Without missing a beat, Kelly said, "Keep calling, sir, we'll find you."

"That wasn't me, it was the seat!" Oh the shame, and she had nowhere to run. Nowhere to hide, and she was too slow for any quick-witted response. And worse, he was quietly amused. "Stop it," she said.

"Your eyes are very blue when you're embarrassed," he noted.

She could say nothing to that: her face was heating again. Something intelligent was needed and fast. "Do you know much about this paranormal testing?"

"Are you nervous about it?" he asked.

"No. Are you?"

"I'm not being tested."

"But you should be. Who's the Indian?"

"Excuse me?"

"The Indian with hair down to his bum?"

"White Raven. My maternal great grandfather. Why?"

"He's with you all the time."

"Yes, I know."

"He's a healer. That's what he used to do."

"Yes, I know. He was a shaman."

"And you inherited the gift."

"Shall we change the subject?"

"What to? Fart jokes?" Rebecca asked.

"If you feel the need. Be my guest."

Had she known him better she may have been amused but he was far too quick for comfort. Rebecca admitted defeat before the battle of wits began. "Do you think John Glover will ever be President?"

"Yes, providing he doesn't get a bullet between the eyes."

That quip killed any conversation for the next couple of miles until they reached Salisbury. "Can I ask you something?" Kelly said as he waited for an old lady to shuffle across the street in the middle of town.

"Is it a 'join the queue' kind of question?"

"Possibly. Faraday said that when you were healing Macpherson, he saw an angel in you."

Rebecca laughed aloud. She was genuinely surprised. "Me? An angel?"

"He swears that is what he saw. Faraday is not prone to fantasy. And Macpherson refuses to say what he experienced."

"Mac was topped with morphine and Jamie must have been hallucinating. And if you think I might be an angel, you are definitely hallucinating. What about you? What did you see?"

"I saw a miracle as it happened, so I'm thinking that maybe you don't realize what you are," Kelly said softly. "Hear me out, Rebecca. You told me about your father and I can understand that. I've come to learn that people as a whole react aggressively to what they fear. People fear anything that's different, out of the norm, extraordinary. You must admit you are extraordinary."

Rebecca couldn't decide if it was a compliment or not.

"The process, which I think I've figured out, is that we, and I mean humanity here, evolve by experiencing many different kinds of lives. You with me?"

"I can't avoid it, can I."

"After a few thousand lifetimes, we've evolved to the point where coming back isn't necessary anymore. But now and then a few do come back, maybe because they have to, there's unfinished business, or they want to. It's by choice. Now personally, I think people like Mohammad and Jesus Christ, I think they came back by choice, not need. Do you believe that?"

He was referring to reincarnation, of course, and the process as she perceived it. "I'm listening."

"So we come to you. All these things you can do, naturally, without any effort, plus your inability to form karmic relationships could be because you do not need any more ties to the earth plane. Have you ever thought that perhaps you've evolved to the point where this is your last time here?"

"Me?" she squeaked. "I'm not evolved. For fuck's sake, I only do what I do because I can do it. Helping people is what I'm good at. It's the only thing I'm good at."

"I've been watching you. Hearing what you say. You're desperate to fit in. To be normal. But you're always distanced. You go through life on your own, because you've always been on your own, and you mistakenly believe you will always be on your own. Maybe there's a reason you never got past a first date."

Rebecca said nothing.

"It's one of two possibilities. Either you're not meant to generate any more karma that'll keep you here, or you've been waiting."

"Waiting for what?"

"Waiting for me."

For a moment her heart stopped beating. She looked away, knowing she'd heard a truth. Indeed, he was the reason she came back. It had nothing to do with John Glover.

"I'll tell you what I know, Commander. I'm here to help you bodyguard a senator who's running for the presidency. That's why I'm here. When it's over, I'm going home. You'll either get that job you want at the Pentagon, or your old one back in Pensacola. Is there any music?"

"What job at the Pentagon?"

"The job you hoped you'd eventually get by marrying a politician's daughter."

"Okay, smart ass. What'd I do in Pensacola?"

For a moment there was silence.

"Buddies? Bud? Buds? I don't know the terminology but you taught warfare. Special warfare. And you dived a lot. Jumped out of planes. You made soldiers crawl through mud while you shot at them and..."

"I've been painting you for fifteen years, Rebecca."

Silence.

"When I was on the Eisenhower—"

"The what?" she asked.

"The Eisenhower. We were in Australia. Brisbane, I think. Yeah, it was Brisbane…"

The hair on the back of Rebecca's neck prickled. "But… I went on board the Eisenhower when it was in Brisbane. I was 15 at the time."

They exchanged a glance.

"I'll never forget it. It was a really hot day. We had to stand in a queue for a long time to get on board. I didn't want to go but I knew if I didn't, I'd never hear the end of it, so I went along to shut her up. To stop her nagging me."

"Who?"

"My mother. She had this thing about men in uniforms, especially Americans. I think she lived for when an American ship came to town."

Silence ruled for quite some time.

"Kelly, I recognized the colonel instantly. He and my mother… Well, she was gorgeous."

Is he right? Has my life been on hold until now? Rebecca wondered. Is the reason I'm on my own because of some invisible RESERVED sign that others have always sensed? She looked at Kelly and thought, him? Me? Nah, he's too good looking.

"Do you like me?" he asked, breaking her reverie.

"Sorry?"

"Do you like me?"

"When you're not in uniform, you're all right." You're all right in uniform too but I won't say that aloud. You're bloody hot if you want the truth…

"Are you sexually attracted to me?"

"Ah..." She'd been shaking inside from being in such close proximity to this man. The past half hour had taken a week to pass. Take your gun and shoot me now, please, she silently pleaded. Put me out of my misery. I can't take any more of this.

"Are you sexually attracted to me?" he asked again, emphasizing each word.

"Why, Kelly? If I said no, I'd be lying. If I said yes, it wouldn't do me any good anyway." She was looking out of the window, trying to focus on the passing countryside. Trying to focus on anything except these soul-shattering questions he was firing at her. Nobody had ever talked to her like this before. She wasn't used to this personal, forensic questioning. He wasn't astounded by the miracles she could perform. He was asking about her. Rebecca Miller.

"So you are attracted to me."

She had to say it, there was no other choice.

"Yes! Yes, I am. At the airport, I wondered what was thumping in my ears till I realized it was only my heart. I am just like any other female you come on to whenever it suits you, and you damn well know it. Are you happy now? Is your ego nicely inflated?"

"Will you trust me, Rebecca?"

"Why are you doing this to me?" It was almost a scream. "What do you want? There must be something on your mind. God only knows why. If you're saying all this shit to make me feel better about myself, don't bother. Please. Don't bother. It's not working. If you really want to know, I feel like I won you in a fucking raffle!"

He laughed so much he had to wipe his eyes.

"Cosmic joke of immense proportion. That's all this is. A big fucking joke..."

They were on the motorway, dodging trucks, cars, and motorcycles in the rain. "Do you want a coffee?"

"No, but you do."

Kelly took the exit to the services, parked, but didn't get out of the car straight away. He sat quietly procrastinating. Rebecca wondered if he was waiting for the rain to ease.

"Your breasts do not offend me."

Rebecca closed her eyes. She was blushing so fiercely now, she thought she'd spontaneously combust.

"Has anybody ever told you how beautiful you are?"

And still she could not say a word, but the truth finally emerged. "No," she squeaked.

"Will you let me paint you?" he asked.

She stole a glance. He meant it. He actually meant it. "Will you make me beautiful?"

"I don't have to."

Rebecca wanted to take that smile and seal it in a jar and keep it in her heart forever. Even if it was the biggest lie she'd ever heard, it was still a treasured moment, words spoken by a raffle prize that would last twenty-four hours only. Better twenty-four hours than none at all. She felt alive when he was around. Alive and confused and embarrassed and shy, but still, alive. As if life was, suddenly, something to be enjoyed and not endured.

And then he was out of his car, the magic of the moment was gone. While she was fumbling for her handbag, he walked to the passenger side and opened the door for her. Rebecca looked up, surprised.

They dashed to the services entry, shook off the rain and went in.

Before he started the car, Kelly dealt with the sat nav, planning the route to the safe-house nestled snugly in suburbia. Squirrel Heath.

She curled in the seat and dozed, on and off, for the rest of the ride. When Kelly got to the mock Tudor high set safe house, three cars and a rental van were parked on the footpath because the street was extremely narrow. Kelly pulled up in the drive and nudged Rebecca awake.

Standing in the doorway, waiting to greet them, was Leon Carter.

"What if I was wrong about him?" she asked.

"What if you were right?" Kelly replied.

The carpeting was thick and soft. A staircase led to what presumably were bedrooms on the second level. Leon led them through an ante room and into the living room, set up in such a way that video cameras would run simultaneously from eight different angles. Rebecca had never seen cameras like these before.

The investigators came in—three men of varying ages and nationalities, and, Rebecca was pleased to note, a woman, too. She looked Hispanic, dark eyes, bottle-auburn hair.

Rebecca was directed to sit facing the corner, and was hooked up to an assortment of machines that monitored brain activity, heart rate, stress levels. Finally, she was blindfolded.

The first questions were controls, so that a sense of normality could be gauged from her physiological reactions. It was, basically, an intricate lie detector.

The woman, who as yet had not been introduced, but was someone Kelly obviously knew, sat at a table the furthest distance from the subject as possible. The curtains were drawn, there were no reflections, no mirrors, no way for Rebecca to know the woman was in the room. The first task was to tell the investigators what symbol was being displayed. The answer came automatically.

"Zener cards. A blue star of David."

The female control lifted a finger, the gesture for affirmative. Next, she picked up two photographs and while she decided which one to show:

"A picture of a child's toy... is it a toy train? No. A truck."

Again, the affirmative gesture of two fingers, but before the woman could choose her next object, she heard, "Dawn, it's your birthday today and no one remembered this morning. You feel forgotten. Abandoned. You're hurting inside because you knows the names you're called behind your back and you feel you'll never gain respect. But that's not the case. Not at all. You'll be the boss soon, Dawn. And you're getting a new house from the divorce settlement and you'll remarry… your first love… Richard? No, Rick. Yeah, Rick. There's another baby here, too, if you so choose to take that path. No, sorry, it's already been offered. You haven't shown the ring to anyone yet. You don't want people to talk, and by the way, Rick hasn't forgotten your birthday."

Dawn Lindsay's face went white. Again the finger lifted, then all fingers splayed in the air. She packed up her objects and vacated the seat, quickly.

"So who's next? Are we going to do this all day?"

A younger man took the seat. There was a deep silence for some time. "I've got a message for Anthony and it's from Claudio. Claudio was an old man when he passed over. He says he is not angry that you weren't there to say goodbye. He's telling me you must look to today. Don't live for yesterday. He says if you hold too tight to yesterday you can't see today let alone tomorrow…"

She 'read' everybody in the room, except Kelly, while she was blindfolded, facing the opposite way and had no way of knowing by physical senses, who was sitting at the table. And there had been few questions and no feedback whatsoever.

Still blindfolded and facing the corner. An hour and a half had passed already. Dawn came in and handed Kelly a mug of coffee. She smiled at him and didn't say a word. She didn't have to. "Who's the unlucky guy?" Kelly asked.

"Rick Newton."

"Congratulations."

"Thanks, Kel."

Dawn and Kelly watched while the chief investigator placed a red stiletto heeled shoe on the table. It was encased in a plastic bag and tagged as police evidence. "Can I see it?"

"We'd prefer you didn't."

Rebecca sat, blindfolded, plastic bag in hand and for quite some time, nothing happened.

"It's a woman's shoe. Size 9. She's… not a she at all. I get a male who wants to be female. He's been through the preliminaries, the hormone treatments, things like that. But not the final operations… I see a fairgrounds. Warwick. Warwickshire? A river, no, it's man made. A canal. A houseboat but it's not what I'd recognize as a houseboat. It's long, narrow. A canal boat? He, sorry she… Oh, Jesus. Can someone please tell me what's expected here?"

"Your impressions only, my dear," came a Germanic voice in reply.

"There's too much fear. But that's not the word. Terror doesn't fit, either. I can't get past it. No, I don't want to do this. Take it away."

But nobody came to take the bag. "Where is the body, Rebecca?" the Swiss investigator asked.

"Scattered," she said quietly. "You will never find all of it. Just pieces. This shoe is just the start… What? Really?" It seemed as if she were having a silent conversation with an unseen entity. "I'm told you're to find the clown. A Croatian at the fairgrounds. Can we break now, please?"

"Yes, soon. Soon."

The physiological reactions eased back to normal moments after the bagged shoe was taken away.

The blindfold was removed, and the first person she saw was Kelly. He was sipping on a coffee, and standing with the Hispanic woman. They were whispering to each other.

There was an assortment of objects on the table. Rebecca knew what was expected without being told. "You may choose," the Swiss investigator said. Of what lay before her—two watches, two rings, a sealed envelope containing a photo of, she knew, John Glover in the days of old when he was a fighter pilot—she immediately reached for the lock of hair tied by a tiny lilac colored ribbon. Child's hair. The Swiss parapsychologist was fully attentive now. She knew he would be.

Rebecca closed her fingers over the lock of hair. "The child was deceased when this hair was cut. I see her in a white casket. Her favorite toy, a red rag doll, is with her. She's telling me the doll's name is... I can't say it. I'm sorry. I don't speak German." Rebecca took a deep breath and continued. "She's dressed in pink. White shoes... Her favorite shoes. She's here now, telling me she died of leukemia when she was six... sorry, seven years old. Her name is Eliza, and she wants to tell you, John, that she's watching her family all the time." Rebecca paused for a moment.

Kelly could not take his eyes from her face.

"She's here now, asking me why you still don't believe. She says that she was at the funeral home when you cut her hair and tied it with this ribbon."

"And when did this child die?" the Swiss scientist asked.

"May third, 1960. She tells me the angels came to take her hand when you and her mother went to get something to eat. You'd been by her bedside for three days."

"Is Mary with her?"

Silence for a moment. To Kelly it seemed as if she were having a silent conversation.

"She knows of no Mary but says Agnetha came last year, just after the wedding. She says it was a car accident. She wants to talk to you, her daddy. She says you want to die now, but it is not your turn for a long time yet." The Swiss scientist caught his breath hard, so hard that everyone in the room heard it. "Why don't you believe? How much proof do you need? The love your child has for you is overwhelming and it still exists. Why do you continue to deny it? Your scientific search for answers is futile because you already have the answers in your heart. Forget the physics and technology. Until there is a science of the spirit, there can be no tangible answers. It's all here and you know it."

Rebecca touched her heart and paused for a moment.

"Believe me when I say your daughter's death was not a reflection of your failure. Her death happened because it was her time. It had nothing to do with you or what you could or could not do."

She put the lock of hair down and picked up the envelope. "Nice try, Leon." She tossed it down again. "John Glover. He's flying an F15 in the Gulf War. If I told you there are too many variables for an outcome to be known just now, what would you say?"

"I'd say I believe you, Rebecca."

"And do you always play Bob Seger in your car? Fire Lake, right? That's your favorite?"

His smile was huge. "How'd you know that?" he asked.

Rebecca glanced at Kelly and the expression needed no analysis. "Don't drive on the M4 in the rain, Leon."

"Okay," he said.

She went back to the objects. "The commander's watch. I don't want that..." She picked up the other watch. "Dawn? You found it by mistake, didn't you. So why are you telling yourself it's not there? If you don't make that call, you know what the outcome will be. You have two choices. You have two paths to follow. Only one path has any viable future. All you need do is use the telephone. Do you understand what I'm saying here?"

Dawn, literally shaken, nodded.

"Good. And when you do make the call, your life changes for the better. You may think it's ending but there's a whole new world waiting for you. It's as if life is only beginning. But if you don't make that call and get... you know what I mean. I'll say no more."

Rebecca watched impassively as the woman retreated to the kitchen.

"Why don't we take five?"

All agreed with Leon's suggestion, and as Rebecca was disconnected from the electronics, she looked down at Kelly's watch. It was two thirty in the afternoon. They had arrived at ten thirty. She picked the watch up and was hit by a wave of love so intense and powerful that it almost took her breath away. And then it changed. He was in a desert. He was using a sniper rifle... She dropped the watch as if it had burned her hand. "I need some air" she said quickly, and grabbing her bag, she went out into the back garden, kicked off her shoes and stood barefoot on the soft grass.

Dawn leaned against the back door. She couldn't look at Rebecca when she said, "Rick found the lump, not me. I've been trying to ignore it but he won't let me."

"Someone once told me the body weeps the tears the mind refuses to shed. It's true for you, isn't it, Dawn."

Dawn nodded. "I'll make the appointment. How did you know?"

"I can see it."

"But how? How did you know all that about me? How'd you know Rick was my first love? The divorce, the engagement. My birthday... I don't understand how you can be so good and we never took any notice until now."

"My question is, what's ahead. What's all this really for?" Silence replied as Rebecca knew it would. "How long have you been working with the CIA?" she asked.

"Eighteen years. I've been over here for six. So what's with you and Kelly?"

"Nothing. Why?"

Dawn laughed, sipped on her coffee and said "I'm not blind," as she walked away, still amused. And she looked at Kelly and laughed. He was coming out with a cup of tea for Rebecca.

"Thanks."

"You're welcome."

Rebecca sipped. Perfect. 'How do you know how I take my tea?"

"I must be psychic. What's wrong with Dawn?"

"None of your business."

"You were talking about me."

"You're paranoid."

Silence for a while. A passenger jet roared overhead on its way in to Heathrow. "I saw the little girl," Kelly said. "They also caught her image on Kirlian video."

"The Swiss guy will find a way to debunk it using his science. Look around this garden and tell me what you see."

"Three o'clock, the window on the left by the chimney, a neighbor watching from an upstairs window. So what do you see?"

"There's enough dead people here to fill a football stadium and if they had but half a chance to talk to me, they would. All at once, too. I might be something amazing to everybody in there but trust me, it's always been like this. It's nothing special for me. Dead, alive, no difference. So what's all this for? Really? Does it have anything to do with John Glover visiting the UK?"

"I doubt it."

"Do they expect me to work for them?"

"I hope not."

"They do. Fine. They've got one more hour and then I want to go."

If she thought he'd object, she was mistaken. He nodded.

So far, what had been caught on the Kirlian and infra red cameras were outline images of the old man who appeared to be relaying a message to his son via Rebecca; a young woman-man in a red sequined dress; and a little girl who had never left her father's side, even after death. But there was one image they could not explain: the figure of a tall, long-haired man, in white robe and reed sandals, invisible to the naked eye but three-dimensional on video: Emmanuel.

"Who is your gate-keeper?" the Swiss scientist asked once she was seated and wired again.

"If a name is necessary, he prefers to be known as Emmanuel."

"Where is he from?"

"He says it is not important."

"He is one of The Nine, yes?"

"He says it is not important and he will keep saying it until you tire of asking ridiculous, irrelevant questions. This is just wasting our time."

"He is your intermediary?"

Rebecca's sigh was audible. "He's my friend and teacher. He's been with me all of my life."

"Why do you use your mediumistic abilities?"

"Why? To help people realize there is no such thing as death. That's the first step towards spiritual freedom—letting go of the fear of death."

"Tell us where you went after you died."

"Somewhere else. Somewhere familiar to me. It was home, I suppose. I can't describe it with words."

"Was it earth like?"

"I just said I can't describe it with words! Even if I could…"

The Swiss scientist waited patiently.

"Language is not enough. I'm sorry."

"Why did you come back?"

She looked at Kelly but he wasn't watching. He was studying his shoes. "I had something important to finish."

"And when it is finished?"

"I don't know. I never know what's ahead for me."

I do, Kelly thought. I know what's ahead for you. You and me, that's what's ahead for us both. If you'll let it happen.

"You called this place home, not heaven?"

"Home, heaven. Just words. How can I explain? While we're here we think this life is reality. But when you pass over you know, instantly, that life here was just a very short dream. Reality is on the other side. It's where we plan for our next dream. It's where we meet our friends, our enemies, where we choose what experiences we'll need to further our evolvement."

"So you tend to lean towards Theosophical philosophy?"

"What is Theosophical philosophy?"

"Are you what is called an angel, Rebecca?"

"Not this again."

"You have been described as one."

"Somebody else's perspective is not mine." How did they know about that? she wondered.

"Your aura, the electromagnetic field surrounding your physical body measures eighty-seven feet from core to extremity, Rebecca, and its primary color is shown to be gold."

"You're pulling my leg."

"This is not a joke. Are you aware that ascended masters have auras of gold which extend over one hundred feet?"

"What's an ascended master?"

"How is it that you were shot in the heart with a large caliber bullet, your body was healed one hour later and you have suffered no physical detriment whatsoever?"

"I don't know, and I don't want to know! I've had every medical test known to man and I'm perfectly healthy. I don't know why. I don't know how. I only know what is."

Impatience was rising. Kelly knew what would soon occur: she'd tell these OSIR researchers to jam it where the sun didn't shine.

"The smell of roses is with you all the time, yes?"

"I don't know, is it?" She looked at Kelly and he shrugged. She smells like apples to me, he thought.

"You heal, yes?"

"I'm a channel for healing energies."

"You heal, yes?"

"Yes. But I do not work alone."

The Swiss psychiatrist nodded to Anthony, who stepped forward, took a scalpel from his pocket, uncovered the blade and sliced open the back of his hand. Rebecca, without thinking, grabbed his hand quickly. It took one and half minutes for the bleeding to cease and scar tissue to form. It was, of course, recorded on camera. The scent of roses and sulfur was very strong in the room, and most of all, the silence was eerie.

With tears in her eyes, Rebecca looked directly at Kelly. Begging for release.

"That's all, folks," Kelly said. "You've got enough. I'm taking her home, Leon."

"You can't do that. We have an agreement. There's eighteen more..."

"I don't care how many more tests there are. I'm telling you, it's over. She's had enough and you have got enough. She's my responsibility. It's my call."

"Kel, it's not like the old days…"

Kelly shot Dawn a warning look from which she shied immediately. Within moments, Rebecca was free from the monitoring equipment and they walked from the house, into the rain. The investigators watched from the door while the BMW drove away.

Rebecca stared from the car window. "Thanks," she said quietly.

"You were right. Nobody's interested in who you really are, only what you can do. So tell me. How many of these fifteen people who go to you every day for help would know what color your eyes are let alone what's in your heart?"

"Most people come to me as a last resort. People in general are too focused on their own issues to notice much else, you know that."

"How many friends have you got, Rebecca? Apart from Annie. How many people can you call on at any time and you know they'll be there for you without question. How many you got?"

"Please don't do this."

"There's fuck all and it's always been that way. You think I don't know? You think I can't feel your desolation? You think I don't know what's causing it? You give, people take. That's it. That's your life. You've been standing on the outside looking in far too long."

Kelly found a safe place to pull over. "Look at me."

She did.

"I've been where Dawn and Leon want you to go. Don't. No matter what they offer you, I can guarantee that after six months you'll wish you were dead, and once you're in, there's no way out."

"But I…"

"Hear me? Now I've done stuff and seen stuff that no civilized human being should ever do or see, and I think you know that already, but I saw you take that bullet and you know what I thought? I thought, no, this can't be happening. I'd been waiting fifteen years for you to come into my life and all I got was half an hour. I never really believed in any kind of God but I prayed anyway. I prayed for a miracle. And you came back. I don't want to know the reason, maybe it is to finish what you started. All I know, Rebecca, you came back to me and it's like I got a second chance to—"

His phone rang. When he saw who the caller was, he got out of the car to take the call. His wife, she thought, as she watched him pacing on the sidewalk. What did he mean about being where Dawn and Leon wanted her to go? She sighed as she watched him pace three steps one way, three steps the other. Dear God he was gorgeous. "Oh, Emmanuel. I finally found a live one I can talk to and he's more psychic than me, he's drop dead gorgeous and he's married and to top that, he kills people, too. Why did I come back?"

"Time and patience my love. Trust in him and have faith."

Kelly ended his call, got back in the car and drove off. When he glanced in the rear view mirror, he saw the long-haired passenger along for the ride, and he heard the words: *Be kind.*

All was deathly quiet.

"So what did you mean about being where Dawn and Leon want me to go?"

"I wish I could, but I can't talk about that."

"You mean you won't talk about it."

"Rebecca, please… I cannot talk about that."

"All right. Show me. You don't have to say a word."

And suddenly he let her in. The wall came down for a brief moment. She 'saw' him, a lot younger, lying on a bed in a windowless room: an older man in an army uniform sitting beside him, clipboard in hand. Then came a brief montage starring George Clooney and a movie poster about men staring at goats.

"Bloody Nora," she whispered. "You used to be a remote viewer."

He said nothing to that. He didn't have to. "I've known some gifted people in my time but you are astounding."

"I don't want to go back to the asylum."

"Sorry?"

"I said, I don't want to go back."

"We've got to."

"I know. But not right now, surely. I'm tired, and I'm so hungry I could rip the head off a rag doll."

"Another hour and twenty we'll be in Salisbury. I got just the place. Get some sleep."

"Aye aye captain." The seat reclined and within moments, she was asleep.

When the car finally stopped, Rebecca woke, disorientated until she realized where she was. It was dark already. She couldn't get used to night falling so quickly at this time of year when at home, the sun stayed in the sky seemingly forever. The car was in a pub's car park and Kelly was checking his cell phone.

"Where are we?"

"Salisbury. The food here's good."

"What's the time? Why is it so dark?"

He slipped his cell phone away. "It's seventeen thirty, sorry, five thirty, it's coming on to winter and I should buy you a watch. Right, here's the plan. We either eat here and head back to the base, or we eat here and get a room, and head back to the base tomorrow morning. Your call."

Get a room? Get a room? One room? Surely he meant two rooms? Rebecca's heart thudded. "Kelly, we can't… you'll get in trouble big time. And what about your…" She could not say the word 'wife'.

Kelly leant over, took her face in hand gently and kissed her, softly. When he pulled back, he saw a thudding pulse in her throat. She was breathing fast.

"Don't do this. Please, don't."

"Why can't you look at me?"

"I know what will happen if I do."

"Is it so wrong?" He touched her face again and turned it. "Look at me." She tried to. "I am not going to hurt you."

Fingers trailed her face, her throat. He didn't fumble with buttons. Fingertips were sliding under the blouse to her shoulder, over the gentle, soft curve of breast and back to her lips. He left a trail of shivers in his wake. And he kissed her again. If he kept this up, she wouldn't be responsible. She wouldn't want to be and he knew it.

"Your call," he whispered.

Kelly took a room at the pub. A double room. Rebecca showered and changed into her purple velvet dress, the one she was intending to wear for her speaking engagement at the non existent conference. But she hadn't brought any makeup in her overnight bag; only a change of clothing. They went downstairs to eat but neither of them had food on their minds. A band was playing cover versions of old love songs.

And Kelly knew he should be driving her back to the base. Was it selfish to want to be in her company as a civilian? No, civilian wasn't the word. Off duty wasn't the word either. Perhaps there wasn't one. He simply knew he shouldn't be doing this, but he threw caution, his old friend, to the four winds.

Kelly took her hand and led her upstairs to their room, letting the band's cover of Nights in White Satin spin into their heads, and into something hopefully as memorable of their own. "If you don't want to do this, we can go. We can go right now."

"No," she said. "I want to be here with you."

Kelly unzipped the dress and she stepped out of it. "I'm not very good at this," she said quietly. But it helped, immensely, that he never looked away from her eyes. His kiss tasted like bourbon and something else, too, something else she remembered from a long time ago; another life perhaps. All she knew at that moment, they'd done this before. Many, many times.

Any fear was long gone.

He eased the bra straps from her shoulders and this time he looked. The gaze was followed by touch, and for the first time, she closed her eyes. His touch was electric. And then it was gone. He was undressing. I should be doing that, she thought.

She reached out and touched bare skin. It was warm and had a degree of softness that belied sight. His eyes were smiling as he took her hand and drew her down to the big, brass bed.

They lay facing each other for a little while. How old are you? she wondered, silently.

"I'm thirty-nine," he said, as if reading her mind. It was strange how someone, who did what he did, could be so gentle when he needed to be.

She didn't know what she should do. Situations like this only happened in movies, or dreams. Or in day dreams when she lay, unable to sleep, soothing her own loneliness by pretense. Always by pretense.

Until now.

Rebecca studied his face as if committing it to a deep, long memory. I can't believe this is actually happening to me, she thought.

"Believe it," he whispered, watching her closely.

"Stop it."

"What?"

"Just stop it. You're spooky."

"And you're not?" He raised on elbow, pushed her to her back and ran his finger over her arm, across her breasts as if he were drawing something invisible there. He kissed her again, and, still propped by elbow, continued the invisible sketching down her stomach, over her hips, thighs, knees, inner thighs, till his fingers were between her legs and she let him in.

And all the while he watched her face. It was good to know he still had the touch; that he could still work some magic now and then. But he wasn't in any hurry. He felt the tension mounting, second by second. Her breathing was hurried, she was close, but it was happening too quick for his liking. She was whimpering, making odd noises, squirming. When her legs spread further and one knee raised, he put his face to her breast and he nipped, probably harder than he should have, and then she came, and she damn near screamed, too. Bulls eye, he thought, as his hand was trapped between pulsing thighs. She was so easy. So incredibly easy. He felt her fingers locked in his hair. He could feel her heart thumping against his face. She held him down so hard he thought he might smother. Yep, it's good to know I still got it in me. Then the thighs released their prisoner, she let go of his hair, and he came up for air. His hand massaged its way up her body. "Did you like that?" he asked unnecessarily.

She smiled at him. It was her turn, now. She pushed him flat and straddled him and watched his face contort as she eased herself down slowly, and once down, tightened every muscle she could. He couldn't open his eyes now. He took it for as long as possible, but if she kept this up it'd be over far too quickly and he didn't want that. So he eased her off and she was about to object. But he kissed her again, hard and fast, and the next thing she knew, she was on her face. Her thoughts were wild, untamed, unchecked but he was too busy to know anything except what was happening inside him at that moment. His hands were hot against her hips, her back, even in her hair. And the old brass bed was squeaking and banging against the wall.

He'd hardly made a sound, except for a sigh when it was finally over. And he lay down, spent. Relaxed, happy and spent. Rebecca lay on her face, doubting she'd be able to move, let alone walk again.

"Hey," he said.

She mumbled something in reply.

Kelly rolled her over and his arm became her pillow.

She half expected he'd take a shower and get dressed and say, we'd better go now. But he pulled her in closer still, and kissed her hair and told her she smelled like apples, not roses.

"That's the sweetest thing anybody's ever said to me."

Kelly kissed her again.

"What's this?" she asked, touching a raised and jagged scar on his collarbone.

"Iraq." His arm? "Afghanistan." His hip? He couldn't remember for a moment, maybe her touch obliterated it, and then memory came back. "Motorcycle, Arizona. Skidded for half a mile on my butt." The nick on his chin? "Bar fight in Norfolk." The back of his hand? "We'll be here all night if you want a detailed description of my battle scars."

"There's not much else to do for entertainment."

"Are you going to let me sleep?"

"No."

Kelly flipped her to her back. "Where are yours?" he asked, ignoring the singularly obvious. Apart from the scar over her heart, there was nothing … Ah. Found one. But only one. "This?" he asked, kissing her ankle.

"I got my foot caught in a fence when I was ten years old."

"Is that all?"

"I've always faced dangerous situations with utmost courage."

They both laughed. Any silence from this moment on could never be uncomfortable. He came back up and offered his arm again. Rebecca snuggled in, close, and wrapped her left leg over his.

"Thank you," she said softly.

"What for?"

"Reminding me I'm a woman." She sighed and closed her eyes. Kelly reached for the bedcovers. As he listened to her breathing, he knew she was sleeping. Her soft, hot body was slowly dulling the sharp edges of his existence, but it wasn't close enough. He needed to feel its every curve against his. Then she rolled over and freed herself from his arms. He drew her back and she snuggled down, almost as if they'd done this a thousand times before.

Kelly woke well before dawn, not from a dream but from the unconscious knowing that Rebecca was not beside him. She was standing by the window, a perfect silhouette, looking out at nothing. She was wearing his shirt. It was unbuttoned, hiding nothing. Why do women always do that? he wondered. Is it some kind of property claim? Some kind of female ritual? Kelly got out of bed and went to the window.

"I don't want to go back. I want to stay here with you."

He put his arms around her and rocked her in a gentle, private, music-less dance. His heart was loud and fast, and she knew he could go again, and again, probably until after the sun rose and she'd not deny him but for now all she wanted was to feel his arms around her. She also wanted to know about his wife and there would never be a moment that felt right.

"Will you tell me about her?"

His body tensed and he pulled away, slightly.

"Do you love her?"

He froze upon hearing the word, love. If everybody had a word to distinctly abhor, Love was Kelly's, especially when it pertained to the woman he'd married. The biggest, saddest mistake of his life.

"Please. I'm breaking my own rules being here with you."

He stepped back, as if distancing himself from her could also apply to a distance between himself and Marianne. "At first I thought I did but… Jesus, Rebecca. It's hard enough already, you know?"

She waited patiently in the darkness, looking up. "No, I don't know. I want you to tell me."

"All right, all right." His voice at first was resigned. He was now facing the inevitable. "She's beautiful, yes. Any guy who looks at her has one thought and one thought only. And that's fine if sex is all there is on his mind, but man, what else can you do for the other 23 hours of each day, right? How do I describe Marianne? She's loud. She's spoiled. She's just spent another five grand on cosmetic surgery because at the end she wants to look like this week's favorite Hollywood starlet. And I can't stop her. I live here and she lives in the States in her daddy's mansion in Georgia most of the time. We've got a nice place a couple of miles from here, and one in Norfolk, Virginia, but it's not good enough for her. Nothing is ever enough. That's my wife. Are you happy now?"

Rebecca folded her arms, a perfect mirror of the way he was standing and she studied him in the same way he was studying her. "Ah, ya. Ya. Happy is me. You see, I, too, hav many vays of making you talk and dat vuz but vun of dem."

"You little shit," he said.

"Betcha can't."

She tried to escape, dodge him somehow. No chance. The room was too small and he was too fast. For a moment in time, she had forgotten who she was dealing with. Rebecca, in a split second, was on her back on the carpet and his long foot was on her chest. It was a spectacular view from down there and she could not stop laughing.

"Say, I'm sorry."

The more she giggled and tried to get his foot off, the more pressure he exerted.

"Say I'm sorry, Kelly, for making you tell me things you never knew how to say."

"Get your smelly foot off me or I'll turn you into toad soup."

"I can't hear you."

"I'm happy, Kelly, that you finally told me these things you needed to say."

"Close enough." Kelly helped her up and kept hold of her hand.

The silence in the car was comfortable until Kelly turned the BMW into a street on the outskirts of Salisbury. He saw the car in the driveway of his cottage, and he knew whose it was. Suddenly his spine decalcified from Rebecca's high-pitched squeal.

"Don't do that!"

"There it is! There it is!"

"What?"

She'd turned in the passenger seat and was all but scratching at the window to get another glimpse of the thatched cottage. "That cottage. Where the Mercedes is. I've dreamed about that since I was a little girl. Honest, Kelly. Truly. My God, I didn't think it existed! Can we go back? Please?"

Kelly stopped the car in the middle of the street.

"That cottage?"

"With the bramble roses and the cottage garden. Yes."

"Are you sure it's that particular cottage?"

He had a strange look on his face. Was he teasing?

"Of course I'm sure... you're joking. It's yours? Is it really? Can we go in? Can I see it? Please?"

"Now's not a good time. Trust me on this."

And at that moment, Gene Samperi came out of the front door, got into the Mercedes and drove away. Marianne Nolan, in a negligee that left little to the imagination, waved goodbye at the front door before going back inside.

If that's his house, then that's his wife. Rebecca glanced at Kelly's face. "Maybe another time then," she said quietly.

Kelly drove back the long way, via Stonehenge, but it was early in the morning and the facility hadn't opened yet. There was a fifteen minute wait and already two buses packed with tourists were queued for entry. He slowed, hoping she'd decline, hoping she'd see it through the fence and that would be enough.

"No, I don't need to go in. I see what you mean now."

"The view's better from the air. I'll fly you over it one day."

"In a chopper? No thanks. I'll pass on that."

Kelly slipped his passkey into the main gates, and they opened. He wasn't in a great rush to get to the car park. He acknowledged Alpha team as they jogged across the drive in front of the car, and there was Macpherson, giving Rebecca a huge grin as he ran by. A small wave of jealousy rose. "I don't particularly want to say this but we can't... I'm not supposed to get emotionally involved here."

"I know that."

"So don't take it personally. All right?"

"You're saying this was another first date."

"I hope not." Kelly reached for her hand and squeezed it tight. When he parked the BMW, he said, "I need to tell you something. Please do not take this the wrong way because last night was very special."

Your wife's shagging Gene Samperi but in an hour's time you're taking her to Ireland to celebrate your tenth wedding anniversary.

"I have to go away for few days."

"Oh. Is it work?"

"No. This has been planned for four months. I can't cancel." He said nothing more and she asked even less. Kelly took her bag from the trunk.

"I'll go talk to the boss. It won't matter if I get in trouble."

"There's no need for that."

"Try and stop me, Commander." Rebecca took her own bag and

used her passkey to unlock the main doors. The party was over.

Chapter 7

"It was my idea. Not the commander's. He was a perfect gentleman the entire time."

Yeah I bet he was, Pete thought. "They're not finished with you, Rebecca."

"I know. But if they want to test me any more than they already have, they can do it here. Their equipment is transportable and I'm sure there's somewhere in the dungeons they can set up."

"Why did you walk out?"

"I'd had enough after the first two hours. But having someone slice open the back of his hand and thrust it under my nose was the last straw for Kelly. He ended the session, and I'm thankful he did. I know we should have come back straight away, but…" Her words faded.

Pete didn't have to be psychic to know what went down. "You know the commander's taking a few days rec leave, and Leon Carter's coming to talk to you again today."

Rebecca closed her eyes and sighed. "Pete, can you please get through to these people that I do not know circumstances yet? I won't know until closer to the time the senator decides to visit. If he decides to come at all."

"If what you say is true, you'll have to be more convincing."

"I honestly can't tell you people anything that you don't already know."

"But, of course, you will when it's time."

"Probably five minutes before his plane lands," she mumbled.

"You said?"

"Look, Colonel. Pete. Whatever I'm supposed to call you. I want to be here as much as you want me here but we're stuck with each other. I want this over with as much as, no, probably more than you do. So is there anything in the rule book that says we have to be nice to each other?"

He tried not to show any amusement. "A little civility would be refreshing."

"Good. Can I go now before I fall into the hole I'm digging for myself here because I tell you, the damn thing goes all the way to China."

Pete nodded and watched her walk to the door. "Rebecca?"

She looked back.

"Kelly's a friend of mine."

"I know that."

"He's also married."

"I know that, too."

They gazed at each other for a moment longer than necessary. No further words were needed until Rebecca said quietly, "I can't help it."

"Then you should endeavor to try harder."

Rebecca wasn't sure what he meant and she dared not ask specifically. "Can I ask you something?"

He was non-committal, but his eyes held a deep curiosity.

"Were you on the Eisenhower fifteen years ago when it stayed a few days in Brisbane?"

"Anything's possible. You're proof of that."

"John Glover was on that ship, too, wasn't he. So was Kelly. I was, too, for about an hour. I was with my mother. She was a very beautiful woman. She always looked ten years younger than she was. She had her photo taken with a blond fighter pilot who looked just like you would have looked back then. He called her and they disappeared for three days and two nights."

The blue gaze never wavered but a half-smile creased his face. Perhaps he was remembering. "Thousands of civilians have been on board the Eisenhower, Rebecca. And thousands of defense personnel have served on her." But he was watching her closely. "What was your mother's name?"

"Jenny Miller."

Pete pretended he was searching his memory, and finally, he shrugged.

"You know him, don't you, Pete. You know John Glover."

"I was best man at his wedding. But I think you know that already."

"He smiled at me once. I saw him in a coffee shop near Circular Quay in Sydney."

"And if I told you he remembered you?"

"Pull the other one, how could he? We never spoke. I talked to his wife. He thought this psychic stuff was all mumbo-jumbo. He probably still does."

"And you believe that?"

"I don't know what I believe anymore. Do you?"

"It's refreshing to know we agree on something even if it's indecision. You can close the door on your way out."

She closed the door on her way out, took four steps down the hall and heard a drawling female voice emanating from Kelly's office.

The Wife.

Gene Samperi's lover.

Rebecca knocked once and walked in, confident and assured externally. Her hair was tied up but already it was falling out of the hair band. She wore no makeup. Her bracelets were rattling. She felt like a rag that had been used too many times to clean grimy windows, and there she was. Marianne. A picture of sheer, elegant, expensive perfection. It took a lot of cash, effort and practice to acquire that look. She was perched on her husband's desk as if she'd been carefully posed there by a celebrity photographer. Her hair was perfectly platinum, trailing softly over massive enhanced breasts that would remain forever upright, defying gravity until the end, and her face was expertly painted. The designer dress was a blue that matched the color of her contact lenses. Even the toenails extending from the high heeled, open-toed, expensive Italian shoes were perfectly manicured and glittering.

Fuck me, Rebecca thought.

"Rebecca, my wife, Marianne."

In a camouflaged Deep South accent, Marianne said, "I've heard a lot about you."

Although she didn't want to, Rebecca took the extended hand. Not a great deal of information passed at the fleeting touch. I will not look at Kelly. I cannot look at Kelly.

"Is my honey takin' good care of you?"

"We've had our moments."

"Yeah. I'll bet you have."

Rebecca needed a hatchet to chop through the tension in the atmosphere.

"So you're the psychic everybody's talking about, huh?" Marianne got off the desk. She did not walk around the room. She floated. She stopped at Kelly's painting and made a quick comparison and then she smiled, but there was no amusement in the smile, just confusion. "I guess you guys got some stories to swap. He's sure got it, haven't you, Kelly. You can't lie to this man of mine, but I guess know that already. Well, hon, don't know if he told you, but I'm stealing him for a couple of days. Sure hope you don't mind. But after all, he is still my husband."

Rebecca said nothing.

"So tell me, who's gonna win the election?"

Rebecca remained quiet, deciphering the barrage of impressions she was receiving from the woman. She could clearly see a mansion: it seemed like something straight from Gone with the Wind. She saw Republican banners, American flags. Crowds of people and the usual pre-election mayhem. "The election? Too soon to say. It's been nice to meet you, Mrs Nolan. Have a great time in Ireland, Commander. Bye."

And she was gone.

Rebecca watched from her window as Kelly, in civilian clothing again, got into that dark blue BMW with his wife, and the car drove away, down the tree-lined drive, and into what, she had no idea. She stared for a long time with some thoughts vying for superiority.

He made love to me but he's married to her. Rebecca looked at herself in the mirror. Not even passable, especially not today. She pulled out the hair band. Her hair hung limply halfway down her arms. The only reason it was unstyled was because she never had time to find a hairdresser—it was easier to tie it back. She wondered where the nearest hairdresser might be.

She turned side on to the mirror and lifted her chest. It looked passable for a moment but once she expelled the breath everything dropped again.

Perhaps Love has nothing to do with appearances?

Rebecca sighed. *Emmanuel, go away. Can't I even have private doubts anymore? Look at me.*

I see not what you see and perhaps he sees more than I.

You're a right comedian today, Em.

Rebecca sat at the small desk and picked up the defense department pen she'd permanently borrowed from Kelly's desk and stared at the blank paper in front of her.

Leon. She'd shaken his hand again yesterday morning, and nothing had changed. What lay ahead for Leon was a blank canvas, touched with gray. And there was nothing she could do about it, either, except warn him. Had it been enough? Don't drive on the M4 in the rain. But this was England. It never stopped raining.

The line between interference and destiny was mostly intangible. How many times had she overstepped it? How many times had she told strangers things they should never have known?

She wrote down her thoughts for a few minutes before walking away. She was too confused. She couldn't think properly. Rebecca made her way down to the mess. Maybe a coffee would help.

"Rebecca."

"Hey, Frank. Anything special for lunch?"

"Everything's special for you," he said with a smile.

"I bet you say that to every girl who's been here."

"And lots who haven't."

"Stop boasting. You, Frank, are every woman's dream—a man who can cook." Rebecca was pouring a coffee when, in her mind's eye, she saw Leon Carter, driving in the rain, and then… She overfilled the cup. Hot coffee spilled onto her hand but she felt nothing.

"Rebecca?"

She didn't hear Frank's alarmed voice.

Leon stood, bewildered, watching as the paramedics and police threw a tarpaulin over the wreck. Someone said, at least it was quick. Poor bastard.

Hey man, I'm here, I'm fine, he tried to say but nobody could hear him.

One minute he was cruising along, singing Fire Lake, and the next, the vehicle in front swerved. The rest was slow motion. He saw the first car bounce off the eighteen wheeler's middle wheels and spin to face him and Leon, in the space of a heartbeat, knew he had nowhere to go. He glanced in the rear view mirror. Peak hour on the motorway. Oh, Jesus, somebody help me here, he thought and he closed his eyes.

The pain started then. At first it was a dull ache in her chest, an ache bad enough to become a sudden tearing inside. She dropped the coffee pot and the cup and fumbled for the nearest chair. She couldn't breathe. The room spun. Rebecca held her head in her hands. Incredible, searing pain. She didn't know what was happening.

"Rebecca?"

The sound of her name came from peripheral, from the edges of a dark haze, but she couldn't make her way through to answer. Something else was pulling at her spirit. And at that moment, freedom came and she understood. She understood it all as the floor reached up and seized her body, hard.

Frank didn't realize how quickly he could move, or how loud he could call out one magic word: MEDIC!

Leon?

Rebecca? How'd you get here?

That's not important.

Look at those guys. I keep telling them I'm okay but no one can hear me.

Yes, I know. There's a reason for that. Why don't you come with me? She held out her hand and he seemed to know what he should do. He should go with her. But he tried to turn back.

No, don't look back. You should never look back... I'll take you home, now. Come with me, that's it. Come with me...

A paramedic was on his belly under the jackknifed truck, retrieving Leon Carter's head from what was, once, the red Ford's backseat.

The Scottish captain stood by the hospital bed, arms folded, deep in thought. The lassie was on the cardiac monitor, the shock cart within reach. He had exhausted every possibility but Rebecca was unresponsive and the doctor did not know why. He stood there for a further fifteen minutes, thinking and theorizing.

"What have we got to lose, sir?" Jamie Faraday asked.

"Kelly won't be grateful. Is his first days off in months."

"He'll be less grateful if Rebecca dies again." Jamie stood by the bed for a little while, looking down at Rebecca. He hoped, just this once, he wasn't wrong. Rumor was that the commander, a long time ago, was a remote viewer. He'd go places in his mind and report back and apparently he was good at it, too. Psychic spying, basically.

Jamie touched her hand. Her skin was cold, her breathing imperceptible. The body was alive, but the spirit had vacated. That much he knew. Where are you, he thought. Where are you?

When he turned to the captain, the captain wasn't there.

Kelly was at Heathrow check-in, standing in a queue for the two o'clock flight to Dublin and hoping for a way out of this, a way out of three entire days of torture, when the Yellow Rose of Texas blasted from his back pocket. "Yeah?… Mike?… She what? When?" There was a pause. It seemed eternal. His heart nearly stopped when he listened to the MO's words. He glanced at Marianne beside him and knew from the look in her eyes that this would most likely nail the lid on the coffin of their marriage—what little of it there was—but he didn't care.

He wasn't being ordered back to the base. He had a choice here. It was not a difficult decision to make. "I'm on my way," he said, disconnecting the call.

"No, you're not going anywhere. I've had this planned for months."

"I'm sorry, Marianne. I truly am sorry. I have to go."

Kelly took his bag and ran, leaving her in the short queue for first class on her own.

"But what about me?" Marianne called, so loud that a hundred people turned and stared. "Don't you do this to me again! Don't you dare!"

"But I was talking to her this morning. She was fine. What time did this happen?"

"According to Frank, ten forty five," Mike replied. It was ten forty five when Carter was decapitated on the M4. It was now two thirty in the afternoon. "Kelly's on his way back."

"Why?"

"You know not to question my authority down here, Peter."

Pete knew it had something to do with Kelly's past: remote viewing. Astral travelling and other such bullshit. "Page me when he's back."

Pete walked from the infirmary's isolation room an unhappy man and Mike knew he'd page the colonel when he felt it was time and not before.

Mike sat by the bed. "You'd be a worry, then, hen. That's what you are. Nothing but a worry."

Leon? Don't be afraid.

But I can't stay here. I don't like it here. Why's everything so gray? I've got to see Susan. I've got to see my kids. They were all asleep when I left this morning. Oh man, I didn't even kiss her goodbye. I've got to say goodbye. I have to, Rebecca.

Leon, listen to me. Please. Listen to me. You're dead, Leon. You won't be able to say goodbye. After a little while, you might be able to go back and try to let her know that you're all right but often it's futile. It's too distressing because you're able to feel what she's feeling but its tenfold stronger for you, and poor Susan, she'll think she's going crazy. Yes, she'll know you're there but if she tries to tell anybody about it, they'll tell her it's nonsense. That it's wishful thinking, or a part of the grieving process. She will eventually believe them, and get on with living without you. But Leon, you will, too. And you will see her again. You'll be waiting for Susan when it's her time. Leon? Look at me.

Leon looked at the angel.

Susan knows you love her and it's all that matters. Truly it is. The love is all that ever matters. Don't bring sadness or regret or anger with you. Just bring the love you gained while you were alive. It's all you need.

Kelly came to a skidding stop only a few feet from the main doors and he threw his keys to the nearest soldier. "Park the car, buddy."

And he was away, the doors not opening quickly enough for his liking. It had been the longest three hour drive of his life.

Mike was dozing when he heard the commotion. And in the commander came, skidding on the tiles.

Now, Mike had known Kelly for six years and in those six years, he'd not seen fear like it. Best, he thought, to leave them alone now. "I'll be in my office if you need me."

Kelly looked down at Rebecca. Her skin was white. The only sound was the annoying beep of the monitor. His hands were shaking. A well of emotion was bubbling. The volcano erupting. "Don't do this, girl. Not now. Please, not now."

Nothing. There was no reaction.

Kelly sat down and let out a shaking sigh. His eyes were stinging. The words were there, words they both needed to hear but they were caught fast in his throat and he was choking on them when he said, "What am I supposed to do, huh? What do you want me to do?"

He touched her arm. Her neck. Her face. She cold even though she was covered by a mountain of blankets. Her spirit had flown.

And then he knew what he had to do. He kicked his boots off and climbed onto the bed, put his left arm under her head, and he held her close. She was limp. A heavy, dead kind of limp. And what he'd done in the past reared again. Kelly had no choice but to find her, wherever she was, and lead her home again.

Home to him.

But I can't be dead. I don't feel dead. And who's going to look after my family now? If I'm dead, if what you're saying is true, how come my mother's not here to...

She is Leon. She is here. See?

A woman stepped from the gray shadows and as she did, she smiled and reached for Leon's hand. Only when the colors appeared, when nothing was gray anymore, when Leon Carter was nearly peaceful in the arms of his beloved mother, did Rebecca retreat.

From somewhere far away, she heard a familiar voice calling her name. Who is that? she wondered and followed the sound back into the gray mist. A light was shining, showing her the way. A familiar voice was calling her name.

Kelly snapped back to reality. The room was full of bright, gold light. It narrowed into a swirling spiral and it circled the room, like a beautiful, miniature tornado funnel, once, twice, before it touched his forehead. When it did, for a moment in time, he was complete. He knew all. He had done all. A love so encompassing illuminated every cell of his being. It was the love of eternity. In an instant, Kelly recognized it, remembered it, and then the funnel of glistening, golden white light found its true home.

Rebecca took a deep, jagged breath. Kelly felt the movement against his body. She made a noise. Kelly wasn't sure what it meant. "Rebecca?"

She opened her eyes and blinked a couple of times, trying to focus. "Kelly?" She strained to tip her head back and look into his face.

"What are you doing here?"

He held her tight for a moment longer, before he kissed her head and got off the bed. The last thing he needed was for anyone to see this.

But it was too late for that. The three medics had been watching from the other side of the isolation room window.

"Nobody saw that, did they," Mike said.

"I didn't see a thing, Captain." Jamie offered.

Mitch was the only one who did not comment. He followed his colleagues into the isolation room. Kelly was regaining some composure and Rebecca was endeavoring to get out of bed. It wasn't allowed. Mike's large hand pushed her back down again. "Welcome back," Mike said. "Tell me the last thing you remember."

"Watching Kelly leave for his days off." She couldn't say, with his wife. The words refused to come.

"And then?"

Rebecca tried to think, tried to clear her mind. Mike shone a bright light into her eyes and it hurt. "I wrote for a bit before I went to the mess and got a coffee." And in a wave of illumination, she realized the reason for the medic's concern. She'd gone to Leon. She had heard his call for help. Her body must have shut down when her spirit had vacated so suddenly without any warning.

"Nothing else?"

"No."

After five more minutes of fussing, the medics retreated.

"Did you think I was dying again?" she asked, once she was alone with Kelly.

"I don't know what I was thinking."

"You've still got time to get to Dublin."

"It's no use."

"Go to your wife. You need to do this."

"And if something like this happens to you again?"

"If it does, it does. It won't kill me. Go. Take your holiday."

"Where did you go, Rebecca?"

"I helped Leon to the other side," she whispered. "He was killed this morning on the M4. I went to help him cross over, but getting him over took a long, long time. He didn't believe he was dead."

Kelly put his hand on her shoulder and squeezed tight. "I'll see you on Friday. Take care."

Rebecca watched him walk from the room and her heart filled with emptiness. Don't go! she wanted to cry. Instead she lay back on the bed, rolled into a fetal curl and quietly wept.

He got a seat on the final flight to Dublin and took a cab to the hotel. It was one o'clock in the morning. Marianne had checked in, alone, an hour before he'd made it back to Wiltshire.

The plan was to rent a car and drive—her tenth anniversary present to him.

Kelly stood at the hotel room door far too long. He hesitated three times before he knocked.

Marianne opened the door and nothing was said for a moment. She wore a black satin nightgown that was split to the navel. Her platinum blonde hair had been cut to within an inch of its life. Women, he knew, cut their hair when they were in mourning. It was a subconscious thing. But how could she be in mourning when there'd hardly been any love to begin with? Then he realized an awful truth. Maybe she did love him? Maybe she always had?

Marianne looked down at her bare feet and then stepped aside. Kelly walked in and closed the door behind him. It was a big room, five star. She'd had room service. Tequila and ice cream. Here we go, he thought.

Without a word, Marianne resumed her place in the middle of the huge bed. She was watching an in-house movie.

"Do you love her?" Marianne asked.

"Yes."

"How long have you known her?"

"Three and a half weeks."

"How long have we been married?"

"Ten years yesterday."

She turned to him. "Have you ever loved me?"

"Yes."

"The way you love her?"

"No."

"And does she know?"

"I haven't asked and she hasn't said."

"Oh, she knows. Can see it in her eyes when she looks at you. Do you think I'm fucking stupid or something? Huh?"

Marianne took the pillow, held it tight and started rocking. He knew what that meant, too. An explosion was nigh. She'd weep, then she'd cry. The crying would metamorphose into hysteria, and uncontrollable rage would ensue. She'd reach for a knife or whatever else was nearby, and if she didn't try to kill herself first, she'd try to kill him. Kelly was walking on egg shells. Half the bottle of Tequila was already gone. It would be much worse if the bottle was empty, that much he knew.

"What happened to us?" she asked.

"I don't know. But we've got two days to talk about what we're going to do."

"Daddy won't like it. A divorce might come back on him. Affect his campaign."

"I'm aware of that."

"If you leave me, Kelly, he won't help your career one bit."

"I don't care."

She looked up, genuinely surprised. "What you gonna do?"

"I don't know."

"And her, this Rebecca? Does she fit in your plans? Your nothing plans?"

"I don't know. It's up to her."

"It's her, isn't it, doing this to you. You'd do anything for her. Why?"

"I can't answer that."

"But she's… nothing. Nothing."

"Marianne, please…"

She turned to him again and the tears in her eyes were genuine. "I don't know what else I'm supposed to do to keep you."

Kelly sighed. Keep me? He'd seen Gene leaving the house. That's how she spent their wedding anniversary, in bed with Gene Samperi. Then again, he was making love to Rebecca. "You can't keep anybody, Marianne. It's not possible."

"Why can't you look at me? Ain't you even noticed yet?"

"I noticed. I don't like your hair that short. I preferred it the way it used to be."

"Like hers."

"You don't get it, do you, Marianne. It's not about appearances. It never has been."

"My head's killin' me, Kel. I gotta get some… some…" She put the pillow under her head and turned to her side. The movie was forgotten. Within five seconds she was asleep and for that he was thankful. He killed the TV, poured the tequila into the toilet and looked at himself in the bathroom mirror. He did not like the reflection staring back at him. He couldn't even meet his own gaze.

Kelly showered and climbed into the bed beside his wife. He faced the wall and flinched when her hand circled his waist and she moved closer, spooning in.

His body did not react.

He spent the rest of the night staring at the wall, knowing that the next few days would be the longest of his life. So he thought about Rebecca instead. But not what had happened that day. No, his thoughts were of their shared sleepless night. Taking her soft and slow. Again and again. Finding her by the window. Wearing his shirt. He couldn't gauge the depth of that well of sadness that lay beneath her surface. Even when she smiled it still lay there in her eyes. But you're married, she kept saying. You're married.

Not for much longer, Kelly thought.

Rebecca watched the basketball game and cheered for both sides—it was easier that way even if she secretly hoped Mac's team would win. When it was over, a draw, and the guys went their separate ways, only Mac remained. He'd asked her to come to the gym and she'd obliged.

"How are you feeling?"

"I'm fine. You?"

Mac shot a hoop and bounced the ball her way. Rebecca caught it, wondering now, what he wanted. Mac was like Kelly in that he never joined a queue to talk to her. So she dribbled the ball over, avoided his defense and scored.

"You should be playing on my team."

"Nah. I'll sit on the sidelines and cheer for everybody."

"You always sit on the sidelines."

"Safest play, sarge." She tried for another hoop but he intercepted. He didn't shoot. He held the ball. "What?" she asked.

"The commander's asked me to teach you some basic self defense."

"Me?" she laughed. "Why?"

"I don't know. I just do as I'm told."

"But why did he choose you?"

"Because I teach it when he can't."

"What if I don't want to?"

"He'll make me cut the grass with nail scissors."

At first she thought he was joking. "Kelly wouldn't do that."

"Want to bet?"

There was something in his eyes she couldn't read.

"What does he want you to teach me?"

"How to defend yourself. How to shoot. It'll pass some time. Maybe you won't be so bored." He tossed the ball and dragged out a huge mat.

Mac wasn't a large man. He stood only five eight tall and was perhaps sixty pounds heavier than Rebecca. He didn't look as if he could fight. But neither did she. They were perhaps, the same age.

"Why do you shave your head?"

"Twenty of us did it for charity a couple of days before you got here."

"What charity?"

"An orphanage in Romania."

"Big tough guys, aren't you." Rebecca caught him off guard. She lunged, grabbed, twisted and he was flat on his back. "Junior karate brown belt."

"Does the commander know?" Mac asked, trying not to laugh.

"No, he doesn't. And he won't know, will he. Here endeth the lesson."

Rebecca sat beside Mac on the mat as he lay there, staring up at the ceiling. "What other hidden talents have you got?" he asked.

"I used to play Skirmish."

"Any good?"

"No. I was always covered in paint. I'd last five seconds in a real situation."

"Five seconds is good."

"Not when you're screaming in terror and it isn't even real."

He laughed at that. "It must be hard for you being here with us."

"It would be hard if I let it be. I don't see the uniforms anymore. That helps. And the guys are generally nice. I feel like everybody's little sister."

"Would you have dinner with me tonight?"

"I have dinner with you every night."

"No, I mean away from here."

"Sergeant Mac, are you asking me on a date?"

"Would you?"

"I'd like that."

"Come on," he said, sitting up, taking her hand. "I'll give you a coat. It's cold outside."

The jacket he gave her was black and heavy. Mac took no notice of the wolf whistling and lewd comments as they walked through the woods, past three training grounds and into the building that housed the indoor firing range: ten booths and paper targets.

"Ammo," Mac said with a nod to the sergeant at the door. He signed in and so did Rebecca. They were handed their respective weapons and obligatory ear muffs. "This is called a Glock 21. It's a forty-five with slider action and takes twelve rounds so remember to count. My father used to say it's not the weapon that kills. It's the idiot holding it. You watch me. Watching?"

Mac loaded it, more slowly than he normally would have, and sent seven quick shots into the paper target—three in the head, four in the chest. Then he released the clip and stood back. Rebecca then saw him differently: this is what Mac did. What he was good at. Reservations rose. She didn't want to touch the weapon.

"I don't know if I should do this, Mac."

"There's acres of grass, Angel. You wouldn't do that to me, would you?"

Angel. Why did he always call her that?

"You can do it. I know you can."

The target was fifty feet away. He had to be joking.

The Lear stops, engines cut. The door opens. Glover appears. He lifts his hand to wave to the school children assembled on the tarmac, behind the cordons…

"Not now," she whispered. "Please not now. Go away."

"Now's the only time we've got and I can't go away. I've got orders."

"I wasn't talking to you. I was talking to… myself."

"Oh. Sorry for interrupting."

Rebecca put the clip in, disengaged the safety and held it, as she thought, the way Mac had held it. "No. You've been watching too much TV. Your grip's wrong. It's got a recoil and you'll lose it if you hold it like that. Shoot yourself in the foot. This way."

Hands came from behind and she felt his hot breath on the top of her head as he adjusted her hands on the weapon. He let go. She aimed, jerked the trigger and the bullet ricocheted with a ping, then a thud. God knew what it hit but she ducked at the sound of the ricochet.

"Again. Easy this time. Steady."

"I can't do this."

"Sure you can."

"No, Mac. Any kind of intent is as harmful as the act itself."

"And if you think like that, you're dead. He's got a gun on you. He's going to use it. It's you or him. You've got two seconds."

Rebecca eased it this time, knowing what to expect. She hit the target low. Very low.

"You've got one shot and only one shot. Twenty five people depend on you to use this bullet wisely. What will you do?"

"Delegate?"

"What will you do?"

"Cry?"

Mac sighed. "Angel. That grass is long and there's a lot of it."

"I don't want to do this, Mac," she whined.

"If you're not sure of a head shot, you aim for the heart. Anywhere on the chest will do."

Rebecca lowered the gun and stepped back.

"What?"

"What you just said. That happened to me."

There was an echoing silence.

"Why, Mac? Why would someone who doesn't even know me do that to me?"

"Maybe he had orders."

"If you had orders? Would you?"

"There would be no hesitation."

"You can't mean that."

"That's the way it is."

"I don't understand it and I never will."

"So get mad. Get angry." Mac pointed to the target. "He's the bastard that shot you. No, he's every bastard who's ever harmed you. He's everybody you've ever hated. Do it. Now's your chance."

Rebecca lifted the gun and fired and kept firing until nothing happened except a successive, empty clicking. The paper target was in tatters but she didn't see a thing. Her sight was blinded by tears. The futile triggering only halted when Mac took the gun from her hands and ejected the magazine. She was shaking. Crying. Arms around her now were automatic. "I think we've had enough for one day," he said softly as he handed the weapon to Ammo and guided her out into the October chill. "Who'd you shoot back there?" Mac asked.

"My father," she said softly.

Kelly drove across to Galway. She talked a lot this morning, the usual shit he wasn't listening to. And then she dragged him along while she shopped. He spent most of the day waiting, wondering whether Macpherson was making a start or not. Wondering if he'd hurt Rebecca yet. Or she him.

Kelly waited on the street for his wife to emerge with yet another carry bag she'd pass immediately to him. Across the cobbled mall he saw a jewelers shop. He went across.

Marianne soon appeared and picked her way across the cobblestones. She put her arm around his waist as he perused the window. "That diamond there'd be nice for a divorce present." He went back to the gold claddagh studded with emeralds. "You want a drink?" he asked, knowing that if he took her into the nearest pub, he could slip out, get the claddagh and be back before she realized he'd been in the men's room too long.

At seven (she'd asked Joel to call her at half six) Rebecca walked down, via the mess, to the front entry and did not acknowledge the succession of wolf whistles trailing in her wake. She knew she looked good. Unfortunately Kelly was not here to see it. But if Kelly had been here, she'd not be having dinner with Mac, would she. For a moment she wondered if she was doing the right thing. But Mac was safe. Mac was gay.

Rebecca could not remember a time when she'd had as much fun. Mac kept her laughing for three and a half hours, and he knew it was time to go when he had to stop her from dancing on the table again.

He had to have her back on base by eleven. He didn't drink. He said he was stupid enough sober anyway, but she knew that was only an excuse, because he had full responsibility for her tonight.

He poured her into his red MX5 and closed the door. Rebecca rested her head back. The world was swimming but she didn't care.

"Jeez, it's a waste."

"What is?"

"You. I'd snap you up in a flash, Mac. I'd never let you go. Ever."

"Promises, promises."

"No, I mean it. You're so sweet. You really are."

"I warned you about the first black velvet."

"And the fourth. I know. I don't care."

"I have to get you home now. Are you going to be sick?"

"Oh, it's not fair."

Mac glanced at her as he reversed out of the car park. "What's not fair?"

"You. You're gorgeous, you really are. I'd have half a dozen kids with you but you don't like girls. How come? Tell me. You have to tell me."

"I do like girls, Angel. But not the way you'd like me to like girls right now if you know what I mean."

"You said I was beautiful."

"You are."

"But not even a …? Not a thing?"

"Not like this, no."

"Why am I always everybody's little sister?"

"You're not my little sister, that's for sure."

"Mac? Stop. I think I'm going to be…"

He came to a skidding stop on the side of the narrow road and just in time, too. She was out and throwing up into the long grass.

"I warned you about those black velvets," he said to himself as he got out of the car and stood at a safe distance.

Once safely back at the asylum, Mac siphoned his angel from the front seat of the car and even though she said she had legs, not that he'd notice though, she could make it up the stairs without falling on her face. But he hovered close by all the same.

It was ten to eleven when he accessed the front doors. Rebecca, swaying on her feet and still nauseous, regarded the old elevator with fondness.

"No. We only use it for training."

"So let's pretend we're stuck in it."

"If we get into it, we will be."

"But I'm… there's too many stairs."

"I'll carry you."

"My hero," she mumbled and fell into his arms.

Mac hoisted her over his shoulder and took the three flights of stairs, pleased no one was about but knowing too that security would be watching, and probably laughing. "Don't throw up on me."

He put her down in the corridor outside her room. "Where's your key?"

She looked at him, grinning. "If you body search me you might find it."

"Rebecca…"

"You're no fun." She gave her tags to him. The door was already unlocked.

"Did you close this?"

"I don't know. I can't remember."

He put the tags around her neck again and went in, turning on the light. The room looked fine.

"You get some sleep."

"Put me to bed and tell me a story, Mac."

"I'll see you in the morning." He planted a kiss on her forehead and retreated.

"But I only wanted a…"

"Goodnight."

The door closed.

"Hug," she said and lay face down across her bed. "I only wanted a hug."

Rebecca felt the universe closing in. She rolled over. The world spun. She sat up slowly and waited for the room to be still again.

It was the last time she'd drink Guinness and champagne. No, it was the last time she'd drink. She couldn't remember much. Except laughing a lot. Dancing? Yes, belly dancing. A few hip drops, a shimmy or two. A good offbeat was all she needed for an improvised lead and follow, even if she was doing it all on her own… Now that was something Kelly didn't know about. The dancing. It blew Mac away. Most of the band, too, if she remembered rightly.

A shower. Yes. A shower. Brush teeth. Pulling her clothes off as best she could, she swayed her way into the bathroom and drew back the curtain.

That was all she remembered.

Chapter 8

MAC LOOKED AT THE TIME. She'd never been this late before, but he guessed she had a reason. She'd have a glorious, Technicolor hangover. But still he wondered why she wasn't down, at least for a heart-starting coffee. Maybe I should have waited until she was in bed, he thought.

No, she'd have tried to get me into bed. The idea wasn't repulsive. Far from it. But he had orders from the CO. Take her somewhere. Let her enjoy herself. Let her get drunk if she wants to. And besides, he couldn't encroach upon the commander's territory. If he so much as thought about making love to Rebecca, he was a dead man walking. Five more minutes, he thought, concern rising.

The second breakfast sitting was nearly over. This wasn't like Rebecca to miss breakfast. She was the only girl he knew who never made a fuss about what she should or should not eat.

Mac went up to her room and knocked. There was no answer. He couldn't hear any movement. He went downstairs again and asked Joel to phone her room. There was no answer. The only person Mac knew of who knew her access code was the commander. He wasn't here.

Trepidation rose. Mac didn't like the feeling. Kelly had said not to let her out of his sight and told him why. He rang Kelly's mobile but it was either out of range or switched off. So he spoke to the next in command.

Mike came up from the infirmary, knocked on Rebecca's door. No answer.

He had no choice but grant permission to break the door down.

And when they gained entry there was nothing in the room except a trail of clothing. The bed had not been slept in.

Rebecca was nowhere in the complex.

The colonel watched dispassionately the taped footage of an empty corridor followed by a blank screen.

"We had a total system shut down at twenty-two thirty hours."

Pete closed his eyes. The timing was impeccable.

"However, there is my own hybrid GPS device, sir. It's something I've been working on for a few months now but it's only 96% accurate."

Barry Mannett, systems tech, all round tinker.

"The commander approved it for use with Miss Miller. Maybe he had a premonition something like this would happen."

For a moment, Pete said nothing.

"And?"

"This way, sir." Barry showed the colonel into his small, cramped office. He touched his personal laptop screen, and a map of southern England showed. A red light was flashing. He touched the screen again and the map zoomed in on a location in farmland east of Salisbury.

The curtains on the windows were of heavy, red velvet. There was no other furniture in the room except for a fold up table and two plastic chairs. The only scent was twenty years of accumulated dust and decay mixed with rising damp.

Rebecca was alone and cold even though she was wrapped tight in a blanket. She felt half paralyzed. The pain in her head was excruciating. Her wrists were bound with a plastic tie. When she moved her hands it dug into her flesh. But she touched her head anyway. Blood. The cut above her eye would need stitches. She had no idea how it had happened. Her last memory was of Mac, departing.

She'd been drunk. Black velvets. Just the thought and she almost threw up again.

Outside, a car door closed. Footsteps. Someone came into the house. She dared to look.

Gene Samperi.

"Not you again."

"Yeah. Welcome to my nightmare," he said.

"I need a bathroom."

"Now that's the trouble with needs, Rebecca. You need something for your head? Sorry. Maybe, just maybe, we can compromise. But first, you and me, we're going to talk whether you like it or not."

"I can't tell you anything you don't already know," she said, her current mantra.

Gene stepped from the shadows and crouched in front of her. Rebecca flinched away when he pulled the blanket off. Underwear only. Nice one, he thought. Not bad. The scar where she'd taken the bullet was bright red. No use questioning. She was here. She was alive and he had a job to do. He took a switchblade from his pocket and again she flinched because he flicked it open close to her face. Terror in her eyes now. She was breathing hard. He cut through the tight plastic. Her hands were free. Then he threw a parka to her. Rebecca put it on and kept the blanket around her lower body. Her legs were freezing.

"Coffee?"

"Yes." She almost said 'please'.

He poured steaming black coffee from a thermos into a styrofoam cup and handed it to her. It didn't matter that it was black and unsweetened when she took hers white with two, or NATO standard as the boys called it. Where were they? Did they even know she was gone? Probably not. Mac would assume she had a hangover and could face neither him nor breakfast.

There was only one face she wanted to see now: Kelly's. Had he known something like this would happen? Only yesterday, in the gym, and at the firing range... Self defense, shooting, it was all his idea.

"You know about Leon?" Gene asked.

"I knew about Leon the first time I touched his hand."

"Yes, I heard. Don't drive in the M4 in the rain. Isn't that what you said? Dawn's impressed. All the researchers are."

"I will not work with them or for them."

"Rebecca, don't be so defensive."

"Defensive? Why all this? There's no need for this."

"You refuse to talk to me."

They were being polite... But she couldn't remember what else Kelly had said.

"I need the bathroom."

"I need answers. Like I said, compromise."

"I can't help you. I know nothing yet."

"You can't lie to me, so stop this crap right now. I would prefer this to remain civil and I'm sure you would, too."

Rebecca sipped the coffee again. It was bitter and strong. "So let me go to the bathroom. Please?"

Gene took her coffee, put it on the floor, and led her from the empty room, down the hall and into a dirty old bathroom. He stood at the door, waiting.

The mirror was cracked and blackened at the edges. Rebecca saw the deep cut, the black eye. She looked far worse than she felt, which was possibly the reason he was being, for now at least, human.

The tiny window was stuck fast and she could not have squeezed through it anyway. Her bum was too big.

Rebecca came out, blanket flowing like a train on a wedding dress.

This time she preferred to sit on the floor, by the tattered velvet-covered window. She knew it was a mistake, that sitting low gave him the balance of power, but it was less distance to fall. "What do you want?"

"What can you tell me?"

"About?"

"Rebecca, I'm patient enough to stay here for a week if I have to."

She did not doubt his words. "Be specific."

"Glover will be here in two weeks' time. It's a goodwill visit, a stopover on his way to the Middle East. He wants the military vote."

"I know that. I knew that two years ago."

"So you did. So you did. Clever girl, aren't you." He was taking a wire bound document from a briefcase by the door. It looked like a script from where she sat. He plopped it into her lap.

Gene offered her a cigarette but she shook her head and watched while he lighted his. Their gazes met over the top of the Zippo flame. She trusted him as much as he trusted her. Maybe I can bluff my way out of this, she thought.

He indicated the document. "Do you recognize it?"

She looked down at the wire bound booklet, and flicked through it. It would have helped if she'd been able to focus properly. The cut on her forehead was still oozing blood.

November 15. Two years ago. Sydney.

She was back in the hotel room, sitting across the coffee table from Elizabeth Glover, holding the woman's hand. What was supposed to have been a private consultation had been transcribed, word for word. Until she actually read it, Rebecca had only remembered the gist of the reading and not too many details. Not that there'd been many to begin with.

Fifty pages of neatly-typed conversation lay on her lap, one page for every minute she'd spoken with Elizabeth Glover. What had

Elizabeth done? Kept the original recording of the reading and passed it to one of her husband's secret service bodyguards when he wasn't looking?

"I need to know how you knew."

"I knew nothing until I touched her hand."

"Like you knew Leon was going to die in a car wreck before it happened?"

"Yes. I get pictures, in here." She touched her forehead, between her eyes. "Feelings, here." Her mid section. "And the voices, too. It's a combination of all three. Interpreting the impressions correctly is the key factor. Getting it right is the hardest part."

"You have seen John Glover die, is this true?"

"Yes. But what if the vision merely symbolizes the death of his ideals? That when he takes office and finds his hands are tied and he can do diddly squat? That his only job is to do what he's told? Perhaps that is what his death means. It may all be symbolic."

"My ass it's symbolic. You said when he takes office. Not if."

"If he doesn't die in England, he will be President."

"Remains to be seen, don't it."

"All I know is that an American woman came to see me for advice, I told her what I got at the time. She loves her husband and it wouldn't matter if he was the President of the United States or a garbage collector. Can you comprehend what I am saying here?"

"I'd like you to look at page 20."

She turned to the page, and as she began to read, she could almost smell Elizabeth Glover's musky perfume. It had been strong, but not as strong as the fear in the woman's eyes.

EG: Please, you have to help me. I'm prepared for whatever you say. I've sought out psychics all over the world but they always tell me what they think I want to hear. I need to know the truth so I can be prepared for what eventuates. Please. I can take it.

(Five second pause)

RM: Your husband is going to run for the presidency. He feels it will make his life complete. He's ... very idealistic. Your husband is a well-respected man, and I hate myself for saying this, but there are a lot of people who would rather die themselves than see another African American in the highest office. When your husband succeeds in pre-selection, it's only a matter of time before he does become President. A lot of ill-feeling will be generated by his candidacy, but when he takes office? Oh, dear.

(Three second pause)

RM: Much of this ill-feeling will come from those closest to you. Those you thought for many years were good, trusted friends. There is betrayal here, Elizabeth. A lot of it from a source you never expected. Your main fear is that you will never know from one day to the next if your husband is going to come home to you alive. That's your fear now, but it's always been your fear. Especially when he was flying.

EG: I've put up with him for twenty eight years but I still love him to death. I can't imagine life without him.

RM: I know. I can't say this any other way, and I hope I am wrong, but yes, your fears are, for once, justified. It's not your imagination. You're being warned.

EG: Is it what I've been seeing almost every night since he retired from the air force and stood for the senate?

She squeezed my hand so tight then, Rebecca thought, that I felt bones crack in my fingers.

I have to know. Please. Tell me.

RM: I see your husband, with you standing behind him.

You're both walking down the stairs of an aircraft, but it's not Air Force One. It's smaller. Much smaller.

EG: A Lear. My husband's got himself a Learjet and he flies it himself. He won't have full secret service protection even though he's entitled to it.

RM: Then perhaps it's time you told him he needs this protection. You tell him to stop being such a stubborn son of a bitch. Convince him. You'll be able to. He listens to you.

EG: He doesn't make it down the stairs, does he. I dream it all the time.

(Six second pause)

But he's a good man. He's a good man.

RM: The warning is here. It can be avoided. Let him hear this.

EG: He'd say, Liz, honey. It's a crock. That's what he'd say. I asked did he want to come in with me, but he laughed and said it's all mumbo jumbo. Said I was being silly. I just want to stop this. I don't know if I can.

RM: You can't stop him running for office. It's destined that he will do this. He must do this. No matter what you say or do, your husband is going to become the next President. The question is, for how long. Liz, I will tell you this.

(Two second pause)

If someone attempts to assassinate your husband, it won't happen in America. It's going to happen in England. Let's see, the north east?

EG: England? But why would he go back to England?

RM: It's not clear. Perhaps he's visiting defense personnel – troops, airbases or something like that... Lake? Water? No, that's not it... Heathlake? Lakeheath. I'm told you know it. Do you?

EG: Lakenheath?

RM: Yes. That's it.

EG: It's a USAF base in Suffolk. John was stationed there during Desert Storm. But why would he go back to visit?

RM: I think he's on his way to the Middle East. To see troops.

EG: What am I going to do?

RM: Believe me when I say the future is never set in concrete. Many people have been able to change what were once predestined outcomes. Perhaps now that you know what may be ahead, you can take measures to avoid it.

Rebecca closed the document and put it on the floor. Giving the recording to the Secret Service had been Elizabeth's Glover's measure of avoidance. And now I'm here, stuck in the middle. Drowning.

"Don't tell me you know nothing."

"But I don't. Yes, there's this, but ultimately, it's of no help to anyone who is there at the scene, is it. The details. The little things. Where. When. How. All these things you expect me to know but I don't know and I won't know until…"

"Until?"

"The time is closer. Or I meet with the senator myself."

"You're getting more images, though. Every day there's some more."

"It means nothing. It's nothing anyone can use."

"During your conversation with Elizabeth Glover, you mentioned some kind of personal betrayal. How relevant is that?"

"I'd forgotten I'd said it till I read the transcript."

"Pete Hamill?"

"I don't know!"

"They're friends. They served in the Air Force together."

"He was best man at the senator's wedding. He's told me."

"Kelly Nolan?"

"Oh, come on."

"Who kept you out in the open at the airfield? Who gave his man plenty of time to take the shot?"

"Kelly? You can't be serious."

"You're trusting the wrong person. You're in love with the wrong person."

"I'm not in love!"

"You are trusting the wrong man, Rebecca. You should be talking to me or to Pete. Or to Dawn. Not Kelly Nolan. You know who his wife is, don't you."

"Yes. She's a politician's daughter."

"And her father is?"

"I don't know. I don't want to know."

"Well, I think you'd better know, honey. Corey Lorber. You heard of him?"

She looked up quickly. "But Lorber's another candidate for the presidency. I didn't know he was Kelly's father in law. He never told me his name."

"Why would he, huh? How can you trust him if you don't know whose side he's on?"

Silence. The pain in her heart was agonizing.

"Do you really want to know the reason you are here, Rebecca?" He didn't give her time to reply. "You're being used as a decoy, no more no less."

"Decoy?"

"Drawing out possible conspirators, honey. That's why you're here. So let's talk about this, okay? Glover's flying his own LearExec into Lakenheath airbase in two weeks' time. Pete's going to take you there a week or so beforehand. Kelly will, of course, be there, too. He does most of the operations planning. Okay, it's a goodwill visit. We know for a fact that Glover only tolerates the bare minimum of secret service protection. John Glover is a security nightmare. He's already got the military vote, he knows that. He's simply assuring himself of it. Hell or high water, honey, he's coming. We don't know as yet if his wife is accompanying him. So you saw what exactly?"

Her voice was flat as she said quietly, "The plane stops. He gets out and he stands on the second step. He sees a lot of school kids on the tarmac and he lifts his hand to wave at them. And that's when… when gets a bullet between his eyes."

"Who is responsible?"

"I don't know."

"Where does the shot come from?"

"How should I know?"

"Is it one shot?"

"Yes. Only one."

Gene sighed and rubbed the back of his neck. "Am I there?"

"How the fuck should I know? There's a sea of faces. People everywhere. A lot of screaming. It's chaotic."

There was a moment's silence. He lighted another cigarette and this time when he offered her one, she almost accepted.

"What if I'm wrong?" she asked.

"I seriously doubt you are ever wrong. I want to tell you something. It's about the testing you underwent. The best in the world, that we know of, reached a top score of 87 and that was eight or nine years ago now. Plus, that individual completed all tests necessary at the time. Do you know what your score was, Rebecca? 98.9 and you walked barely halfway through. We cannot afford to ignore you, but I'll tell you what I know and I sure ain't no psychic." He sat beside her on the carpet, but he did not sit close enough to touch. Not yet at least. "Nolan's the assassin at Lakenheath."

"No. You're wrong. I know him."

"And I don't? Me and Kelly go back a long way, Rebecca. You've seen what he drives. You've seen his wife. Whose money pays for that? You think he'd give her up for you? Look, I don't want to be too invasive here, but how long did it take him to fuck you?"

Rebecca said nothing.

"The guys were running a book on it, Rebecca."

Rebecca tried to get up and Gene made the fatal mistake of touching. He grabbed her arm and pulled her back down.

At that moment, she knew that nothing had changed.

It was still Gene at the airfield. It was still Gene in bed with Marianne Nolan. He loved her. He wanted Kelly out of his way. It was Gene taking orders from Corey Lorber. Rebecca could see the palatial mansion again. Topiary in the garden. Marianne swimming naked in the pool, Gene watching. He didn't want her. He wanted her father as President. He was on his way to becoming some kind of Presidential advisor.

And from the edges, Kelly's voice returned. Mental, emotional, physical. You'd be easy.

"How long did it take him to fuck you, Rebecca? Because if you're thinking it was making love, honey, you're seriously mistaken."

Perfect reaction. Tears. He had her.

"He wants you to love him because if you love him, he is safe. He's covered. He has your trust. He has your loyalty. He's feeding on your weaknesses, girl. That's all he's doing."

Silence. She had ceased defending him.

"He would put a gun behind your ear and stand to the side so he wouldn't get hit with your blood, honey. He would not hesitate to kill you when the time is right. And he will. He'll do it in the confusion. The chaos you've already seen. That's when he'll do you. After he's done Glover. He is a soldier. He does what he's told when he is told. But he has more than one agenda here, and you should be aware of that."

The silence was strong and complete.

"Just because he's fucked you don't mean he won't kill you. Think about it. Use your head. You've seen his wife. Why would he want you?"

Rebecca turned to Gene and said, "You shouldn't touch me, Gene. You should know better than that."

Confusion was alive in his eyes now. He had misjudged. The situation was beyond repair. He let go quickly and was on his feet in half a heartbeat. Rebecca scrambled to get up. Run. The head wound upset her balance but she tried to get away. He was too quick for that. Rebecca tried to kick, knock him off balance. There was contact. Her foot hit his chest but it was not forceful enough. He grabbed for her long hair as she tried to flee and the knife he'd used to free her initially was against her throat. It stung.

The Cliffs of Moher. Kelly moaned aloud when he saw how full the car park was. Half a ray of October sunshine and there was a tourist flood. "You can't walk to the cliffs in those heels."

"You never know, Kelly. I might slip. Then you'll get the insurance and the other woman. That'll make you happy. God knows I can't anymore."

"Knock it off, Marianne. Please. Enough is enough." He got out of the car and closed the door harder than he should have. Marianne waddled off across the car park towards the stepped pathway leading to the top of the cliff. Kelly stood for a while, taking in the view but it didn't last long. He felt a sting at the base of his throat as if something had bitten him and he rubbed at it.

"Are you coming or not?" Marianne spat.

And he thought, as he walked, that maybe, just maybe, she might fall... the tragic death of a presidential candidate's daughter in Ireland. Probably get the old bastard sympathy votes. No, Kelly knew for a fact that what you wished for the most never eventuated. He knew hundreds of ways to end life, but most of them were quick and clean. Not one of them was slow enough for Marianne today. Her sole mission in life was to make his existence as miserable as was inhumanly possible.

On she tottered in her high heels. She never listened to a word he said. Now she'd moan all night about blisters and aching knees.

He took most of the stairs quickly and easily, and stared at the view, trying to concentrate on the changing hues of sea and cliff face. He tried to clear his mind totally but it didn't work.

She was walking fast to begin with, not at a steady pace. She didn't stop to admire the view. No, she'd promised her daddy that she'd walk it, and she'd take a photo when she got to the top. Marianne never stopped to gaze, meditate. She never stopped to see, feel, hear, touch or smell.

Kelly knew he could stand here in silence with Rebecca. That he would be the one to tire of it first. I'll bring her here, he thought. I'll bring her to this place. I'll take her anywhere in the world she wants to go.

He looked for this wife amid the tourists. She was chatting. Always chatting and saying nothing.

Kelly ached for the phone to ring. For some kind of emergency call. For some kind of action. Something. Anything. Marianne had the phone in her designer back pack. She said it was on. Of course it was on. Yeah, right.

Kelly caught up with her, fumbled in the bag and took out the phone.

It was off. "I could kill you right now, woman."

And she thought he was joking.

He went down the shallow, long stairs two at the time, dodging and weaving to avoid the tourists, skipping around teenage girls and tossing two Euros into a violin case. The busker was a pretty thing and she played well, too. But he didn't stop to see the smile.

In the hillside shops he bought a can of Coke, then he strolled back to the car. He knew he was in for a long wait. She'd make him wait, too. Hours if need be.

He put the phone on the dash.

The battery was charged.

He only wanted to hear her voice. Maybe he could phone? It was sixteen hundred. What did she do at sixteen hundred? She sat in the bar, sometimes. Played Pearl Jam or Chris Isaak on the juke box. Sometimes she was in her room, lying on her bed. Meditating, she'd said.

He couldn't get her out of his mind. "Damn it." Kelly took the mobile and yes, there was a signal. He input the numbers for the base and then her extension. "Come on," he mumbled, checking to see if Marianne was returning. Not yet.

It rang half a dozen times before Joel intercepted the call. "The person you wish to call is unavailable. How may I help?"

"Nolan. Where is she?"

"Jesus Christ, we've been trying to reach you all day!"

"What's going on?"

"She's gone."

Silence.

"You there?"

"I'm here."

"She's gone. We're out searching but so far nothing."

"Find Samperi and you'll find her. Talk to Mannett. We put a tracker in her tags. I'm on my way." Kelly got out of the car and felt another sting.

A thin trickle of blood was flowing down her neck and staining the collar of the parka. "It's meant to be, Gene. Glover will be President. You're dispensable. You're dispensable to both Corey Lorber and his daughter. You're a means to an end as much as I am. Don't do this. You can't do this. You know it's wrong."

Overhead, the thuck thuck of rotor blades split the air.

He cursed, quietly, and terror flooded in, so much of it that it swept into Rebecca as well.

Gene spun her. The back of her head crashed into his shoulder. He had the point of the knife under her ear. She knew it would be quick, relatively painless. A blanket of calm draped her spirit as Gene ungracefully danced her towards the back door.

The sun was setting. Rebecca saw farmland out there: acres of rolling, fallow ground. But a black chopper dropped from the sky and billowed up choking dust.

"Let me go, Gene. Let me go or they'll kill you."

He dragged her back inside and slammed the door.

They were back where they started.

He's going to kill me, she thought. Why am I so calm?

Rebecca closed her eyes and imagined. She imagined a headache, so intense, that Gene would lose his grip on the knife, and he would drop it. Then he would fall to his knees, screaming from the pain.

She imagined disabling him without spilling blood.

That was the reason for her calmness.

A moment passed.

Gene made a noise: more animal than human. His grip loosened slightly. The knife dropped from his hand. He thudded to his knees, both hands gripping his head.

His screams began, then suddenly ceased. Gene fell face first on to the floor and lay there, eyes wide, gasping for air.

Rebecca took three steps back. She was light headed. Nauseous.

Glass shattered. Heavy boots upon the floor. Someone touched her. Spoke. It was a voice she knew and trusted. Mac?

"Mac?" She started crying. Strong arms enfolded her. "Did I kill him? Oh, God, no, Mac, I killed him. I killed him!"

"No. He's still alive."

Rebecca dared to look. Jamie Faraday was crouched beside the helpless form of the man who was once Gene Samperi, whose body now did not comply with his damaged brain's wishes.

The commander rang from Shannon airport. He hadn't been able to get a flight out and the ferry from Rosslare was long gone. "Okay, Joel. Fine. That's fine. You're sure she's all right?… Somebody's got to get her to talk… No, it can't be Macpherson if he was on retrieval…"

Marianne sat in the VIP lounge, sipping on a Baileys, antipathy turning to hatred with each intake of breath as she listened to Kelly talking to God knows who about her.

"Was it Samperi?"

She turned her head quickly at mention of the name.

All was quiet for awhile. Kelly glanced at his wife. "Are you sure? I'll be on the next available flight but I don't know when that will be."

Kelly disconnected the call and stared at the phone for a moment.

"Well?" Marianne asked.

Kelly studied her for a little while. "What were you planning to do? Divorce me? John Glover's out of the running, your daddy's in the White House, you marry Gene and all's right in your perfect world?"

Marianne thought that was amusing until she heard, "Gene's had a cerebral hemorrhage. Right now the only thing he's good at is goldfish impressions."

All color drained from her face. Tears filled her eyes and for a heartbeat of time, Kelly almost felt sorry for her.

Almost.

There were three butterfly closures above her left eye and dressings and skin tape on her throat. Mike had said there wouldn't be much of a scar. But she didn't care.

"Lass, will you talk to me?"

Rebecca stared from her window into the night, over the wooded skyline. Which direction was Ireland?

"You've got to talk, pet."

"Leave me alone, Mike. Please." Her voice was shaking. "I just need to be on my own for awhile."

She'd not said a word at the debriefing. Mike knew she'd not say a thing until the only person she could trust was present. He did not know when that would be.

"Lass?"

Rebecca turned and looked up into the doctor's calm, kind eyes. She'd never had a father, not one who loved her. This man was the closest she would ever get.

"I want you to come closer."

Rebecca stepped closer. She didn't hesitate and it was a good sign. Mike reached out and held her tight, and for a second, felt the tension in her body. It was not easing. It would not for some time. "You been to hell and back today, pet. Aye?" She nodded. "Gave you a hell of a fright, aye?" Again, she nodded. His hands were warm and strong and reassuring. He holds his daughters like this, she thought. That's how he sees me: another daughter. The thought was very comforting.

"There'd not be a law says you have to pretend you'd be someone you're not." She was relaxing. "So you talk to me. Aye?" Mike drew her away gently and she looked up into his eyes.

"I only wanted to give him a headache. I didn't think it would… he would… Is he going to die?"

"We all die, pet."

"But…"

Rebecca rested her face against Mike's chest. His heartbeat was loud.

"I'm sorry, hen. I'm sorry this has happened to you."

Rebecca retreated from the offered comfort, gripped her arms, tight, and slowly turned back to the window. "None of this would be happening if only I was…"

"What?"

"Normal," she said with huge tears in her eyes.

Rebecca settled into her narrow, hard bed and rolled to her side. "I just want to be normal."

"No such thing as normal in this world and if there was you wouldn't want it. You've a gift from God. When you've a gift from God, not using it is spittin' in his eye. You're different, that's all you are. But when young James Faraday says he sees an angel in you, then by God who am I not to believe him? If I could touch people the way you do without even knowing it, then I'd die a happy man. You've done somethin' here, Rebecca. You've changed us all. We'd not know how and we'd not know why but had something happened to you out there today, there'd not be one man in this place who'd not blame himself. I saw it for myself, lass. Forty-two men volunteered for the retrieval."

He looked down. She was asleep. But he sat there for a good five minutes more and in that time he wished, how he wished, he was twenty years younger. And for the first time in his life, Mike McLaren envied another human being. He envied Kelly Nolan because he knew what the future held for them both. And it was about time, Mike thought. It's about time they both had some joy. The joy of each other. For however long it was likely to last.

He pulled the covers to her chin, touched her hair and left the room. It was late but he phoned his wife. There was no reason, of course, and Mary couldn't understand it, but when he said he loved her and he always had and that he'd be home soon, she was well pleased to hear it. He'd not said he loved her since they courted. Was not something his Mary could take without asking what it was he wanted now. So he'd not said it aloud again.

He didn't know how much longer he had for this world but he knew he needed, now, to live it surrounded by his own—his wife, his girls, his wee grandson. A grandson who was six weeks old and Mike hadn't seen him yet. Yes, he was sent photographs every week, ever since he picked up the phone and called Peanut, but he'd not yet held the boy. He'd not yet been able to personally share the light of this new life shining into his family's heart.

Is time I resigned, he thought.

Kelly sat in the dark, the emerald-encrusted rose gold claddagh rolling between his fingers. He'd watched Marianne take four sleeping pills with a full glass of whiskey. If she expected him to stop her, to say, that's too many, she was disappointed.

She'd finally admitted that she'd taken him away so they could talk about divorce and the best time to do it and not have it interfere with her daddy's ambitions. She was going to marry Gene. And they'd planned on living in Washington because with John Glover out of the way... But now Gene was damned near brain dead, and life wasn't worth living if it had ever been worth living.

How long had it been going on behind his back?

Nine years.

Nine years and they'd been married for ten.

He watched her sleeping. How could he have believed he had ever loved her? Just the thought of her name now was enough to twist his gut into a tight, strangling knot.

Marianne cried out in her sleep. He turned to where she lay. Kelly felt nothing. No pity. No love. No hate. Nothing.

Chapter 9

SILENCE REIGNED SUPREME WHEN REBECCA walked into the mess the next morning. She tried to ignore it but it was impossible. Fifty pairs of eyes pretended not to stare.

"It's... different," Frank, the ration assassin, said.

She looked at him and tried to smile.

Rebecca took a tray, a bowl of cornflakes and coffee.

There wasn't even a murmur yet.

Mac didn't have to clear any kind of space that morning. Rebecca sat by the window at the far end of the long mess, her back to everybody, alone, until one man rose and weaved his way between tables. Uninvited, he sat opposite. BRANNAGH was embroidered on his pocket. "I'll fix it for you if you want."

"Fix what?" Rebecca mumbled and tried not to look at the inquisitive face.

"Your hair. I know how."

Mac went back to his breakfast. At least now he didn't have to wonder what he'd say to her today. She had relieved them all of that duty.

"I'm sorry... Brannagh?"

"Steve'll do."

"Steve. Don't take this personally but fuck off and leave me alone, all right?" Rebecca sipped her coffee and started on the cornflakes.

"No, it's not all right. Lunch time, or I will find you. Clear?"

"Is it really that bad?"

He nodded. What had she done? Taken paper scissors to fistfuls of her hair? "Here." He put his Nighthawks cap on her head. "I'll get it later." He went back to his table.

The cornflakes tasted like cardboard so she didn't finish them. Rebecca stood up, left her tray on the table—something she never did—and she departed, coffee mug in hand.

A low cloud of thunderous murmuring blanketed the mess the moment she left the room.

Rebecca rounded the first flight of stairs and the body coming down did not see her coming up. Half a mug of hot coffee splayed across a uniformed crotch. "F…f…far out."

Pete. Shit. "Sorry, boss."

"I didn't see you."

"I wasn't watching where I was going either."

"Rebecca, I need to talk to you. Just the two of us."

"Today is a new day, Colonel Pete. Yesterday's long gone and whatever happened yesterday can stay right where it is, thank you very much."

"You need to talk."

"I talked to Mike last night."

"No. You need to talk to me. Not Mike. Not Kelly. Me. Zero ten hundred, my office."

"Do I have to?" she whined.

"Yes. You have to."

Rebecca was glad to finally close her door. She looked from the window. It was raining hard today. She touched the peace lily on the window sill. She'd seen it in the mess and asked Frank if she could save its life. He didn't care. He hadn't known how it had gotten there anyway.

The single white flower was shadowed with green now. Soon the stamen would wither and the flower's beauty—its very life—would perish. But another one was coming to take its place in this world.

She looked at her reflection but not for long. She had a black, swollen eye a prize fighter would be proud of. She took off the Nighthawks cap and put it on again, quickly. She looked down at the garbage can, full of hair. She'd cut it at four in the morning and she'd been crying as she chopped and hacked. And now one of the boys would fix it for her. Steve. She'd not uttered a word to him until now.

Again she looked at the reflection. Mirrors never lied.

Has he fucked you yet? If you think it was making love you're mistaken.

But it wasn't a mistake. It would never be a mistake. Rebecca closed her stinging eyes and fought back the feeling. It was as if he was there. She could almost feel his fingers on her face, tilting her chin. Looking at her closely as if he was committing every line and curve to memory. His touch. His body. The way he held her so tight that even in sleep he seemed afraid to let her go. How she pretended to sleep when all the while she was listening to the sound of his breathing… and thinking, most of all, he's here. With me. I don't scare him. He believes in me.

She returned to the moment. This introspection was achieving nothing. Damn the romanticism, what did he care for that? He was a soldier for God's sakes. He's a man. I'm a woman. We did it. So what? Millions of people are doing it somewhere in the world every minute of every day. What's so special about us? Just because I feel I've met him before. Known him forever. It was as if meeting him now seemed like meeting him all over again, and perhaps they were picking up where they left off. Last time.

Reincarnation. Yes, she believed in it, and she knew the differing spiritual theories, but in reality, she had too many issues with this life to bother about what had already been, in another time, another place.

Her thoughts kept returning, for some vague reason, to the aircraft carrier, to the day her mother dragged her along to Fisherman's Wharf. The US military was in town again.

This time her memory did not falter. She obediently tagged along after her mother, aware of the looks she received but too shy to acknowledge anyone. She was fifteen, she looked eighteen. And it seemed that wherever she went on that big ship, there was someone following. A Native American.

Go do something, Jenny Miller said the moment she saw the blond pilot. She was such an extrovert. A flirt. A tease. Rebecca did not want to admit this woman was her mother. She stood there, ashamed, watching her mother chatting to the blond pilot, while the tall, half Cherokee with dark, dark eyes, in turn watched her. She just couldn't bear to look while her mother posed for a photo. The only time she smiled like that was when she was trying to get herself a man.

Rebecca glanced at the dark haired one dressed in white. His face creased with a smile and he nodded, however slightly. The man beside him was a tall African American wearing the same uniform as the guy her mother had claimed. Why not, she thought. Rebecca fumbled in her shoulder bag for her trusted instamatic camera. Ten shots done, two left. Gathering all of her courage, she stepped forward, unsure of herself, or which of these men to ask.

"Could I… would you…" but her heart was beating too fast, and now she was shaking. Words failed.

The African American said, "Sure baby. Stand here between us. We won't bite."

And a passing marine was ordered to take a photo of the Aussie teenager standing between the two American servicemen. The marine handed her camera back, and she took it shyly.

Rebecca's heart lurched. She reached for the phone. "Hey, Joel, I need to call Australia. Can I do that?"

She asked Annie to go to her apartment, and in the garage, in a sealed plastic box, labeled Really Old Pix, find a photo of her, aged

171

fifteen, standing between two uniformed men. Please scan it and email it to her private address ASAP. No, she didn't know when she was coming home…

"Enter."

Rebecca walked in.

"Sit."

"Woof."

Pete looked up from the paperwork on his desk. "What did you just say?"

"Woof. Well, you said 'sit'."

Pete tossed his pen impatiently. "What's your problem, Rebecca?"

"How long you got, Pete?"

Pete sighed and rubbed long fingers through his very short blond hair. "Coffee? Tea?"

"Coffee. How do you want yours?"

"There's no need for you…"

"I know. But there's no need for me to be here period." Rebecca said as she went to the coffee machine. "Black? White?"

"Black. Thank you."

She picked up the cup she presumed was his with an insignia on it:

She poured black coffee and set it down on his desk. He was a little wary. Not that she blamed him. She went back to the machine and got her own. "How did you know where I was?"

"GPS."

Rebecca turned to Pete, cuddled the coffee mug between her hands, and studied him for awhile. "I'm not very good at this military stuff, am I."

"You're not expected to be."

She walked about the office—it was twice the size of Kelly's. She tried to imagine Kelly sitting there in the colonel's executive chair, but the image would not come successfully. He must have been happy as 2IC. Being 2IC wasn't quite as alienating an existence as being 1IC. But the men would still like and respect Kelly no matter what rank he held.

Pete, too, had framed photographs on his walls. Aircraft. Fighter jets. Plaques, awards, commendations. Rebecca wasn't surprised, though, to see family photographs amid the military. His wife was a flaming red-haired beauty who wore green satin and he was in a dress uniform. It was a relatively recent photo, because standing between them was the current President who would, in time, yield to John Glover.

History was in the making again and she was playing a part in it, a part the senator probably never even knew about. There were times when Rebecca almost forgot why she was there.

Another photograph on its own. A little girl with dark hair and blue eyes. One front tooth was missing. Her bike still had training wheels on it. The camera lens had picked up refractions of light around the child's head. Some would say it was the angle of the sun, a trick of the light, but to Rebecca it seemed that she could have been looking at herself, aged five. This child is special, she thought. She has the knowing, too. It was difficult to imagine Pete playing games with his daughter, but maybe he was like Kelly. The moment he drove from the gates, he metamorphosed into a real human being. "What's her name?" Rebecca asked.

"Jennifer. Will you please sit down? I can fully understand your reluctance to talk openly about yesterday…"

"You understand nothing. You are not me and I am not you. Agreed?" But she sat down anyway and sighed. "Thank you," she said quietly.

"For?"

"Finding me. Hindsight's a grand thing, isn't it."

"Tell me what occurred the night you were abducted."

"I don't know. I was pissed." She caught the look. Again, a misunderstanding. Pissed in American meant angry. In Australian, it meant drunk. "I had four black velvets in Salisbury and I'm a one pot screamer at the best of times."

"Yes, I know what pissed means. There has been the occasional Australian in this unit therefore most of your language I comprehend. So you were shit-faced drunk, right?"

"Oh aye, that would be correct."

"Does being under the influence heighten or lessen your abilities?"

"Wipe out, Pete. Absolute wipe out."

"You're telling me you have no idea who may have taken you from this compound?" He was sipping his coffee now but watching keenly over the rim of the black and gold mug.

"Not a clue. I was on my way to the shower because I'd thrown up on the way home. That's all I remember. I woke up with a sore head in a strange place with red curtains and he came in."

Pete put the mug down and traced the gold insignia with slow deliberate strokes of one fingertip. "Samperi was alone?"

"Yes. Just him and me. He was nice at first. He was. Truly. But I couldn't tell him any more than I could tell you. He had a transcript of Elizabeth Glover's consultation and he asked me questions about it. He even said how impressed the researchers had been. How I scored higher than anyone, ever. How nobody could afford to disbelieve. Don't get angry with me for saying this, but the first time I saw Gene Samperi, from the moment he touched my hand I knew he was the one who shot me at the airfield."

"I know this, Rebecca."

"Kelly told you?"

"Of course he told me. Leon Carter died just as you said he would and Samperi took Leon's position. We never allowed him access to you and perhaps that was my mistake. I misjudged the situation and for that I apologize. I do. I should have seen it coming."

Was he sitting there, admitting a mistake?

"Am I gullible, Pete?"

His smile touched his eyes as well as his mouth. "Tell me why you think you are gullible and I'll consider my response carefully."

"For a while, I believed him." Rebecca sipped the coffee and sat back in the seat, extending her legs again. "It was as if he were sailing a yacht. Tacking this way, then another and another and before I knew it, he had me so confused I barely knew what my name was. I usually know my own mind. I know right from wrong. I know when somebody's lying to me just by looking into their eyes. But I didn't know with him. He was very convincing."

"In what way?"

"He told me I was only here as a decoy to draw out potential conspirators. Maybe that's true. In a weird kind of way I can understand it. But he made Kelly seem like an enemy of the state. And at one stage he thought you were going to put a bullet into the senator."

Not a flicker of expression passed over his face when he asked, "Me?"

"It was just a lot of circumstantial bits and pieces but it was the way he put it all together. He said he and Kelly went way back."

Pete nodded. "I can't comment on that, Rebecca. You'll have to ask the commander yourself but be prepared for an ambiguous response."

"I guess he can't talk about Navy SEALs and snipers and black ops and stuff."

"Like I said, ambiguous. Now, is there anything you need to tell me?"

"Nothing that will help."

"If that changes you will speak to me immediately."

"Of course I will. That's the deal."

"John Glover will be flying his own jet into Lakenheath Monday fortnight."

"Yes, Gene told me."

"He knew?"

Rebecca shrugged. "He told me."

A curse was surfacing but it never emerged. "Great. I've only just got word myself." He mumbled to himself and she thought she heard him cursing under his breath; something about being the last to know. "We'll be flying out to Lakenheath in a week's time for security preparations. I want you there."

"I know."

"What, did he tell you that, too?"

"Yep."

"Anything else I should know?"

She thought for a moment. "No, I don't think so."

"Commander Nolan's chief training officer for this unit in hand to hand and close quarters combat."

"Yes, I know."

And Pete continued, regardless. "On Monday morning I want you out there. Learning."

"What, exactly?"

"How to survive in less than ideal situations."

She almost said Kelly had already started but she stayed quiet. It was the best choice under the circumstances. This man gave the impression he knew what was happening within the outfit he controlled, when in fact, he hadn't a clue.

"And you will not give me any new age love light and laughter bullshit about this, okay? It needs to be done. We do not, I repeat, do not want to relive yesterday's unfortunate events. I want to get through this without any bloodshed, especially yours."

"Aye, aye, captain."

He was surprised she'd be so obliging. The quick agreement caught him off guard but he soon regained composure. "Washington wants you in uniform for Glover's arrival at Lakenheath."

She stared at him, blankly. "Why?"

"You're not the only person here who would like to know why. Rebecca, I'm as happy about this as you are. The commander will teach you only what we both feel you need to know to act the part. Do you understand what this means?"

"I'm going to be a soldier? Fark, are you sure?"

His phone rang. He ignored it.

"No, you are not going to be a soldier. You are going to be a Nighthawk for a day. But I warn you, the next fortnight will not be easy for any of us. That will be all for now." He picked up the phone. "Hamill." He waved her away as he said, "John? Yes, good to hear from you. Thanks for getting back to me so quickly."

Rebecca looked at the time before she left the office quietly. He was talking to the senator. As she walked down the corridor, she wondered if she'd ever meet him: this man who would soon be king of a nation who had not a king to its name.

No, she didn't think she would get to meet him. All of this, for a few minutes at an airbase, so one man might make it to the bottom of a few stairs without dying.

Until the next time, of course.

She went down to the mess to wait for Steve Brannagh, but discovered he was waiting for her. And he said nothing as he walked up to her room, two steps behind her all the way.

She unlocked the door and he waited for her to enter first. Rebecca did not close the door. Nor did he ask her to.

Steve hardly said a thing except to tell her what he'd thought he'd do. As she sat in her tiny bathroom, in front of a mirror, with a towel around her shoulders, and she could not help but look at her reflection, she decided that anything at all Steve could do would be an improvement.

He sprayed her hair with water and combed it. She saw the look in his eyes and hoped he'd talk to her soon. The men now knew what he used to do and his life at the moment was tortured.

"Any relation to Kenneth?"

"Who?"

"Kenneth Branagh. The actor."

"Why do you ask?"

"Curious."

"Not a good enough reason." He was quiet for a while as he fiddled with her hair. 'Different spelling," he said, eventually.

"What do you do here, Steve?"

"I'm into explosives and that's all I can say."

"And the hairdressing? Where did you learn this?"

"I used to work for a movie production company. Special effects mainly. Makeup and hair sometimes."

"Wow. Really?"

"Keep still." Fingers clamped on her scalp. She dared not blink. "I don't believe in it, you know," he said as he began to cut.

"What?"

"Life after death. This psychic stuff."

"At least you're honest."

"And I don't like the idea of a woman here, either. It's no place for a woman. Never has been. Never will be." He wasn't exactly gentle as he pushed her head to the side. The scissors were cold and sharp against her cheekbone. Little snips.

"I'm leaving in a fortnight," she said. "After the senator's been."

"Good," he said.

"I've got to become one of you guys though. Next week, actually."

Steve stopped cutting and looked at her in the mirror. "What the fuck for?"

"I don't know. Upstairs Management has decreed."

He pushed her head the other way and nothing more was said until he was done. Steve Brannagh took the towel off, rolled it up and put it in the wash basin, then he ran his fingers through her hair, a final touch, and stepped back.

It wasn't an improvement. It was a transformation.

"Jesus Christ. Is that me?" she asked.

Steve smiled, picked up his scissors and retreated.

The central heating had been reset for the early winter that was settling in. Rebecca wasn't sure what to wear now. She had a couple of summer dresses in the closet, mainly because it would be summer when she arrived home again. There was the black velvet, but that was too hot.

Rebecca chose a blood-red halter necked jersey that had cost a small fortune in a boutique on the Rocks in Sydney. It was somewhat see through, but what the hell. No one looked at her anyway. She showered, added a touch of perfume and a splash of makeup. Lip gloss. Mascara. She ran her fingers through her hair, just as Steve had done.

She had never believed she could ever look like this. All dressed up and nowhere to go: a celebration of what, exactly, she did not know.

Rebecca floated into the mess, picked up a tray and realized there was yet another loud silence. Then someone wolf-whistled. Rebecca picked up her tray, and turned to face the sea of staring faces.

"And who was responsible for that sexist gesture?"

Forty two men raised their hands.

"Rat bags," she said and chose her food. Mac cleared space when she approached. He'd been reading his Kindle. It wasn't a bad story either but it paled into insignificance the moment his angel walked in. And she was coming towards him. Thank you, God, he whispered. His heart was loud and he was on fire. He wanted to stand but he couldn't. Please, he prayed silently. She'll beg for it tonight, won't she. Please God, say she'll beg for it tonight… "You look great," he said as calmly as he could.

"So do you, Sarge."

In jeans and a tee shirt? She's joking. He watched the way she picked up the paper napkin and anchored it into her cleavage. But so did everyone at the next table, too. Please, please let me be that paper napkin. "Brannagh did that? It looks great."

"And if breasts could talk they'd say, thank you for noticing my hair, Sarge."

Eyes up. "Sorry." He went back to his meal. It had no taste, and as for the story—what story?

"Guess what?"

Mac waited. And while he waited, he wondered what it would be like to…

"I'm going to be a Nighthawk next week."

Mac choked, almost spat. Composure returned, eventually. "This is a joke, yeah?"

"You're safe this time, Mac. The commander's going to turn me into a lethal weapon, not you."

There was a huge smile that he tried very hard not to release but it kept coming and coming until it was out and he was laughing so hard he was almost crying.

"I see you don't think it's possible," Rebecca said as she returned to her meal. A silent dare lay in her eyes.

"True. I do not think it's possible."

"Why not?"

"You're a girl."

"So?"

"Girls can't."

"Girls can't what, exactly? Come on. Be specific."

"This is a joke, yeah? You've been watching too many movies, love."

"No joke, Sarge. Dead set. The boss said something about not wanting a repeat of yesterday's unfortunate events. Besides, I have to be at Lakenheath and I have to be in uniform and I'm supposed to know how to act the part. And I'll do it. I appreciate a challenge."

"Challenge… We'll see."

"Yes, we will. Fifty quid?"

"You're throwing it away, Rebecca."

"Fifty quid, Sarge. Put your money where your big mouth is."

"You're on." Hands reached across the table and when they shook, she knew. Oh, dear, how she knew. Mac was not gay. The clouds of pure pink emanating from him were based solely on love. Love for her. She let go quickly and resumed her meal. Be normal. He was still Mac. "Sarge?"

"What?"

"I'm sorry."

"For?"

"Getting drunk, dancing on tables, and being an idiot."

"Don't worry about it."

"No. I was wrong about you. All along I've been wrong. I'm so sorry. But I meant what I said. About you being sweet. You're one of the nicest people I've ever met."

Mac felt that magic word looming. "But?" he asked. She couldn't say it, so he did. "The commander."

She nodded.

"He doesn't have to know."

"I couldn't do that to him and I couldn't do it to you, either."

"But you wanted to when you were drunk."

"Mac, I thought you were gay."

Her words hit very hard. "Why the fuck would you think that?" There was pain in his eyes. Disappointment. She'd kicked where it was never wise to aim: male pride. "I'm not fucking gay!"

Faces turned at mention of the word. Did he have to yell?

"I'm sorry. I really am," she said softly. "I shouldn't have said anything."

"Jesus Christ. Is that the only reason you sit with me? Was that the only reason you had dinner with me? Because you felt safe? You thought I was some fucking fairy?"

"No, Mac. I've always liked you from the moment I first saw you."

"Because you thought I was gay."

"No! Because you never want anything from me!"

"Well, you're wrong about that one, Rebecca. You are so wrong because making love to you has been the one constant thought in my head ever since I first laid eyes on you. You have no fucking idea what you do to me."

Tears stung. "If you want me to sit somewhere else, I will."

"Rebecca, I don't…" want you to sit somewhere else. Too late. She didn't sit somewhere else. She walked right out of the mess, leaving her food untouched.

Mac sat for a little while, unaware of the quiet amusement around him. Why would she think that? Why would she think I was gay? All I've ever wanted to do since the first time I saw her… He picked up his Kindle and went in search. She was in the bar, at the table where she always sat and she was staring down into the night, chewing on her thumbnail. As he drew closer, he saw the inevitable: a tear-stained cheek. Her makeup was running.

"I'm not gay," he said. "But I am too slow."

She looked up and wiped at her face quickly.

"From the first moment I saw you, I knew I had no chance. May I?"

She nodded and he sat opposite.

"You were… I don't know how to say this. Is familiar the word? It was as if I'd known you all my life but there you were, a complete stranger."

"And I saw the way the commander, looked at you, and, man, I knew then I didn't have a chance. It was worse for him because he'd been painting you for years."

Mac sighed and gazed out into the dark.

"And I'd see what was in your eyes when you looked at him and I knew it was wishful thinking on my part. And then I took that fall and… You want to know what I saw? I saw what you really are. I couldn't take advantage of you when you were drunk because I am not some opportunist. Now I understand it was just some ego thing of your own at work, it had nothing to do with me. But I need to know one thing. Will you please tell me why you thought I was gay?"

"Your colors," she said softly.

"What colors?"

"Your aura. What I see around you. All the time. The colors you show when you look at me. I misjudged because I'd only seen it around mothers with infants. I'd never seen it around a man before. Well, maybe once. He was homosexual."

"Angel, is there any way I can turn the fucking thing off?"

"I don't think so, unless you'd rather hate me. I don't want that."

Mac searched her face for a clue, but all he found was sadness. Sadness, shame. Discomfort. "You don't feel safe with me anymore."

"I'm still here, aren't I?" She tried to smile. It didn't quite work. She'd thought she'd lost him, forever, but he was sitting there, opposite, and about to apologize unnecessarily. "Of course I feel safe with you."

He reached for her hand. "Rebecca, if I told you I…"

"I know you do, Mac. I know."

His intake of breath was shaky. "Can we go somewhere? Can we talk in private? Just you and me?"

And she looked at him and didn't need to be psychic to know what was on his mind and it wasn't conversation. "Oh, Mac…"

"He doesn't have to know."

"We would know."

"Rebecca, he's married."

She had a choice. She could get up and walk out and he would follow her and they'd meet in a corridor, down in the bowels of the asylum, and it would be dark and his hands would be hot and he'd make love to her against an ancient stone wall and … Dear God, he'd be good at it, too.

She looked into his eyes. From a simple touch of his hand, there was a fire smoldering in her heart. Was it real or born of loneliness and desperation? Would it be wrong? What was this word, wrong?

What did it mean? They were both consenting adults and she needed some kind of human touch almost as much as he did.

Mac's fingers touched the gold cross around her neck. The back of his hand grazed her soft skin, leaving shivers in its wake.

"What do you say?" he whispered.

She looked into his eyes.

"Yeah? Please?"

Rebecca stood, looked down at him and stepped away.

She hadn't said no, she hadn't said yes. Mac sat there for a moment, watching as she walked to the door. When she turned back, he hoped that what lay there in her eyes was the equivalent of what raged within his body. She smiled.

He waited for a little while before walking out. Nobody noticed.

Rebecca was waiting at the bottom of the stairwell. Mac took her hand and led her towards B block and his own private office. There were no cameras down here. He locked the door, reached out and held her for a little while. She didn't object. Perhaps that was all she wanted, all she needed? It would never be enough for him. Mac kissed her, softly at first, and hesitantly, too. If there was any passion in response, he did not recognize it. He wanted to touch her breasts, see them, hold them, feel the heat, the weight, be a child again. Enter fully into a oneness for which he ached but his hand was only on her arm. It was as if he had not the courage to venture further. She was so small, almost delicate. His fingers would meet if his hand circled her throat. He traced her collarbone, her ribs. Oh yes, how easily she would break. How easily she had broken. A scar remained. It was plainly visible. It was damn ugly. He looked down into her blue eyes and saw again that wide, surprised, dead stare.

Tossing her into the back of the chopper. The commander using his own knife to cut the shirt off. Help me, Mac! Both on their knees, Mac on the breaths, the commander the external compressions. Mac could hear the crack of ribs under the pressure. But he knew it was futile.

"She was dead before she hit the tarmac."

What?

"That was what you said."

He stepped back. He had to. How could she know what he was thinking?

"And you threw a blanket over me, and you sat back, and because you didn't want Kelly to know you'd seen him crying, you turned your face to the window. Women would have cried aloud. Held each other. Wailed. Got rid of it. But men? No. No, sit back, say nothing. Let nothing show."

Mac stared at his angel. No wings, no lights, no magic. There was only Rebecca, leaning against the wall, hands behind her back. It was as if she knew she shouldn't be down here, as if she knew this shouldn't be happening.

"What do you see when you look at me, Mac?"

Someone else's woman, he thought.

"Exactly. We can't do this. He'll know. We will know. We can't."

And any hope he had died a slow, lingering death. "He's made love to you, hasn't he."

She nodded.

"It's not going to work, is it."

Rebecca shook her head. "Not the way you want. No."

"I'm sorry."

"Sorry is what three of us would have been, Mac."

"Oh, Rebecca," he said and held her again. She rested her face against Mac's shoulder, and for the second time since Kelly's absence, Rebecca felt truly safe. "Time we reappeared," Mac said. "We don't need any search and destroys right now." He kissed her forehead tenderly and led her away.

Music was blasting from the Wurlitzer.

Mitch Stafford went to the juke box, chose a song, and got a can of Fosters from the bar. When Chris Isaak had finished with his *Ring of Fire*, Cold Chisel began. *When the War is Over.*

Rebecca sat, fondling the crucifix around her neck, listening to a song she used to love as a kid but had never really heard until this moment. When the sad guitar finally stopped its crying, she heard the can of beer thud to the table. She didn't have to look up to know who it was: she recognized the antipathy.

"I was all right until you played that song." She looked up at Mitch. Jekyll and Hyde, first aid kit in one hand and deadly weapon in the other, a stethoscope around his neck and a volcano of anger bubbling away inside. Just what she needed.

And Mitch looked at her hair, the makeup, the dress with a split to the thigh. She was cold. Braless. Her nipples were scabrous. "If the commander saw you now he'd kick your arse."

"Go harass somebody else."

"You're needed downstairs. It's the captain."

"Who's with him?"

"Faraday."

Mitch finished his beer and led her down to the infirmary. They didn't get far.

"I've something to tell you, Sergeant Stafford," she said on the stairs. "And I'd like you to listen because it's important."

"Save it. I don't want to know."

"I'm going to tell you anyway."

"I said I don't want to know."

She pressed on, regardless. She knew she had to. "The only judgment in this life comes from within and you have nothing to fear except your own…"

"I'm not listening to this shit, you hear me? I am not listening!"

"Maybe you should!" she yelled back. "There's a woman here who looks like me and she has two little boys with her and she's been waiting years to get this message through to you! She won't fucking leave me alone so you hear me."

In the blink of an eye, Mitch pinned Rebecca to the wall, his arm across her shoulders, his face too close. "And I said, I am not listening. Are you deaf or do you have a death wish? Which is it?"

Ordinarily such anger would have forced an entire battalion to retreat. Not Rebecca. She wouldn't back down. "You did not kill your boys. Jeanie did. Jeanie took the twins and put them in the car and used the hose from the exhaust pipe, Mitch. You did not." And still he stared at her but the hate was disappearing, fast. It was replaced with confusion. "You were in Timor when it happened. SAS, yeah? You were with six other guys long before our troops were sent in. You did not kill your family. Why in God's name are you doing this to yourself?"

"I wasn't fucking there!" He walked away.

"She was disturbed."

"You think I don't know that?"

"The war is over, Mitch. It's over."

"It's never over."

"Forgive her and it will be over. That's all she wants from you. Forgiveness."

He came to a standstill. "How can I forgive her? How can I? The psycho bitch murdered my sons."

"Let it go. Please, let it go. She's begging me."

"Good. Keep the psycho bitch begging and shut the fuck up. I don't want to hear anymore of this shit. I don't believe in it."

"Don't walk away when I'm yelling at you!"

Something hard hit the back of his head and he turned, quickly. A shoe? She'd thrown a shoe at him? Rebecca met his death stare with an equal amount of determination.

And suddenly, Mitch almost laughed. This girl was as welcome as a fart in an elevator, but her persistence was admirable. Rebecca hobbled down the corridor and put her shoe back on. "She says her name only had one 'n' and you always spelled it with two, just to annoy her. She says you used to sing that song to yourself all the time. When the War is Over. You take it with you wherever you go. She says that song was in your head when they finally tracked you down in Timor and gave you the news."

"How can you know that?"

"She's telling me, Mitch. Jeanie's standing beside you. She's…" Rebecca paused, as if listening to words no one else could hear. "Mitch, you saw me and you thought I was her, didn't you. And what you said to me in the mess. If I said something would you hold it against me. That's what you said to her when you first met. But she didn't react like I did. She looked you in the eye and said that was the worst pick up line she'd ever heard but at least it showed some originality."

He couldn't meet Rebecca's gaze. "It wasn't original."

"The boys. They're with her. But they're also with you. Two little boys. Identical twins. Three years old. One is playing at your feet. He's got a yellow truck. His name's Sean. The other, he's drawing. Jason? Yes, Jason."

Mitch swallowed a rising lump. Sean. Jason. For three years they were his reason to live. "My boys are dead because I wasn't there. I was in Timor. If I'd been home, they'd both be in school now."

Rebecca reached out and touched Mitch's arm gingerly. Some of his volatility was easing. "You loved her but it wasn't enough. Sometimes it's not enough and she knows that now. But she did love you, Mitch. She just couldn't cope on her own. Even if you'd been there, with some nine to five job in a hospital, she'd still not have coped. She had some serious mental health problems."

He nodded, eventually. Now it was hard to look this girl in the eye.

"So let it go? This minute. Right now. Let it all go. They love you as much as you love them but let them go now."

"I don't know how."

"Tell them it's all right. Tell them they can go."

Rebecca touched his hand and he felt an electric charge from her fingertips. And then she smiled. At that moment, he too, saw what Faraday had seen. And when he could breathe again, the tightness that had gripped his heart for the past twelve years was gone. And so was the hatred he wore like a favorite overcoat in all weathers.

A weight literally eased from his shoulders. When he breathed, his lungs filled. But tears clouded his vision.

He had let his family go.

The black ops commando wiped his face on his sleeve. "Enough of this shit. Mike needs you," was all he said. When Rebecca turned, the woman and the two little boys were walking into the Light. Hands were reaching for them.

Chapter 10

REBECCA STOOD BY THE BED, knowing Mike was not going to be a willing party to this. Physician, heal thyself? she wondered as she pulled a chair closer. Mike didn't wake. She pulled the covers back and put her hand flat on his heart. His hand clamped over hers quickly. "What are you up to, pet?"

"I thought you were sleeping."

He squeezed her hand in reply. "Aye, I am. Off you go now."

"Let me help you?"

"It's mine to deal with."

"Let me help you."

The hand was still closed on hers. She looked about. Mitch and Jamie were watching. They were both leaning against the wall in a mirrored pose—Mitch with right arm over left and left foot over right, and Jamie, left arm over right and right foot over left. The umbilical brothers.

"You didn't want me to know about this. Too bad and too late."

"No, it's God's will," was all he said.

"You stubborn old fart, it's your will. Keep God out of this."

He grunted but kept hold of her hand. "Calling me an old fart now?"

Mitch and Jamie both glanced at each other and tried not to laugh.

"I'll tell you something else, you stubborn old Scottish shite. It's God's will that I'm here with you now, holding your bloody hand, aye?"

"Get off with you. You cannae talk to me like that."

"Oh really? What are you going to do about it?"

"Put you across my knee and slap your arse. That's what you need."

"You're too sick to sit up let alone slap my arse. Admit it."

Mike turned to look at her and he closed his eyes. "Would you put some clothes on, hen. You'd be as bad as my girls."

This was the funniest thing Jamie and Mitch, combined, had heard for weeks.

"Let me help you, Mike."

"I cannae."

"Why not?"

"It hurts you. That's why."

"Rubbish. It doesn't hurt me. I just get a little, I don't know… Dizzy."

"Dizzy, my arse. Get off wi' ye. I don't want you here!"

"Mike, you're a stubborn old…"

"Scottish shite. Aye, I know. Get off with you."

It was a point blank refusal. "All right. Suit yourself. Suffer. Vomit buckets of blood. Be in indescribable pain. If you think that'll get you home sooner, you're wrong."

"You're talkin' rot."

"I know where your resignation's stashed. Top drawer, right hand side. But I'm sure Mary doesn't want you home sick like this. Or the girls. And what about little Hamish?"

Mike huffed. How'd she know Peanut had called the boy Hamish? The grandson he'd not seen yet?

"I want to help. It doesn't hurt me. My blood sugars drop and that's all."

"You won't leave till I say aye."

"Captain Mike, you must be psychic."

The medics watched the angel at work. There was no light show today—it happened very quietly. The room filled with the scent of roses, obliterating the disinfectant.

After six minutes Rebecca sat back and stretched.

"Here," Jamie said. "Try this."

Rebecca took the glass of glucose willingly. She didn't pass out. But nor did she move from Mike's beside for the rest of the night.

It was two thirty in the morning when Jamie woke, not knowing he'd been asleep, to find Mitch, standing arms folded at the end of the MO's bed. He'd thrown a blanket around Rebecca. No sense moving her now.

"How's he doing?"

"Better."

"I heard a rumor."

"And?" Mitch asked as they walked back to their station.

"The CO wants her in uniform for the Lakenheath gig."

Mitch did not react like everybody else. He did not laugh, choke, become aggravated or lay any bets about failure. "Who drew the short straw?"

"Kelly."

"Does he know?"

A shrug came in reply. Only then did Mitch's smile appear.

"You look different. Did you get laid?" Jamie asked.

"Faraday? Shut up."

She was still in the red jersey dress when she came in for breakfast. Mac wasn't at his table and guilt rose again. Too much damage had been done. Sure, they'd parted friends last night, but she knew their relationship was cracked now. It wasn't, however, irreparable. She ate alone and took her coffee upstairs.

Pete was waiting near her door. "Morning," she said.

"Where have you been?"

"In the infirmary. The captain's not well. What have I done to deserve this visit?" she asked as she let herself into her room and Pete followed.

"You? Nothing."

"That's a change."

"I've just had a call from Kelly. He'll be back tonight."

If he was expecting some joyous reaction, he was disappointed. Rebecca's heart skipped, but she hid it well.

"And... there's a dinner party at my home on Friday. You and Commander Nolan are invited."

"A dinner party?"

Pete had a curious look on his face: something about her had changed but he wasn't sure what it was and he certainly wasn't going to ask. When Sheila seemed different, it was usually something to do with her hair... "I like your hair, by the way."

And then he was gone.

The minutes to hours took eternity to pass.

The captain was almost recovered, but resting. There was nothing for Rebecca to do but wait.

Wait, and think.

Would she still feel the same when she saw Kelly again?

Yes.

Would he still feel... whatever it was that he felt?

Unknown.

It was the longest day of Rebecca's life. She lunched alone. She had dinner alone. By ten pm expectation had turned to exhaustion.

She sat on the stairs near the main entrance, waiting.

At midnight, Kelly parked in his space. He got out of the car, took his bag from the trunk. He glanced up to the officers' quarters. Rebecca's light wasn't on. Disappointment settled, unfairly, yes, but still it settled. For some reason, he hoped she'd be waiting.

He used his passkey and stepped inside.

She was asleep, sitting up, her head resting against the bannister. Her hair was short. A cut over her black eye. Jeans. Orange pullover. Purple fluffy slippers. His heart leapt on sight alone.

Kelly put his bag down and sat beside her. She didn't wake. "Hey. You're snoring."

Rebecca propped awake. "I wasn't, I don't... You bugger."

All she could see was the amused light in his eyes.

Kelly was home.

Rebecca rose to her feet and stood on the next stair so that for the first time she was at eye level with the commander. She didn't know what to say. She wanted to touch, reassure herself that he really was there, that he was not, and never had been, a figment of her imagination. "It's good to see you again. I missed you. I never miss anybody."

"Except Annie."

"Annie's different. It's a..."

"Girl thing." His gaze was intense tonight. Almost frightening. He hasn't slept, she thought.

Kelly picked up his bag and took the stairs. Rebecca stayed where she was until she heard, "Are you coming?"

Rebecca watched while he stripped. She watched as he showered and didn't draw the curtain. He's beautiful, she thought. The way he's standing stretched out with his hands on the tiles like that. I could watch this for eternity and never tire of it. Water cascading, steam rising.

Rebecca turned away and sat by the window near the easel. There was a preliminary sketch, quick and untidy, of her. She was reading, head in hand. She seemed awfully bored. He said he'd make me beautiful, she thought. In this, I look sad.

She glanced back into the bathroom when he turned the water off. She watched the way he dried his body. And then he caught her staring. She looked away quickly. "That's not it," he said.

"What?"

"What you're looking at. That's not it." He came out totally naked and rubbing his head with a towel. "I don't know what I'll do with you yet."

She could have interpreted that in a myriad of ways. He could strip naked in front of her and not care. Did he do this often? Had he no shame? Wasn't he cold?

"No, I'm not cold. And I'm comfortable with you."

"Stop doing that!"

"What?"

"You're reading my mind."

"Now you know how I feel." He hung the towel up. She'd never seen a male actually hang anything up before.

"No, Kelly. I don't know how you feel. You never say a thing. I thought you'd be happy to see me. God knows I sat on those stairs forever waiting for you and then you came in and you didn't say a word except hey, you're snoring."

"You were snoring. I was happy to see you. I am happy to see you."

"So say it."

"Say what?"

And that was the difference between them; between male and female.

"Don't you know yet?" he asked, adding to her confusion.

196

"What?"

"I love you." It came automatically. Naturally. He didn't choke on it. He meant it.

He was about to hold her, undress her and make long, long love to her again until he heard:

"You knew about Gene and what he was likely to do. That's why you asked Mac to teach me self defense. It wasn't necessary because I almost killed a man by thinking about it. And I don't know if I can ever forgive myself for doing that."

"You did that to Samperi?"

"I thought it. It happened."

"Nobody else finds out about this. Do you understand me?"

She nodded. "It's just that—"

"You listen to me. You speak of karma? Gene Samperi got exactly what he deserved, no more and no less. No. You hear me out. If you can kill or inflict harm by thought alone, then be assured I'd much rather you held that power than me."

"But you're always so, so…"

"Cold?"

"Calm. Nothing bothers you."

Kelly almost laughed. "Oh girl, you have no idea. What you see is never what you get. I want you to remember something because for the next few days, you're going to hate me. I will put on the uniform and turn into some asshole who'll make you do things you shouldn't even know about. So you remember that I love you, I would never hurt you. I would lay down my life for you. Are we clear?"

"Aye, aye Captain."

"Good. Now, where were we?" Kelly took her face in hand and kissed her, lightly at first.

"But, but…" Her feeble protests lasted a few seconds.

"I've started divorce proceedings."

Kelly woke to a voice filtering in from the edges of consciousness. There was a warm, soft body spooned into his back; a hand, heavy across his stomach. "Lilies," the soft voice said. "All white. No. No, not you too, no!"

Kelly sat bolt upright.

Rebecca rolled over and all was quiet for a little while. A nightmare? he wondered.

"Flowers. The one with all the flowers…" With a stifled scream, she was wide awake.

"You ok?"

Disorientated for a moment only. "I think so."

Kelly slid back down into the bed and, ignoring the time, cradled her head with his arm. "I need to ask you something."

Rebecca waited.

"What have you seen about my past?"

Rebecca hesitated to say.

"Please."

"Sniper. I've seen you under water, blowing some kind of boat up. I've seen you jumping out of a plane. I've seen all kinds of things. Why?"

With a sigh, he said: "I need to be straight with you, Rebecca. No secrets. But I want you to listen and not say a thing. I was in Iraq in 2004. Fallujah. Gene and I were a sniper team back then. There was an incident where four Americans were ambushed and killed, their bodies burnt, dragged through the city. It was pretty fucking gruesome. We got some intel about the ringleader, a guy called Abed, so we followed it up. We got to the location and there was a young Arab couple there. The guy would have been twenty, max, and his wife, who knows. 16? 18? Pregnant. The young guy said he didn't know Abed. Or maybe 'no talk' was the only English the poor bastard knew. Anyway, Gene's got him on his knees, a gun at the back of his head. I've got the girl and we're gonna make him talk. But all he can say is, no talk, no talk."

For a moment, all was quiet.

"But Gene's impatient. It's taking too long. He shoots the wife, this pregnant woman, and she's convulsing at my feet. The Arab guy's hysterical now, no talk, no talk… I kept saying, he doesn't understand English… Before I know it, he's dead, too."

Rebecca stayed quiet. Silence was safe. He shouldn't be telling her this.

"I've been living with this for too many years now. The intel put us in the wrong fucking house. So that was the end of my SEAL career. Marianne's father had contacts that kept us both out of prison. Having a son in law facing murder charges would do serious damage to anyone's political ambitions. And that's how I ended up here. How to kill a Navy SEAL—put him behind a desk. I'm not proud of it, Rebecca. I may not have shot those two but I was there, I was a part of it, and I am just as guilty as Gene Samperi and as I said, that's something I've got to live with. I'm part Cherokee and we believe in balance. You call it karma. Gene's paid for his part. I'm still waiting for mine."

Kelly looked deep into her eyes. "What I'm trying to say—if you get up and walk away right now, I wouldn't blame you."

Rebecca got out of the bed and reached for her pullover. She put it on, and searched the floor for her undies. Kelly watched, devastated, as she dressed. Then she turned to face him.

"Up and at em, Captain Courageous. You have to turn me into a finely tuned killing machine."

Rebecca had breakfast with Mac. She hadn't seen him about because he'd taken a couple of days leave.

"Today it begins, yeah?"

She looked up as she spread Vegemite on toast. "God help us all."

"Fifty quid, wasn't it?"

"I was hoping you'd forget. Can I ask you something?"

Mac regarded her with extreme caution.

"What do you do here, exactly?"

As he spread marmalade on his toast, he said, "Primary weapons skills training. Hostage rescues, assault and pre-emptive. Chopper insertions. I've done one or two dozen aircraft assaults. Then there's the covert entries, explosives breaching… and you haven't understood a word I've said."

"And everybody does this?"

"More or less. There's specialist teams for specialist situations."

"Kelly's the overall team leader?"

"Once a SEAL, always a SEAL."

She leaned forward and whispered, "What exactly is that?"

"Don't you know what a Navy SEAL is?" Mac asked.

She shook her head, so Mac leaned forward this time and he told her what a Navy SEAL was. Rebecca sat back. "Holy crap. Really?"

Rebecca knocked on Kelly's door and walked in. He was on the phone, so she sat quietly and waited, and tried not to listen to his conversation. It was only a succession of yes, no, okay, and more yes and no. Kelly hung up and looked at her, questioningly.

"It's five to ten. I'm not late." She didn't like the way he was studying her. "What?" she asked. "What?"

"This came for you." He pushed an Australia Post airmail packet across the desk towards her. It hadn't been opened. Rebecca Miller. A post office box in Salisbury. She turned it over. Annie!

Rebecca tore at it as if she were a starving canine. A photograph in a frame was wrapped in bubble-plastic but she read the letter first. Pages and pages of it.

Annie seemed to think Rebecca was never coming home. Instead of scanning the photos, she decided to mail them, mainly because she couldn't remember how to work the scanner. Getting a snail mail address was a nightmare. She had stored the original phone number in her cell and had called back, asking for a postal address for Rebecca Miller. Eventually, she was given the box number…

Rebecca looked at a four by seven photo and handed it over to Kelly. "Annie's boy."

Kelly took the photo. A toddler, playing with toy trucks. "He's the closest you'll get to having a child of your own, right?"

She had never seen this type of look cross his eyes before. It was as if he knew something she didn't. "I only wanted you to see him. That's all." Rebecca snatched the photo back and went on reading the letter. Kelly waited, patiently. She unwrapped the framed photograph, looked at it and said, "Bloody hell. This sat on the wall for years, Kelly. Years. When Mum died, I took it down, put it away. All this time and I never noticed this before." She passed it over and he looked at it. It was the Eisenhower, definitely. He recognized the woman in the photograph only because her daughter was similar. What was interesting was that Rebecca's mother stood beside Pete, who was, at the time, a fighter pilot. Joint operation war games: a stopover in Sydney, then Brisbane and finally, North Queensland and Shoalwater Bay. He remembered it well.

The background of the photograph drew Kelly like a magnet. He could see himself on the deck, feet apart and arms folded. But he wasn't watching the camera. He'd been watching a teenage girl, who wasn't in the photo. His head was inclined towards the person on his right, as if the photo was taken mid-conversation. Kelly was talking to John Glover, the man who would be President.

"If you think that's spooky," Rebecca said, "Have a squiz at this one."

In his hand now, another photo. The hair on the back of his neck stood to attention immediately.

Kelly, Rebecca and John Glover, fifteen years ago.

"When I was still in high school, the US Navy came to town. I had my photo taken standing between an Indian and a black guy. Fifteen years later the black guy is going to be President and the Indian's job is to protect him. And guess what? I'm still slap bang in the middle."

It wasn't often that Kelly was lost for words.

"This is meant to be."

"You're not wrong," Kelly said.

He reached for the intercom and told Joel he'd be back in four hours. "You're coming with me." He took his spare jacket from the hook behind his door. "Leave all that. You can collect it later."

Rebecca left the packet, letter and photographs on Kelly's desk.

"What's he like? Really?"

"Who?"

"John Glover."

"John? He's a regular kind of guy."

"He's going to be President, he can't be a regular kind of guy."

"He was then and he is now. Sorry to disappoint you."

"Don't walk so fast. I can't keep up."

He slowed a little. "What's your time been like, here, with us?"

"In all, better than I'd imagined."

"Because of the men?"

"Nah. Because of you."

There was silence except for his boots clumping and her sandals clacking along the floor of yet another corridor. "This underground passage leads to Stonehenge, doesn't it."

He held the supply room door open. Rebecca walked in, under his arm. A young man stepped forward. Rydell. She'd seen him before but they had never spoken. He measured her for a uniform and the entire time, Kelly watched in his usual stance, arms folded, feet apart.

"This way, Miss," Rydell said and let her further into the cool, clammy depths, showed her into a tiny room and closed the door.

She could hear them talking out there. No one could find any viable reason for this to be happening and neither could Rebecca. There, on the table in a room where she was surrounded by plastic wrapped uniforms of varying colors, gray, khaki and black, lay hers, or at least a substitute until the 'real' ones were available. She was told to wear the black today. The green tomorrow. Gray the next day. Alternate. Get used to it until it became a second skin.

Yeah, sure.

She put the pants on first. They were hard and prickly and were made from a heavy cloth immune to flame or so it felt. The pants were far too long in the waist. A tee shirt. Black. The smallest they had fell to her thighs. Next, the pullover. It had padded, vinyl patches across the shoulders and chest. It was heavy, too. Maybe it had built-in bulletproofing? Again it was the smallest they had in store, the cuffs reaching past her fingernails, hem to her knees. When she tucked this into the pants she looked like the Michelin Man.

She was twenty pounds heavier already. She picked up the belt and wondered how it worked.

"Need some help?" Kelly was leaning against the door, trying to hide his amusement. He stepped forward and showed her how to put the belt on.

Next, boots. "Do I have to?" she whined.

"Yes, you have to. You can't do this barefoot."

She put the boots on. The smallest in the supply room were again too big. They felt like water skis. She regarded her reflection in the cracked mirror and topped it off by putting the Nighthawks cap on her head. It also was too big. She turned to Kelly. "What do you think?"

His face registered nothing but his eyes were laughing at her.

Rebecca followed him from the room, her civilian clothes over her arm as she tried not to trip on the uneven floor.

Rebecca plodded through the mud behind Kelly, and all was fine until she balked at the hill. She knew she'd never make it to the top. He, of course, walked up it as if he was riding an escalator. Every time she'd attempt one step forward, the boots would slide down the narrow muddy track. She was covered in mud already and she hadn't got two hundred yards from the compound yet. It was no use calling out. There was too much noise about to hear a thing.

Kelly looked back from the top. She was halfway up. One more step, her feet slipped and she slid back down the incline on her belly. She lay at the bottom of the hill, her face in the mud. She tried to get up, took a few steps forward, slipped, landed on her butt then rolled back to where she began. He wanted to help her. No, more than that. He wanted to pack her bags and throw her on the next plane home to Australia. She didn't belong here. She shouldn't even be here. "Do we have a problem, Miller?"

"These fucking boots are like waterskis!"

He yelled at her. "Get up. Now!"

"I'm trying. I'm trying." She was too slow. In a split second, he was lunging. Two long strides and he was rolling her aside. Half a second later a dozen fully-armed, black uniformed men ran past. They would not have seen her until it was too late. They'd have avoided her, sure, but they were using live ammunition today and the last thing he needed now was an accident.

Kelly sat in the mud beside this woman, this disaster waiting to happen. "Didn't you hear them?"

"No." How could she? There was a chopper hovering a hundred and fifty feet away, and loud gunfire somewhere else. All her concentration had been engaged on keeping herself upright in the mud. Getting up that bloody hill. It was like Everest.

Kelly covered his face with his hands. I have to stop this, he thought.

And beside him, in the mud, she struggled to get up. She fished her cap out of a pool of muddy water and skidding a bit, he noticed, on flat ground, she regained traction and balance quickly. He took her hand and pulled her up the hill.

She slipped and fell four more times by the time they got to the shoot-house. She was exhausted before she even began.

"Watch," was all he said after he'd prodded her up a ladder. She looked down from the non-existent roof of a concrete structure that was supposedly a house. There were four straw dummies, two at a table, one in a corner and one in the center of the room. Four men, in blacks, kicked the door in. Gunfire. A heartbeat later three dummies were dispatched. One, in the center of the room, remained intact.

"Four seconds average," Kelly said. "Four seconds in which the outcome is either life or death. We train every day of our lives for those four seconds."

She said nothing.

"With me."

Don't make me do that, she prayed as she climbed down the ladder. Don't make me do that.

He led her away from the shoot house and into the firing range. She'd been here before but this time the place was empty. Kelly signed in, just as Mac had signed in and he helped himself to the same type of gun Mac had chosen. He had his own tucked in his belt.

Rebecca already knew the procedure but dared say nothing. She watched him load, unload. Safety. Grip. He set the paper man back fifty feet.

"You first," she said as she took the .45 from Kelly.

He set the target back a hundred and fifty feet and while it was still in motion, he'd drawn and fired five times. Rebecca had blinked twice in that time. Daylight shone through the target's head and chest as it came back to its original fifty foot distance.

She closed her eyes. I cannot do this.

"Yes, you can do this, Miller."

"Stop that."

"What?"

"You're reading my mind."

"No. I'm reading your body language. You will do this. We are not moving from here until you are able to hit that target. Four seconds, max. You shoot to kill, not to disarm, not to wound. You shoot to kill."

"But… but…"

The look on his face, that warrior look, halted any reservations. Rebecca unloaded the .45, loaded, released the safety, held the gun just as Mac had taught, aimed and fired. An ear. A shoulder. A thigh. Three complete misses. It took her one and a half minutes.

"Again," Kelly said.

And again. And again. And again. Into infinity.

And each time she squeezed the trigger, she begged silent forgiveness. Kelly could hear her heart crying in pain. But she did not give in. She kept trying. And he knew there was only one reason she was trying. She wanted him to be proud of her. But this was hurting him more than it would ever hurt her. There was only one thought in his mind: you shouldn't even be here, girl.

Chapter 11

Halfway through breakfast, Rebecca was paged to the CO's office. She looked over to Kelly at the same moment he turned to her. He was obviously waiting for his pager to go off but it did not. Rebecca, wondering what she'd done this time, took her toast and coffee mug and walked to Administration on her own, plodding her way through the corridors, up unending flights of stairs.

Dawn Lindsay was waiting in Pete's office. Rebecca saw the immediate question in Dawn's eyes the moment she saw the oversized uniform. They held hands at first, then hugging seemed the only way to greet each other. Pete watched the touching reunion without much expression. He'd never understand women, period.

"How are you?" Rebecca asked, thinking that she needed a hatchet to slice through the air. Her presence had interrupted an argument. Most of the hostility came from Pete.

"I'll go in for the procedure after the senator's been and gone."

"Good. And Rick?"

Dawn wriggled the fingers on her left hand. Rebecca saw the size of the engagement ring and smiled. Now Pete's expression was interested, until Rebecca caught the silent question and said, "Secret woman-business, Colonel."

Dawn helped herself to the coffee machine, and she didn't ask the CO if he wanted one. Rebecca sat in her greens, balancing her coffee mug on her knees. There was a blank space on the pocket where her name should be. Her 'real' uniform wasn't ready yet, but this one fitted a little better than the black. She'd hoped that when she wore it, she might at least feel like a soldier. She survived on hope.

"Two things and then I'm out of here," Dawn Lindsay said. "We want you at Pete's little get together tonight. I'm sure Commander Nolan will be more than happy to escort you. From what I've heard you two are getting along just dandy." Rebecca said nothing. We were getting along just dandy before he became my teacher. She sipped her coffee.

"Tomorrow at fourteen hundred, you're going out to Lakenheath."

"I know that."

Dawn sat and crossed her legs. She flicked her mane of thick, red-brown hair from her eyes. "Is there anything else you can tell us, Rebecca?"

"Not really."

"Not the answer I wanted."

"That's the answer you get."

Pete watched the two: an unending tennis volley as:

"Will Elizabeth be with him?"

"Yes."

"What's she wearing?"

Rebecca gazed off into the middle distance she saw as the future, capturing images in her mind and relaying them to the foreground of the present. "She's wearing a dark blue suit, with a diamond brooch. She wants to wear her grandmother's pearls but the catch breaks when she's putting them on. She's in the Learjet when the string of pearls breaks. The senator won't help her pick them up. Says he hasn't got his glasses. Says he'll buy her new pearls—they have an argument."

"And what's the senator wearing?"

"Brown suit, white shirt."

"The color of the aircraft?"

"White with pale blue striping. I think."

"How many people are greeting him?"

"Behind the cordons or on the red carpet?"

"Just tell us what you see."

Rebecca concentrated on the bronze eagle but her mind was elsewhere. First, she described the layout of USAF/RAF Lakenheath. She'd never been there before. "There's about thirty kids. Primary, sorry, grade school students. Some have flowers for the senator. There are two TV news crews. BBC. CNN, I think… Yes, the CNN van has a satellite dish on the roof. There are Nighthawks everywhere but the people in the crowd don't realize it. I recognize the faces near me: Mannett, Mitch Stafford. Mac…"

As soon as she said his name, Mac's image faded from the scene, as if his presence there was in some way doubtful.

Rebecca swept it aside and continued. "Some of the lads are in civilian clothing, some in blacks. The ones in black are not visible though. They're up high, looking down. Only a couple of them are in greens."

"And you?"

"I have no idea. I'm not looking at myself. What else is there… MPs. Fire trucks. There's a black limousine that has little Yankee flags on it. It feels as if the people waiting are all Americans. Mostly defense personnel, wives and family… Shouldn't Kelly be here for this, too?"

"Just get on with it," Pete said.

"I'd like Kelly to be here."

"Get on with it!"

Her heart told her no. A hundred times no. Dawn sat quietly fuming, wanting to gag the colonel. "Please, Rebecca."

"On the other side of the barrier, there's Pete. You're in a dress uniform. A blue one. Kelly's in white, beside you. His face is intense. It's that look he gets when he feels disaster's looming. There's a diplomat of some kind. There's also somebody from Lakenheath. He's in the same uniform as you, Pete. He's got gray hair and as many medals. I see three ladies. One's with the diplomat. One's with the other colonel. Your wife… Sheila? Is that her name? I don't think she wants to be there, but she knows she has to be. It's expected. She doesn't like John Glover. Something happened about ten, maybe twelve years ago, and it's as if she's never forgiven him for it. You said you were best man at his wedding, but I'm not so sure your friendship's as strong as it used to be."

Pete rose and walked to the coffee machine. Dawn said, "Why didn't you say something? I would have got you a coffee." But he didn't reply.

I should not have said that, Rebecca thought. That isn't a can of worms I just opened. Worms are harmless. This is a tank full of piranhas and I just let them loose. "I don't see you there, Dawn."

"That's because I won't be there. Go on."

How Rebecca wished Kelly was there. She was able to read his signals, yes, carry on, no, stop there… But he obviously wasn't required. No, he wasn't wanted. There was a difference.

"Please, Rebecca."

Rebecca took her mind into the future, back to Lakenheath. "People are getting nervous because the plane's late. Let me go up there… The senator's not flying it. He's not well. It's his head, I think. It feels like a hangover. He's trying to sleep and Elizabeth's nagging but he keeps waving her away and that makes her worse. She is so scared. Terrified… Something's wrong. Something's really wrong. They're coming in to land and told no. They have to circle and it's the sudden change of plan the senator doesn't like. He swears at the pilot. He's got a temper… There are two bodyguards with him. One's tall and he's got blond hair and the other's short and looks like Tom Cruise when he was young. The short one goes to the pilot. It's something about an emergency landing. Not their plane. Another plane. It looks like one of those jets you flew in Iraq, Pete. One of those. Something's wrong with it. It seems to be on fire. It gives the people on the ground a needed diversion, that's for sure."

It was as if they were sitting around a campfire, listening to a storyteller of old.

"There's a lot of smoke. It comes in and there's something wrong with the wheels. The front wheel—it's a belly landing. The fire trucks go out. The ambulances go out, too."

"Does the senator's plane touch down or not?"

"Yes, but… It's different now. It's changed. That emergency landing has changed everything. Why isn't the commander here? He should be here. I don't understand why he isn't."

"Just tell us what you fucking see and stop this can't do it without him bullshit right now!"

Rebecca looked at Pete, and then at Dawn. She hadn't liked the feel of the atmosphere the moment she walked into the office. She knew they'd been arguing but she didn't know what about. Perhaps it was because Pete didn't appreciate CIA involvement but he had no choice? No, it was more than that. It was Dawn's presence this time, and she was shaking his composure. Why? What the hell's going on here? she wanted to scream but Dawn obliged instead.

"Would you shut the fuck up and let me talk?"

Had Dawn's glance to Pete been armed, he'd be on a morgue slab. The atmospheric tension's frail elastic band was ready to snap, Rebecca knew that. But damned if she'd say another word unless Kelly was present. And she knew that wasn't about to happen. "If Kelly is the chief operations planner, why isn't he here?"

"This is simply an off the record chat."

Bullshit, she thought. "It keeps changing. There are too many variables to point towards one outcome. If I tell you something now, it will be right for now, but it may not be right for tomorrow. Do you understand what I'm saying?"

"I do, Rebecca. Of course I do." And Dawn did understand but Pete sat there, rubbing his forehead. He can't sleep, Rebecca thought. His worries are many. Many indeed. But she still couldn't understand why they wanted to know every last possible detail because Nighthawks did this kind of thing regularly. Nothing made sense.

"There's nothing more you can tell us?" Pete asked.

"No," Rebecca lied.

He believed her. "That will be all," Pete said.

Without another word, Rebecca fled.

Kelly did not ask what had happened, not at first. Perhaps he assumed she would tell him. She couldn't hit the target today. Her mind was definitely elsewhere. "I can't do this."

"Yes, you can. You will."

"Oh, don't you start."

"What's wrong?"

"It's twisting. It's all out of shape."

"What is?"

She unloaded the .45, put it down and stepped back. She walked away.

"You haven't been excused."

She kept walking.

"Get your ass back here, now!"

"Oh, sit on it and spin." She walked out into the cold, and made her way down the greasy tracks towards the asylum. She stopped and braced herself when a team ran by and skirted around her, and Kelly heard the calls: 'Hiya, Rebecca.'

"Hi guys."

"If you were taller we might see you better, soldier," one of them said. She knew not who it was. She hadn't the energy to find a witty comeback and by the time she'd thought of one, he'd be long gone anyway.

Kelly caught up with her. "What is the matter with you?"

"Leave me alone."

Another team was coming. A full pack run. Kelly pulled her to the side and they sat on a log in the middle of the woods. She stared into inner space. He rested elbows on knees and waited for the inevitable.

"Why can't you all just leave me alone?"

"What's wrong." It wasn't a question. "What happened in the CO's office?"

Eventually, Rebecca spoke. "What's between Dawn and Pete?"

"Sorry?"

"Dawn. Pete. What's their story? It's borderline hatred."

"Personality clash is my guess. That woman's got balls of titanium."

"Maybe she needs them. It's not good, Kelly. He is really resenting her presence. I thought we were all supposed to be on the same side here? It's sure going to be a fun night."

"What are you talking about?"

"You're supposed to be taking me to a dinner party at Pete's tonight. Some posh tiara and diamond thing."

"That's tonight?" He took his cap off and scratched his head.

"How long have you known Pete?"

"Sixteen years."

"Did you meet him on the Eisenhower?"

"No. I knew him before that."

"And the senator, too?"

"Why?"

"Has Pete ever said anything about John Glover and Sheila?"

"It's not something I can go into," Kelly said after a moment's hesitation.

"Was it some kind of sexual thing? An affair?"

"Why?"

"I need to know."

Kelly thought for awhile before he said, "This military life, it's almost family. For some, it is family. You're away for months at a time. In a combat situation, who knows how long you'll be away, or when you'll get to see your family again. You with me? You got buddies at home or going home, and they visit. They help out. They go in and fix the cupboard door you never had time to fix. Basically, you trust them with your life."

"And with your wife. I see now. Gene was a friend of yours, once, wasn't he. Before that thing in Iraq happened."

"Yes, he was a friend."

"You've been in a similar situation, haven't you. You've been the one away while a mate visits. Kelly, I need to know what's going on. I'm only trying to understand. I can't afford to guess or make assumptions. I've already been burned by assumptions, so please, talk to me. You once said there was more at stake here than one man's life or death."

"You tell me what you think the situation is here and I'll let you know if you're wrong."

He can't betray confidences, she thought. "Pete flew with John Glover in Iraq. They were good friends back then. Like you and Gene Samperi. A team."

And still, that silence. She wasn't wrong yet.

"Something happened during a mission. A school... There was a munitions factory under it. After the bombing raid, the senator didn't cope. He was grounded and sent home."

"I wish you couldn't do that."

"If I couldn't, Kelly, I wouldn't be here with you now, would I. So, John Glover goes home for psychiatric reasons. He can't cope with the guilt. He has nightmares about those children, even during the daytime. Elizabeth doesn't cope, either. He's not the man she married any more. So he turns to his best friend's wife because there is nowhere else he can go. You said it yourself. Family."

"Something like that."

"It only happened once. And it shouldn't have happened at all. Pete's wife, Sheila. She terminated the pregnancy because she had to, and the abortion should have been straight forward, but it there were complications and she nearly died. She thought Pete would never find out, but he did, because when he finally got home from the Middle East, Glover confessed the indiscretion. He should never have said a word. He knows that now. He has four children of his own, but Pete and Sheila had to adopt their little girl. This is the only thing in the senator's past that could destroy him, Kelly."

Kelly squeezed her hand.

"He's in England now, isn't he."

"Yep."

"He'll be at Pete's dinner party tonight."

"And he wants to meet you."

"There's only one thing I do know about this mess. It's not some faceless conspirator who wants him dead. It's not some unknown entity in the crowd. It's not even a racial issue because John Glover will probably be the one of the best Presidents your country's ever had. It's not a political assassination. It's personal. And it's not a bullet between the eyes. That's changed, too. He does make it down the stairs now. It's Pete, Kelly. Pete's going to kill John Glover."

"Pete? I don't think so."

"Think what you will but I wouldn't trust him as far as I could throw him and he knows that. He's scared of me, Kelly. I know he's your buddy. I know you're close. But don't trust him on this. You can't trust him."

"Convince me," Kelly said as he inspected his fingernails.

"I see the senator, he comes down the stairs. He's smiling at the kids but he's got this line of people to greet. He knows almost everybody there. John Glover shakes hands with acquaintances but if there is somebody he knows, he embraces them. Man or woman, it doesn't matter. He gives them a bear hug. He gets to Pete and they embrace and it's point blank. Nearly a full clip."

"He wouldn't do that. It'd be suicide."

"It's what I saw today in Pete's office. And I tell you what, I got out of there so fast. If I'd been sprinting in the Olympics I'd be wearing a gold medal right now."

"You're wrong, Rebecca."

"I don't think so."

"There'd be a dozen ways to make a hit on Glover at Lakenheath, girl. Quick, clean. One target, one shot, and you're outa there. Pete is not suicidal."

"He can get as close as he wants. He's got nothing to lose."

"Except his life."

"And that's why he didn't want you there today. He's been waiting for that moment when he realizes I do know what's going to happen. That means it'll change again."

"Rebecca, you're wrong about this."

"Please, God, let that be the truth. Let the OSIR's two percent inaccuracy be happening at this very moment."

"If Pete wanted John dead, why would he wait for Lakenheath when he has him in his own house for dinner tonight? Rebecca, what you saw, what you think you saw, is a game they used to play. Two kids wrestling on the floor, that kind of thing. With Pete and John, there's no handshake. They always embrace and shoot each other with imaginary guns. That's what you saw, girl. Two friends saying hello, nothing more and nothing less. But I'll tell Pete to offer his hand in case security gets nervous."

"The senator was on the ground and he was dead."

"Pete's too ambitious to throw it all away. It doesn't make sense."

There was quiet for a little while.

"I don't think I can do this tonight, Kelly. What if, when I meet the senator, he is going to die? What then?"

"You said it yourself, a couple of years ago. It's a warning. We take measures to avoid it."

"I don't know if can do this."

"Yes, you can. You will. And this conversation has never taken place. You've said nothing and I've heard nothing and that's the way it will be until that Learjet touches down at Lakenheath. Is this understood?" Kelly put his arm around her and she rested her head on his shoulder.

"I'm going to miss you," she said, hoping he might say the same, but he didn't. "I don't want to go home when this is over. Yes, I want this part of it to end, but every day I wake and I know I'm one day closer to... You'll be here and I'll be there and..."

Silence.

"I waited all my life for you and all I get is six weeks."

Say it. Please. Say it. Say it!

And he was going to say it, too. But he could not. He held her tighter instead. And then the moment was over. "We need to finish what we started. Back inside. Come on."

But she didn't move. She sat on that mossy, wet log, crying. "I can't do this—"

"What we do with what we've got is the most important thing whether it's a lifetime or six lousy weeks." She wouldn't look at him so he lifted her face. "Are you back with me yet?" She nodded. "Wipe your face and stop that damned sniffling. Rule One. Nighthawks do not cry. They do the job. Rule Two. When the job is done and they're alone, then they can cry."

"I'll never be a Nighthawk."

"You've got it down to eight seconds. I want you hitting that target in four."

"Four?" she whined.

"Four shots, two head, two chest, two seconds."

"Minimum?" she pleaded.

"Maximum."

"Kelly, I hug trees. I save moths from drowning in the bath tub, and..."

"Get off your fat ass, now!"

"I haven't got a fat arse!"

"I haven't got a fat ass, sir."

"Pig's bum! I will never call you sir."

That's more like it, Kelly thought, hiding his smile. "One more hour, then I take you to town."

"Sorry? Did you say you'll take me to town?"

"We've got a dinner party to go to. Tonight you're meeting the future President. New dress. My treat."

Rebecca sprang to her feet, ready for action.

Mac, on his way to report to the CO, watched the Commander and Rebecca drive off. He watched until the BMW disappeared down the tree-lined drive before tapping on the CO's door. "Enter."

The colonel was on the phone, conversation quickly aborted.

"Macpherson. Sit."

One and a half minutes later Mac emerged from the office.

Chapter 12

REBECCA CHECKED THE CORRIDOR AND closed the door after she let Steve into her room. "Thanks for coming up. I really need your help."

"Yes, you said that, but I don't see how…"

"I need a miracle. Fast. I've got this posh dinner party to go to tonight and all kinds of people are going to be there. I need your help. I want to wear this dress, mainly because it was the only one that looked all right and fitted me."

She took the dress from the closet. It was black jersey flecked with gold, and it was simple and elegant, with a low neckline and a lower back. It was one of those dresses that defied the use of underwear. "That should turn a couple of heads," Steve said. "What do you need me for?"

"You said you did special effects and make up as well as hair?"

"I used to."

"Can you camouflage this please? Somehow?" She unbuttoned her shirt. The scar from the bullet wound was circular, about an inch in diameter. "I've tried foundation and concealer, but it makes it more obvious. I'm not sure what to do."

Kelly was waiting in the foyer, and at twenty one hundred precisely he heard the sound of high heels on the stairs. And then she appeared. He swore, for a moment, just a moment, that he saw wings within her massive golden aura. And when she saw him, sparks of red ignited the gold.

"Holy shit," he whispered.

"Bloody Nora," Rebecca whispered.

And that's where they stayed for thirty seconds, both of them unable to move. Kelly, resplendent in dress whites, his hat tucked under his arm. Rebecca in black and gold. He was the most magnificent example of man she had ever seen and he thought the same of her as she floated down those stairs to meet him.

"Wow." She reached out and touched the court mounting on the left side of his pristine jacket. So many medals.

He took her hand and kissed her fingers, trying to swallow his heart back down, not able to say a word. There was some kind of transformation in progress here. Her eyes were huge. The cut on her forehead was concealed by hair. The rolls of soft billowing fabric that somehow, miraculously stayed on her shoulders almost concealed... An adhesive tattoo? A single red rose covered the bullet wound scar. He peeked behind. Her back was bare and smooth down to one, maybe two inches above her ass and on the exit wound, another tattoo of an upward spiraling dove.

"Don't you like it?" she asked. "Do you want me to wear something else?"

"No! Ah, no. No, it's... Jesus. You're stunning. Absolutely." His gaze was on her hair, her eyes, her body, even her golden-shod feet.

"So I scrub up okay then?"

"Sorry?"

"It's what Australians say to each other when they look good. You scrub up okay, luv."

"Oh. Right."

"Kelly?"

"Hey?"

"I'm starving to death. Can we go now?"

Kelly unlocked the BMW and opened the door for her. He was in no hurry tonight. There was something he had to ask but it wouldn't come. Not yet. "You look great."

"So do you," she said.

"The tattoo's not real?"

"No. Of course not. It was Steve's idea. How I look tonight is all Steve's work."

"Brannagh?"

"Yep. Top to toe. He's a makeover magician."

"That's what he was doing in your room?" he asked and hit the ignition.

"What did you think he was doing?"

Kelly remained silent.

"You can be such a big wally sometimes," Rebecca said and watched the passing countryside until the BMW came to a sudden stop very close to a hedgerow on the narrow country road. Kelly killed the engine, flicked on the interior light and turned to her. She waited, wondering what he was going to say. She didn't know if he was happy, disappointed, or simply apathetic. Not a lot flickered across his eyes but something was happening in that head. He almost spoke, but the attempt was a failure. Nothing ever came out, nothing that was important. Nothing that was personal, concerning their future. If, indeed, they had one.

There were another two false starts before:

"All the time I was in Ireland with Marianne, the only damned place that mattered was here because you were here. I stood on the Cliffs of Moher and I wanted you there with me, not her."

He was quiet for awhile.

"I never had any depth of feeling for her. I know that now. I never felt much for anybody until I met you. And I can't talk about it and I can't show it because I don't know how."

The Navy SEAL Commander, his chest so crammed with medals that he rattled when he walked, looked into her eyes, took something from his pocket and reached for her left hand.

Rebecca saw a rose-gold, emerald-encrusted claddagh and he slipped it on to her finger, then leaned across and kissed her. And there was a promise of more to come but there always was in his kisses. "Will you marry me, Rebecca Miller?"

Annie was right all along. You'll meet someone and never come home.

"I'll marry you, Kelly Nolan."

Mac sat in the darkness of his quarters, nauseated, indecisive. Barry Mannett, his room-mate, came in, turned on the light and before he could say a word: "Turn it off," Mac said. "Turn it off and get the fuck away from me!"

Barry retreated, quietly and quickly, and the light went out.

Mac sat in the dark again, thinking.

Kelly parked opposite Pete Hamill's manor house and killed the engine. He sighed.

"You don't like this kind of thing, do you."

"A war zone is often safer." He got out of the car, opened her door and helped her out. "You ready for this?"

"As I'll ever be."

He walked her across the street and knocked on the large blue door.

A middle-aged red head wrapped her arms around Kelly's neck immediately. Sheila, Rebecca thought and waited for the long-time-no-sees to end. Kelly introduced her to the colonel's wife, and when the woman looked at Rebecca she almost made the mistake of touching her hand. "Well, well. I've heard a lot about you." The voice was vaguely hostile and so was the all-encompassing glance that judged the newcomer from her short hair down to her gold-sandaled feet. Obviously, this woman had been friends with Marianne.

"Nice to meet you," Rebecca said, knowing that Pete had given his wife instructions not to touch the psychic under any circumstances. And God only knew what else he'd said. She felt the spears, the arrows, the darts, knives and whatever else lay in the woman's arsenal as Kelly put his arm around her waist and walked her inside.

"I can't do this, Kelly."

"Yes, you can. Just be yourself."

"That's what I'm scared of."

Pete saw them walk in. He saw his wife's hesitation and Kelly's affection for the girl on his arm. And she looked stunning. She'd gone to a lot of trouble for this. Pete poured himself a bourbon. He needed one. He downed it quickly, regrouped, and greeted the late arrivals as if they were both long lost friends. It was a quick, nervous glance at Rebecca as he offered her a drink.

"You can have anything you want, providing you keep your dancing on the table to a minimum."

"I'll keep that in mind."

Pete signaled for a waiter and as Rebecca took a champagne from a silver tray, Pete saw the claddagh on her left hand. His gut twisted so tightly it hurt.

"You have a lovely home, Colonel."

"Thank you."

"Where's your daughter?"

He pointed upstairs. "Trust me, it's the best place for her right now."

"I was hoping to meet her."

"Perhaps another time. If you'll excuse me?"

Rebecca watched him walk off, towards more important people. The house was indeed lovely. It could have featured in a television home decorating show: original paintings, antique furniture. The smell of fresh flowers pervaded the air, mingling with cigarette smoke and free-flowing alcohol. The carpet underfoot was thick and lush, and from somewhere in the house, music played. It was soft. Bluesy. And then a voice, above all others, boomed with laughter from another room.

"That'll be John," Kelly said. "Get it over with, huh?"

He took her hand and led her into the drawing room. There was a large circle of people surrounding one man in particular: John Glover, a tall African American with prematurely gray hair and sparkling eyes. His wife was not with him. The senator saw Kelly and looked twice. "Nolan? Kelly Nolan? Is that you hiding behind that uniform? Who's that with you? Who you got hiding there under your arm?"

The crowd that was gathered about this man who would be President parted as he stepped forward. He took Kelly in an embrace, pulled three quick punches and Rebecca's heart stood still because she'd seen that before. Then he turned to her.

John Glover already knew who she was and most of what she'd endured. He'd seen the photos and knew why she had that rose tattoo on her chest. But he never expected this. Lord, he thought. She's tiny. She's... The senator looked away momentarily and when he looked back again, it was still there. The tiny Aussie he could have stuffed in his pocket was surrounded by a gold fog that stretched right across the room and then some. For a moment, the world stood still.

The senator took her into a powerful embrace and when he pulled away, Rebecca's face was pale. "Are those lunatics from the 32nd looking after you? They treating you good? Turned you into a Nighthawk yet, honey?"

She glanced at Kelly but he offered no help. "Let's just say it's an ongoing challenge for us all."

"Are you as hungry as me? How about we scuttle up something to eat. Just you and me. I don't think I can wait another hour. I could eat the ass off a low-flyin' duck."

She looked back at Kelly as the senator waltzed her away from the drawing room. Two black suited men tried to follow.

"Leave us be for ten minutes. I need to talk to this young lady in private. Do you understand that word, boys? Private?"

"But she hasn't been—"

"Searched my ass. You leave her be." His secret service bodyguards backed off, quickly. One was blond, and the other looked like Tom Cruise when he was younger.

The senator steered Rebecca into a small room near the kitchen where a full complement of chefs and waiters were in full battle mode, and he closed the door, leaned against it and sighed, loudly.

Rebecca was imprisoned in a pantry with the future president of the USA. She'd never seen this coming.

"Don't be frightened of me. It's the only damned place I can be alone except in the john and even then they're waiting by the door. You right there, sir? Every five minutes… A man can't even enjoy a crap these days."

"I'm not frightened, Senator. Just overwhelmed."

"Don't be, hon. And for Christ's sakes, call me John. You talked to my wife in Sydney, right? I know you remember because these people won't let you forget. Now back in those days running for the presidency was just a thought in my mind. It came and went. I woke one morning and the thought stayed. A year passed by before Liz made me sit and listen to what you'd said that day in the hotel. I only agreed to pass it on to shut her up. To give me some peace. I never took it seriously. But a lot of other people did take it seriously. Honey, what I'm trying to say, I never wanted any of this happening to you. By the time I was informed what was happening it was already too late."

Rebecca said nothing.

"What amazes me right now is why."

She looked up into his eyes. "Why? You're going to make a difference."

He was amused by that. "Oh, honey, we'd all like to make a difference but what we can do, even in a position like mine, is severely limited."

"But you will. You will make a difference. You are going to make history all over again. But will you promise me one thing?"

"Shoot."

"Next Monday, will you please wear body armor?"

He smiled again, and then he laughed aloud. "Darlin', with a gaggle of buzzards out there in the next room claimin' to be your friends, what other choice does a sane man have? Let me tell you something. Liz, my wife, you met her, she's got these obsessions. Every day for thirty years she'd said to me, have you got a clean handkerchief? And she always has this thing about my underwear, too. I flew fighters for Christ's sakes. If they's gonna scrape me off some tarmac the last thing they'd be looking for is clean underpants. Now, what was I saying? These last two years, honey, every day, my wife says, you got your vest on John Glover? And it's no matter if I have or haven't, she always looks before she lets me walk out that door."

Rebecca's smile was contagious. Kelly was right. He was a regular kind of guy. He lacked pretense of any kind.

"Can I ask you something now?"

Here we go, she thought, bracing herself for the inevitable.

"You ever play pretend games when you were a little girl?"

The unexpected question took her off guard. "I still do."

"You close your eyes and you pretend you just found some old magic lamp on the beach. You got yourself three wishes. You tell me what they'd be."

Without any hesitation, she said, "I would wish to be normal. An ordinary person."

"Now why the hell would you want that? I'd sell my soul to have what you got."

"No, you wouldn't. Nobody who is half sane would. I'd wish to live each day of a boring, regular life without knowing things that most people should never know to begin with. I'd like the chance to have a conversation with one single human being without seeing a crowd of spirits with them, all screaming at me to be heard first. Knowing the future isn't always the kindest thing for some people, Senator. But there are two spare wishes, so perhaps you should have them. You're going to need them."

"I'm going to be President. You know that, don't you."

"Yes. It's almost a landslide."

"If there is anything I can ever do for you, you'll call me."

"I can't see how I could do that when you're in the White House."

"You call collect from wherever you are, give your name, and you'll get me. And if I'm not available, I'll get back to you, darlin', as fast as I can." And he meant it. "Now I want you to tell me the truth. Am I gonna die next Monday?"

Twenty carefully chosen human beings were seated at two long oak tables in the manor house's ballroom. Rebecca sat between John Glover and Pete Hamill and opposite, Kelly sat between Sheila and Dawn Lindsay.

Only two of the faces at her table Rebecca recognized: an English singer who was famous fifteen or so years ago, and a Shakespearean actor who kept looking at her and smiling.

Rebecca wished Sheila wouldn't stare. Her hostility was increasing, moment by moment. Perhaps it's because of what I'm wearing? Perhaps it's because I'm with Kelly and she and Marianne were friends?

She nibbled on a bread roll and tried to listen to the conversations happening around her but it was difficult because now and then the senator's leg touched hers and she wasn't sure who was trying to play footsie under the table. She suspected Kelly but nothing showed on his face. He was busy holding his own between Dawn and Sheila.

The first course was served.

Quail.

Rebecca looked down at it. She felt as if she was going to eat her budgie. I can't, she thought. The poor creature has died in vain.

The senator leaned close and whispered, "Try it. I know it looks like somethin' that once sat whistling in its cage, but trust me on this. When you're hungry you'll eat damn near anything."

As Rebecca started on the quail, John Glover took center stage.

"So, Rebecca, did you hear the one about the gunnery sergeant who hadn't had sex since nineteen fifty seven?"

Rebecca dared a glance at Kelly, who had obviously heard this one before.

"There's a hot young lady at this major event and she sees this marine, shiny medals comin' out the wazoo. Now we know that young ladies like uniforms, don't we, Commander, so she walks up and starts talking. Has he always been a marine, has he seen much action, what's the body count today, stuff like that. Then she asks, are you married, gunnery sergeant? No, ma'am, never married. Duty to my country always came first. That's how marines talk, but I guess you know that already. Anyway, this hot young lady feels kinda sorry for him, so in a roundabout way, she asks, when did you last make love to a woman, gunnery sergeant? Why, ma'am, I believe that'd be round about… nineteen fifty seven. 1957? Oh, my Lord! She grabs his hand and off they go. And yeah, well, the short version, the young lady, she's lying there, exhausted, staring at the ceiling and she manages to say, gunnery sergeant, that was amazing, specially for somebody who hasn't had sex since 1957. Why, thank you, ma'am, he says and looks at the time. Best be on my way now. It's almost twenty one forty five."

Laughter split the room.

Rebecca was the only person who didn't get the joke and that, to Kelly, was funnier than the damned joke itself.

The second course seemed more inviting, but still Sheila's gaze was icy and directed at one person only.

"Rebecca, how old were you when you first started seeing the future?" Sheila asked, a little too loud. Sheila, who was afraid to touch her or get too close. Perhaps she thought the distance across the table was safe?

Curtain up. The show really begins. Rebecca put her fork down. "I was about five years old. I knew my grandfather was going to die."

"And how did you know that? Did some kind of angel tell you?"

Angel. Pete's told her everything.

"Yes. That's exactly what happened."

"How did your parents react?"

"With fear. They always reacted with fear."

"So you're saying they either knew you were different, or they thought you were weird?"

Sheila appreciated a challenge and Rebecca knew it. Pete attempted to silence his wife with a glare, but she ignored it.

"My parents were agnostic school teachers who could only believe what they could see and what they could not see frightened them, and that, I'm afraid, is what is wrong with humanity. We believe only what our physical senses can perceive."

"You know how and when people are going to die, don't you," she said and looked directly at John Glover.

Rebecca nodded and picked up her fork but had to put it down again when she heard:

"And all these miracles?"

Rebecca tried to ignore that one. "I don't know what you mean."

"Of course you do. She came back from the dead, folks. She touches people, she heals them. Who do you think you are? Jesus Christ come again?"

Beside her, Pete was dying, slowly. His edges were fraying. He was barefoot and naked in a minefield, and he needed some reassurance, but Rebecca knew if she touched him now, he'd probably hit the chandelier.

"No, I don't think I'm Jesus Christ. Why would I think that?" Rebecca said calmly. "The Christ Spirit is an ideal, and acquiring it is the ultimate goal of human endeavor. His only purpose in coming back was to heal humanity's alienation from God. Any person in this room will ultimately be capable of attaining the Christ Spirit and doing what He was able to do, if they believe it is possible. That was His message. He lived by example. We can all be that, if we believe we can."

"Next you'll say you've met God."

Will this woman ever stop? Why didn't she take her Prozac? "How can you meet what you've always known?"

And then a voice she recognized cut through Sheila Hamill's hatred. "Give it a rest Sheila."

All eyes turned to Dawn Lindsay.

"My life changed the day I met Rebecca. So let me tell you about that day. She sat blindfolded, facing a corner, and she couldn't have known I was even in the room, but she told me things that nobody and I mean nobody could have known. You want the truth? She scared the hell of out me until I asked myself where did this come from? It's got to come from somewhere."

No more, Dawn. Please, no more, Rebecca begged silently.

"What the hell would you people do if Jesus Christ himself walked through the door now? How would you know who He was? How would you recognize Him? What would He have to do to get your attention?"

"Dawn, please."

"Shush, girlfriend. You had your chance. I tell you what He'd have to do. Something extraordinary. Something no one else could do. Turn some water into wine maybe? Raise someone up from the dead? Put His hand on somebody and heal them? Speak a truth or two that you thought you'd forgotten until you heard it again? You'd believe it then, sure, but you can't believe it now. Why? Because a woman sits here? That's all she is. Look at her. She's one of us except maybe she can do a few things we don't think we can. I am not going to sit here and listen to you throw crap at somebody you're frightened of, Sheila. You're scared because you don't understand and you don't understand because you don't want to understand. What are you scared of? She might know something about you? Who here doesn't have some deep, dark secret? I know I did. But I tell you now, this woman saved my life and she hadn't a clue who I was. If that isn't Love in action—saving a complete stranger's life—then I don't know what you're supposed to call it. Do you agree with me on this, Senator?"

"Oh yes," was all John Glover said.

A deafening silence split the air but it lasted a little while only.

"So Rebecca, have you heard the one about the fighter pilot and the UFO?"

"Got a surprise for you," Kelly said. "Close your eyes."

Rebecca wasn't sure she could handle any more surprises in one day. All she really wanted was to get back to the base and sleep. Impossible.

Kelly guided her from the car, up the path. Eyes closed, she heard a key in a door. "You can look now. Second thoughts, don't. Jesus."

Rebecca opened her eyes.

Kelly's place. The cottage.

Marianne had moved out and not a lot was left except a really dreadful smell that wasn't coming from the litter spread all over the carpet.

Rebecca, hand over face to stifle the stink, followed as Kelly kicked a pathway through to the kitchen. He opened the fridge. The power was off and it was empty except for one large dogfish decomposing on the middle shelf. Kelly closed the fridge door quickly. He opened the pantry. Empty. There was nothing in the kitchen cupboards. On the breakfast bar, jammed into a Nighthawks coffee mug was a packet of rat poison, open, a teaspoon protruding. The mug sat in the middle of a solitary plate, one knife and one fork on either side.

Some messages could not be misconstrued.

"Could you live here?" he asked, eventually. "Once it's cleaned up? Refurnished?"

She touched the shiny buttons on his jacket.

"Home is wherever you are," was all she said.

Chapter 13

THE SHOOT HOUSE'S CONCRETE WALLS were pitted and scarred, as were the assortment of targets and bullet scarred mannequins in different types of dress and pose. Rebecca had sneakers on, no boots today, and for some reason, the black uniform was making her itch like crazy.

It was distracting, but worse was Kelly's mood. Last night he'd been fine, but today... He'd barely spoken. After breakfast he barked the order, with me, now.

His preoccupation had been daunting but this. This was *eerie*. He kept circling.

Stalking.

"What are you up to? Would you stop that?"

Kelly put his arm around her as if to hug, and in one quick movement, the gun was out of her belt and under her left armpit.

"You're dead. Why didn't you try to avoid that?"

"I thought you loved me."

Kelly closed his eyes, let go, handed the gun back and stood directly in front of her with his hands on his head.

"I want you to shoot me."

"Sorry?"

He tapped his chest. "Kevlar. Blanks. Shoot me."

"No way."

"Forget karma, thought, word and deed and anything else you believe in. Shoot me. Draw and fire at will."

"Will's not here. Will has left the building. Will went home. Lucky

Will."

"It's not gonna hurt me. Like I said, Kevlar. Blanks."

He patted his chest again and put his hands back on top of his head.

"No. I can't. Blanks or live ammo, it's the same thing. I can't pretend any more. This is killing my soul."

"I need to know if you can shoot at a living target."

"This is your world, it's not mine. I've had enough. I quit. It's not worth fifty bucks." Rebecca unloaded the handgun, put it on the ground, and walked away.

"What do you mean, fifty bucks?"

"Mac won the bet. He said I couldn't. He was right."

"Get back here, now!"

Rebecca turned and gave Kelly the finger.

Mac folded a letter, sealed it in an envelope and addressed it to ANGEL. He slipped his dog tags from his neck and placed them on the envelope. Without any hesitation he took a 9mm from a box in his otherwise empty closet, checked it was loaded, and tucked it into his jeans. He looked back at the door, at all of his possessions packed neatly into four labeled boxes on his bed.

He walked, neither fast nor slow, down to the main car park where his Mazda waited. Mac unlocked the car, took the 9mm from his jeans, and sank down into his pride and joy.

He put his head back against the headrest, took one deep breath, put the 9mm under his chin and pulled the trigger.

Rebecca was in the mess, helping herself to the coffee machine, when she heard, "I'm going away."

Mac?

She turned.

"Goodbye, Angel."

"Mac?" She sensed something amiss, especially when he reached out and touched her hair, her face. But she didn't physically feel the touch.

"I'm sorry," he said.

Then she heard the commotion in the corridor. "It's Macpherson!" someone yelled. "Main car park, now!" She turned back but Mac wasn't there.

Rebecca's heart froze. No. Oh dear God, no. Not Mac. Not Mac…

The following minutes passed by in a blur of disbelief. She followed a succession of uniformed men down to the car park where she pushed her way through another mass of soldiers until somebody gripped her arm, tight, and would not let her any closer. "No, Rebecca. You don't want to see this."

But she fought free and breached the crowd. "Mac! No!"

"Get her out of here!"

Hands gripped her shoulders and spun her about but she struggled to see. Mac was being pulled from his car — a bloody great hole where the top of his head used to be.

"No. No. No!" She started screaming then, and kept screaming until her voice failed and she vomited, and the world was lost in a wavy, shimmering fog.

When she woke, a hand was on the back of her head, her face pushed between her knees. Her mouth was sour. Acid. Her memory returned and she slapped the hand away.

"Mac?"

"He's dead."

She looked into Mitch Stafford's face. Tears welled and fell but she didn't make a sound.

The library was empty, except for Rebecca, who sat curled up on a sofa by the window. She had an envelope in her hand, ANGEL written on the front of it. But for a long time she couldn't open it. Holding it was enough. She thought she knew already what lay on the paper inside until courage rose and she tore the envelope open. The first thing she saw was a fifty pound note.

Angel,

I want you to know that you changed my life. For a few weeks you made living worthwhile. I wanted to tell you how I felt every damned time I saw you, but the words wouldn't come.

I'd have given anything for a chance to make love to you and have you love me, and I mean anything, but the Commander got there first, and I knew by the way you looked at him I had no chance. I figured being your friend was the most I could hope for. Lovers come and go but a good friend is forever. We were that, weren't we.

I hear you're a Nighthawk now so you keep on fighting for the light, soldier. The world needs more people like you in it. You won the bet.

Yesterday I got orders I can't carry out. Don't think you could have stopped me. There's no way out for me now. There's no exit. I'm not scared of dying so no tears for me, Angel.

I love you.
Mac.

Rebecca folded the letter, put it back in the envelope and wiped her eyes with her hand. She gazed from the window, down to the car park. Military police were there with Kelly and Mike, a tow truck nearby. Pete was nowhere to be seen.

"You ok?" came a voice from the door.

Rebecca turned. Mitch again. She shrugged, reached for a tissue and blew her nose. Mitch sat down beside her and studied his fingernails for a little while. Rebecca hoped he wasn't going to offer some kind of meaningless consolation: 'It'll be all right' when it would never be all right.

"I need to thank you."

She looked up, quickly. "What'd I do?"

"You helped me see the light, excuse the pun. Six more weeks and I'm out of here. I'm going back to Perth. Been accepted into med school. It's just that... if you hadn't... if... ah Christ, I don't know what to say."

"You'll be a great doctor. Might even have your own Emergency Department one day."

Mitch stretched out and cracked his knuckles then relaxed with a big sigh. "Listen, about Mac. He'd been on the edge for a while now. Sure, he was a nice, quiet guy, and I know you and Mac were pretty tight, but we all knew it was just a matter of time."

"I don't understand it, Mitch. Life's a gift, an opportunity. He threw it away."

"Maybe it's a gift for some people, Rebecca. Everyone I know is fighting some kind of battle. Dry those tears, soldier."

"Nighthawks never cry?"

Mitch patted her leg and got to his feet.

"What do you mean she's not coming?"

"She's under light sedation."

"Took it bad, I guess?"

The question did not warrant a response from Kelly.

"Can she defend herself yet?" Pete asked.

"Yes."

"To what degree?"

"She's quick enough, she's accurate enough."

"Thank you."

"But…"

"No buts. You've either done your job or you have not."

"Done."

"Good. Did Macpherson leave a note?"

There was something in Pete's eyes Kelly couldn't read. Could it be that Rebecca was right? Don't trust him? "As far as I'm aware there was no suicide note," Kelly lied. He'd yet to see Rebecca let alone read the letter if he was able.

"I'll see you downstairs in, say, thirty minutes. If Miller's unable to attend today, we'll fly blind on Monday. We've never needed her anyway. I'll be on leave from tomorrow but I will be back for Lakenheath." Pete leaned towards the intercom. "Barrett. Get me Macpherson's father on line 6."

"His father's dead," Kelly said.

"Oh? When did that happen?"

"IRA car bomb when Mac was seven years old."

"Barrett? Make that the mother."

When Pete looked up again, Kelly was no longer in the room.

Kelly, in blacks, knocked on Rebecca's door. He heard the soft footfalls and the door opened. Her eyes were red, swollen. Her face was pale except for dark circles under her eyes, and she was running on empty. "I couldn't get here any sooner."

She didn't respond. She stared, zombie like, through him.

"I've got to fly out to Lakenheath in fifteen minutes. You are not coming."

"Can I go home now? Please?"

"Rebecca…"

Tears welled in her eyes and again they escaped but she didn't make a sound.

Kelly ached to hold her. "Mac's letter?"

Robot-like, Rebecca took Mac's letter from where she had it folded and stored, in her bra, near her heart. She gave it to Kelly and turned away. She lay on her bed and rolled to her side. After a little while, when he'd finished reading, she said quietly, "One of three people gave the order. It wasn't Mike. It was either you and if it was, Gene was right about you, or it was Pete, and if it was Pete, then I was right. So do you believe me about your bosom buddy now, Commander Nolan?"

Chapter 14

"It's open."

Rebecca came in. She still looked pale. Today she was wearing a dress. Kelly never wanted to see her in another uniform as long as he lived. "You'd better sit down before you fall."

"I feel ok."

"You don't look it."

She sat anyway. "It's all wrong now. All of it. It's all wrong. I can't see any more. I can't see anything." A silent tear escaped her eye and rolled down her face. If she'd had the uniform on, she'd have wiped her face on her sleeve, but she wasn't in uniform so she didn't act the part. "I don't know what I'm going to do now. It's all gone. What I could do before, it's gone, Kelly. There's nothing there now."

Kelly looked beyond her head, refocusing. Her aura was still gold but it wasn't as bright, as sheer, as pure. The fog reached twenty feet instead of the usual eighty. There were shafts of yellow, orange and blue there now as well as an awful mustard color he'd seen around people who were so deeply mourning they couldn't find a way out.

"Kelly?"

"Hey."

"My wish has come true."

He came around to sit on the edge of his desk, in the same place where, she noted, his wife had posed herself. When was that? Forever ago.

"You were born with it. You can't will it away that easy. Trust me, I've tried a thousand times."

"No. It's gone and there's this emptiness inside, it's like some massive black hole where my heart used to be."

"You're grieving."

Just a couple of words, but he always used two for every fifty of hers. She hadn't thought of the pain as grief until this moment. "Is that what it is?"

"Absolutely." You're grieving for Macpherson, for the life you once had. Your beliefs. Who you thought you were. Nothing will ever be the same for you now. "You've lost nothing."

"How can you tell?"

He shrugged. How to say that the shimmering ball of gold light energy she called Emmanuel still circled her head faithfully?

"It's all been a waste of time, hasn't it."

"Absolutely not."

Another tear. And another. "Kelly, I've tried to see but everything's black."

"Good," he said.

"But I'm supposed to help you and…"

"We don't need your help. We've never needed it. You go on back to your room now."

"I want to be at the airbase. I need to be."

He shook his head.

"But that's the reason I'm here."

"No," he said.

"Please let me go? Let me come?"

Again he shook his head. "Go now. I've got a lot of work to do. I'll be along later when I finish up here." Kelly leaned across his desk, hit the intercom and told Sam to escort Rebecca back to her quarters.

Sam appeared within sixty seconds. He led Rebecca away and Kelly went back to work. The contents of the in tray were breeding by the hour, but they were mostly leave applications awaiting signature.

He caught movement on peripheral. The gold light was back. Beware the one bearing flowers came directly into his mind.

Emmanuel?

Who I am is not important.

What do you want?

She is to be there. She must be there.

But not in uniform.

That is not my concern. Beware the one bearing flowers.

Why?

And Kelly was given the future. A glimpse of it was loaned to him. He was not in dress whites but in assault blacks, perched on a roof at Lakenheath with a sniper rifle. It was a cold day and raining. The waiting crowd was impatient and most faces were obscured by umbrellas. That didn't help. Kids with flowers for the senator, the presidential candidate, fought and played in pools of water while their mothers talked.

Rebecca was in the crowd, wearing exactly what he had expected to see her wearing from the beginning: black velvet and rose quartz beads. She was unarmed.

She raised her head seconds before the alert split the air.

A crippled F15 Eagle came in, one engine on fire.

And then there was nothing. The gold light disappeared.

Four days to go.

She wasn't in the mess at dinner so he presumed she'd eaten at first sitting. She wasn't in the bar, either, but she hadn't ventured into the bar for almost a week now. Kelly went up to her quarters and knocked.

"Hey, sailor."

"I had a visit from a friend of yours today."

"Who?"

"Emmanuel. You will be at Lakenheath. But you won't be in uniform and you won't be armed. We'll have a body mike on you which means we'll hear you but you won't hear us. You'll wear body armor and I don't care if you look like the Michelin Man. I'm not taking any chances. And come Friday next you and I are out of here. I've got four weeks of leave well overdue. What do you say? Scotland? Ireland? Spain? Italy? Wherever you want to go, you got it, including home."

She finally smiled.

Chapter 15

ONE DAY LEFT.

Since Mac's death, Rebecca had to spend her time in the infirmary with Mike, Mitch and Jamie. At night she shared Kelly's room whether she wanted to or not. He was acting CO now. She never saw him. She was asleep when he came 'home', and he was gone well before she woke. Last night she'd wanted to wake him—too much on her mind, too many unanswered questions, but each time she attempted to, something stopped her. He was exhausted and it showed. But Rebecca could not wait any longer. It was now or never.

Kelly didn't look up when she walked in. "Can you get me a coffee?" he asked. It begins already, she thought. Get me this. Get me that. No please, no thank you. Just do it. "Please?" he added.

Rebecca poured him a coffee, sweetened it and put it on his desk. "Thanks." For the first time since she walked in, Kelly noticed the expression on her face. This was a female preparing for battle. Oh shit, he thought.

"Is it true that you're independently wealthy? That you own half a casino in Las Vegas?"

Kelly sat back, studied her face, then picked up his coffee. "Why?" he asked, watching closely.

"I want to know."

"Now's not the time."

"There will never be a time. Is it true?"

"Rebecca, what's wrong…" It wasn't even a question. It was a half-bored acknowledgement.

"Just fucking tell me!"

"It's none of your fucking business." His eyes were cold. She'd seen that ice before but she wasn't about to back down. People always backed down when he heralded that look. It wasn't going to work with her and he knew it.

"You asked me to marry you but it's none of my business? Who is your business partner?"

"No."

"Try again. I don't like that answer. Who is your partner."

"Out." He nodded towards the door.

No, that won't work, either. "There are a hundred people here you can boss around at will, but I am not one of them." She folded her arms defiantly. "What exactly are you going to do, Commander, while you're lying up on some roof hiding behind your uniform? What are you going to do in the confusion after John Glover's finally dead? What are you going to do?"

"You get your ass out of here, now, go take a pill and come back when you're human. I'll pretend I never heard what you just said."

"You've got four seconds." She was twisting the claddagh off. She meant it. "Who's your partner."

"My partner has nothing to do with this."

"Who is he!"

He couldn't read her. He had no idea what was happening in her brain so he took a guess. "It's not my father in law if that's what you're thinking. My partner is my sister."

"Whose side are you on?"

"Whose side am I on? Nobody's. I do the job…" He watched her face, closely. He thought he knew what was happening in her head now. She'd been with Samperi for six hours and slow cooking for three weeks. "What did Gene say to you?"

How could he do that? His question disarmed her, totally. "He said… he said things that made sense."

"That'd be a first."

"He said, how your father in law was also running for office so who's side are you really on? Who was waiting for you, here, Kelly when we got back from London? You never told me you were going away with your wife."

Her logic, if she used any, made no sense to him. "Until she called, I'd forgotten."

"Loss of memory? You? What did I do the very first time you spoke to me?"

"You turned around to see if I was speaking to somebody else. What is this?"

"You've got a photographic memory so don't you dare bullshit me about forgetting a tenth anniversary present from your wife. How did Gene know about us?"

"He was a trained interrogator, Rebecca. He read you like a book."

"Rubbish. He asked how long it took you to get me into bed. And that didn't take long, did it. He said how you needed my trust, my loyalty. Just because you fucked me didn't mean you wouldn't kill me. That's what he said. So if it's true that you've got more than one agenda here then maybe what Gene said is correct. Maybe he was right all along. And you know what? Right now, I don't know whether to believe it or not because you won't fucking talk to me!"

Kelly looked away briefly. She waited for an explanation. She waited for something, anything would do.

"Talk? What for? You don't listen to a word I say. Is there something wrong with your short-term memory? Who believed you about Leon Carter and who took you to London? Who put a tracker in your tags so that we'd find you if we had to? Who tried to tell you what assholes like Samperi might do? Who's been trying to protect you from getting a bullet in the head? Macpherson was under orders to kill you. He couldn't do it and that is why he topped himself. It's called death before dishonor. You heard of it? Yes, he loved you. He loved you so much he killed himself instead. He disobeyed a direct order and that is what no exit meant. And don't you fucking cry!"

Rebecca wiped her face quickly.

"Why have you been in the infirmary adhered to Captain McLaren? Why have you been living in my quarters? I'll tell you something right now. There are two people I can trust here, girl, McLaren and myself because to be honest, I don't know if anybody else has been given the order or not. Every moment of the day when you're not in my sight I'm wondering what the fuck might be going down."

"I'm sorry," she said softly, hoping he was finished.

"And furthermore, if I'd simply fucked you, Rebecca, you'd know about it. What we've got, no, what we had, is, sorry, was a lot more than that. Don't look away from me!"

"I said I was sorry!"

"And you should be because if I wanted you dead you would not be standing here right now. Do you understand me?"

Rebecca couldn't say another word. Her mind was adhered to his words, what we had. What we had. He was talking in past tense.

"Are you listening to me? If somebody's home in there I'd appreciate some kind of acknowledgment. Even a flicker of recognition would suffice."

She looked up and transfixed him with her huge blue eyes. "I'd rather you hit me than yell at me. It wouldn't hurt as much."

He looked away. He had to. "You will not be in uniform tomorrow, because if you wear the uniform in a situation like tomorrow's, it's assumed you are armed. We've both been fucked, here, girl. I was teaching you crap that you never wanted to know and you should never have known to begin with, for one purpose only. It'd be easier to eliminate you when the time is right. I saw it, too. Your Jesus lookalike buddy showed me. So the scene will be changed to suit a new set of circumstances. All right?"

She nodded.

"Rebecca, I know who's going to do Glover and I also know how it will happen. All along you have been correct, until a few minutes ago when you waltzed in here and started throwing accusations at me. But I'm glad you did because at least I know where I truly stand. Right now it feels like quicksand. So you tell me, right now. What do you want?"

There was only silence. Silence, riddled with a lifetime's worth of guilt because she hadn't trusted him and she should have. She was fighting tears. "You," she said softly. "I want you in any way I can get you. I only want you."

"Good. How about we start over." He picked up his coffee mug as if nothing at all had happened. But yes, it was true that she knew nothing about him. "You want to know about me? Fine. Joanna, my half sister, is ten years older than me. We grew up in North Carolina, a place called Snowbird. I was fifteen when I enlisted in the Navy and fought my way up. What I'm trying to say here is that Joanna's father was Cherokee. She's not a half breed like me. I don't know who my father was, but our maternal grandfather was…" He sighed. This was as enjoyable as having teeth drilled. "He was an actor. He made a hell of a lot of money from B grade westerns—Gene Autry and Will Rogers, that kind of stuff. He never came back to North Carolina, and he died long before I was born, but he left my mother all he'd acquired over his years in Hollywood. The casino is only part of it. There's also a cable movie production company in LA, and a few other things, too. My mother died a few years ago… There's not much else to say. Look, I've already talked to Joanna about you and she wants to meet you. I was going to tell you when the time was right."

"I feel so stupid now."

"Good. I'm happy."

"It's just that Gene…"

"I warned you about that."

"Only because you knew it was coming." She was quiet for a little while. "Tell me about the remote viewing."

"I can't talk about that, Rebecca. I wish I could."

"Are you going to tell me what you see happening tomorrow?"

"No, I am not."

"I need to know."

"No. You do not need to know. You'll be there because your presence is expected and for some reason unknown to me, required. So all you will do is observe and let us know anything that you feel may be relevant."

It was a long, loud silence.

"We just had a fight."

"Nah, that wasn't a fight. A fight's when you're coming at me with a busted whisky bottle. Not all my scars are work-related."

"It doesn't matter to me if you're stinking rich."

"Yes, it does. It matters."

"It's bloody hard to lie to you, Kelly."

"You're not the first to tell me that."

She picked up a pen and played with it.

"Feeling better now?" he asked because her colors were pure again, bright.

"Yes, I am. Thanks. You're a good therapist."

"You can go now."

But she put her arms around him and slipped cold fingers into his green shirt. His skin was warm, unbelievably soft.

And she saw the air base at Lakenheath. The limo with the American flags on it was waiting and it was raining, and…

"I know what you're doing."

She kissed his cheek, hugged him again and walked from his office.

Chapter 16

SHE WALKED INTO THE MESS at zero six fifteen hours and there was hardly a soul about except for Frank and Nick Mancuso who was reading the paper. Nick was in blacks. He looked up. "Aren't you supposed to be in uniform today?"

"Aren't you supposed to be with everybody else?" she replied.

Nick went back to his newspaper. "You wearing body armor?"

"You wearing clean undies?"

He finished his coffee, tucked his paper under his arm, shot her a death glare and walked out.

"What a charmer."

"Only you could get away with saying that to Mancuso," Frank said.

"Thanks." She knew she had to eat something but nothing took her fancy—far too nervous to have an appetite. She chose an apple, got a coffee and sat by the window, on her own, looking out at the woods, thinking of how she was going to miss this place. She felt almost like a hostage, her loyalties twisted beyond recognition. This, to her, was normality now. Surrounded by commandos, listening to their conversations, occasionally being drawn into their lives.

Frank, who was rarely seen out of his kitchen, sat down opposite and shattered her reverie. Winter was coming, fast, but he had another tiny red rose. It was perfect. It had no scent, but its form was beautiful. "It's been good having you here. I'm going to miss you. It's like the sun shines again whenever you're around."

"You're sweet, Frank. You really are."

"Word is you're going to marry the commander."

"How'd you know that?"

"No secrets around here."

"I'm going to miss you too, ration-assassin." She leant over and kissed his cheek. It was the first time she had ever seen him smile.

Rebecca waited by the closed gym doors for the briefing to end. She was now where she was told to be and at the right time, too. Sixteen men came out of the gym and almost each one greeted her and she them, by name. She thought, I know their names now without having to look at their pockets.

Mitch was the sixteenth to appear and the eighth in civilian clothing. "Gidday," he said.

"Hey, stranger."

"You're with me today so don't lose me or I'll kick your arse."

"You couldn't run fast enough to catch me. Got your brolly, sailor?"

"It's not going to rain and if you call me sailor I'll do some nasty things with the biggest hypodermic I can find."

"Is that a promise?"

"You stick close to me."

"Super glue, Mitch. I'll be super glue."

Mitch rarely smiled but he did that morning. "See you in the huey."

Rebecca wondered what a huey was as Mitch walked away. Since his wife had moved on, there'd been a dramatic change in him. Oh, he was still gruff and grumpy, and he still kept the pretense of apathy alive, but the negativity, the hatred, was gone. Her time here hadn't been wasted. At least she'd helped one man across the abyss of grief, guilt and misery that had plagued him far too long. And he was leaving too. Going back to school. Going *home*.

It must be what freedom felt like.

Rebecca wondered if she would ever experience that.

Kelly, the seventeenth man, appeared in his blacks, and as usual, the moment their gazes met her heart flipped and an electric buzz hit the backs of her knees. Will I still feel like this in five years when he walks in the door, takes a beer from the fridge and adheres himself to the football on TV? "Walk with me," he said and they made their way to communications. "Are you wearing Kevlar?"

"No, this is velvet."

"Are you wearing body armor?"

"You're like Elizabeth Glover. She's obsessed by body armor, too. Body armor and clean underwear."

"John told you that?"

"He certainly did."

"Are-you-wearing-a-vest?" Kelly asked, slowly, emphasizing each word for greater comprehension.

"Yes, Commander. I am. Can't you tell?" She wanted to take Kelly's hand but he wouldn't voluntarily do such a thing. He wasn't much of a hand-holder. There'd be no romantic walks in the park with this man.

And to prove her wrong, Kelly reached for her hand and he didn't let go, not even when a soldier passed carrying a rather large weapon. All Rebecca could see beneath the balaclava was a pair of gray eyes. "What was that nasty looking thing?" she asked.

"Nick Mancuso," Kelly said.

"I know it was Nick. I meant the weapon."

"Sniper rifle. You're with Stafford today."

"Yes, he told me."

"You do exactly as he says, when he says."

"Aye aye captain."

Kelly opened a door and she walked in under his arm. Joel was on duty, stuck between a computer and a telephone system, and surrounded by close circuit TV screens. Joel with the pale eyes, the one who always told her the time. He had a lot of clocks here to choose from. Every time zone in the world was on display. "Body mike, sir?"

Kelly nodded and to Rebecca, said, "I want you at the helipad in forty minutes."

"Aye aye captain."

Kelly made his way across to the armory to collect a Super Magnum for his own use.

"Are you nervous?" Joel asked as he stuck an earpiece into his ear.

Rebecca raised her hand. It was shaking.

"You'll be fine. We do this kind of work a lot. This way." She followed him into another, smaller room where he taped a tiny microphone to her shoulder.

"I don't know if this is going to work, Joel. I do terrible things to gadgets. I was politely asked to leave my one and only job because I kept blowing up the electronics."

"It works."

"How do you know?"

"The commander wants to know what the job was."

"K Mart checkout."

Joel listened again and smiled. "The commander says you'd have been a knockout checkout-chick."

"I knocked out the electronics, that's for sure."

Kelly had said they would be able to hear her but she wouldn't be able to hear them. All kinds of possibilities opened wide. She could sing and drive them all crazy; she could declare undying devotion to their commander and he'd never have another moment's peace. Anything would do. Anything to take her mind away from what this day might bring.

Forty minutes later, she walked from communications to the helipad. The first chopper was lifting off, another was on the ground, blades engaged. She choked back some of her fear.

This is it, she thought. I've got to get into that chopper now.

Kelly was giving her hand signals to hurry up. She swallowed down rising fear again and stepped closer. A hand extended. Steve Brannagh, the hairdresser, helped her into the chopper. There were nine people in it, including herself and only she and Mitch Stafford were in civilian clothing. Two seats were spare, away from the open door. Heavy helmet on her head and buckled in, the chopper lifted, banked. Rebecca clung tight, knuckles white and eyes closed, not daring to look down.

After a minute or two, Rebecca, face pale and nausea rising moment by long moment, felt a hand clamp on her ankle. Her squeal of fright was over-ridden by the hellish noise inside the chopper. She looked down. Kelly was pointing.

Stonehenge from the air.

Two hundred feet down, the circle of ancient stones stared up at her. She could see the wide pathway around the perimeter, and tourists were like ants down there. Harlem, the Negro chopper pilot, hovered for awhile and then the chopper banked again for the north east.

Beware the one bearing flowers.

Is that all you're going to tell me?

Trust. Faith. Patience.

Trust, she thought. Yes, I have that now. Faith? Always. Patience? That was a tall order because she wanted, desperately, for this to be over with. She did not want to endure the next few hours which would be nothing but a tortuous hell. She wanted the clock to jump ahead. She wanted to see John Glover and his wild-haired wife get into that limousine and ride away, and she wanted to turn the television on one night in the future, and there on the news he would be: John Glover, President of the United States.

You call me. You give your name and you'll get me.

Why did I go to Sydney anyway? If I'd not gone to Sydney, none of this would be happening. I'd be working from home right now, helping people deal with their messy lives whilst overlooking the fact that there was never anybody there to help me deal with mine. If I hadn't gone to Sydney, Elizabeth Glover would never have found me.

And the man who would be President would not be alive to do what he was born into this life to do.

She looked at Kelly, sitting there on the side of the chopper as if he'd been born in one. I love him so much, she thought. This wasn't just about the senator, not really. It was about Kelly, too. He turned to her then as if he'd caught her thoughts mid-air. He was good at that. He said it was a case of reading body language. Rubbish. He's more psychic than me, she thought.

He winked at her and took something from his pocket. A cell phone. He played a game: one way to clear the brain, or aid focus, or obliterate boredom.

Rebecca looked at the faces surrounding her—each man was off in his own little world. If they were nervous about the immediate future, nothing showed. It was another day at the office for them.

It was just a job.

But…

She looked again, heart in mouth for a moment. Yes, she hadn't been seeing things. Mac was sitting by the door. She glanced at Kelly. If he'd seen Mac, nothing showed on his face.

Mac? What are you doing here?

My job.

Then Rebecca realized that the chopper held only five living people. The others, along for the ride, were spirit. Only Mac knew he was dead. But she'd spoken to four of these guys, on and off over the past six weeks.

Was that the reason most of the Nighthawks thought she was crazy? She talked to people no one else could see?

The chopper set down hard due to a strong crosswind from the building storm, and the teams dispersed to take up their pre-arranged positions.

Rebecca was so nervous, all she wanted to do was pee. When she made it to the nearest toilet, she fell to her knees and vomited instead.

An hour to go. Kelly had to take position soon. People were arriving, women, school children with flowers, airbase MPs searching everybody. "Stay with Mitch at all times."

"Aye aye captain."

There was a look in his eyes that was unmistakable. He couldn't say what was on his mind because they were both wired and sixteen other people would be listening.

"See you later," she said.

"Remember, we can hear you."

After a look she hoped was not a final one, Kelly was gone, towards his position on a nearby rooftop.

There was a deafening roar from a distant runway as four F15s took off. "One of those planes is going to come back in with one engine on fire the same time the senator's plane has clearance to land."

Sixteen heads turned to the F15s. Kelly didn't bother. He'd seen it himself, already. Mancuso, on the roof opposite Kelly's, a position with a direct view of the crowd, said, "How does she do that, Commander?"

"NFI," was all Kelly said in reply. He looked up. The wind straight from the North Sea was picking up and the air was chilling, quickly. The senator's aircraft was going to be delayed. He knew it. He felt it.

"Bloody Nora, it's cold," Rebecca said, jumping from one foot to the other. Had a North Sea oil rig worker strolled by she'd have mugged him for his jacket.

"This isn't cold," Mitch said.

"My nose is numb. It's going to rain ice." Rebecca opened her bag and took out an umbrella. "What time is it?"

"Five minutes after the last time you asked what time it was."

She popped the umbrella thirty seconds before the heavens opened. Kids squealed, mothers called them to cover. Most of them preferred to run riot in the icy rain. It was too much for some. The waiting crowd dwindled.

TV news crews were setting up. Military police were more numerous now. Rebecca recognized a few faces in the crowd around her and Mitch's constant presence was easing her agitation. Then she saw the RAF car pull up, followed closely by the limousine with the American flags flapping in the near cyclonic wind.

Pete and Sheila, and the airbase commanding officer and his wife emerged from the car. Sheila was having trouble with her skirt. Pete searched the waiting, sheltering crowd but he did not see Rebecca. He was looking for a woman wearing his unit's uniform and not one wearing black velvet.

The diplomat stayed in the car and offered the women some respite from the rain. Pete and the other colonel sheltered under umbrellas each fought to control.

And it was all so very different to what Rebecca had previously seen. "He's coming in," Rebecca said. "But so is the F15."

Elizabeth Glover only flew when she had to. In her mind, there was something wrong with people who liked being in the air. John was catching some shut-eye and she hoped he was suffering. She'd told him to take it easy the night before, but would he listen? No. He never listened.

She clung to her seat and wished the plane wouldn't toss about so much. God, she prayed. Just get us down in one piece. On the carpet at her feet were strewn her grandmother's pearls. The flight was too rough to unbuckle her seat belt and pick them up.

"It's all right, baby. We're not going down. If we were going down you'd know about it."

How could he sit there, sprawled out like that? He was enjoying this. "You wearing your vest, John Glover?"

He unbuttoned his shirt like he did every day of his life when they were together, and he buttoned it again.

"Jesus, Mary, Joseph and every saint I can think of, this is killing me."

"Calm down and shut up, baby, you're scaring the kids."

Glover's two Secret Service bodyguards, Baker and Williams, looked at each other.

The aircraft suddenly gained altitude and banked hard, right. Elizabeth screamed and the senator cursed. "The hell's going on up there?"

Baker scrambled his way to the cockpit and came back, relaying the message that there was an emergency landing—an F15 coming in on one engine. It was also having trouble with its landing gear. "Sorry, sir, but we have to use another runway." John Glover looked from the window at the storm, sat up straight, and tightened his seat belt.

"Fire trucks will go out in a moment and then an ambulance. The senator's jet is going to use another runway."

Two fire trucks departed the station, sirens screaming. Ten seconds behind, an ambulance joined the cacophony.

In the pouring rain and high crosswind, the Lear touched down, hard, on a runway it was not destined to use and its engines screamed.

"Mrs. Glover is having a nervous breakdown because the senator wants to check on the pilot. They're fighting. She says he can't. He says he'll do what he damn well wants. Okay, the blond bodyguard will open the door. He'll use a red umbrella."

She was telling the Nighthawks what was happening at least one minute before it occurred but that was good because they were used to four seconds of opportunity, or no opportunity at all.

The Lear taxied to a stop at the VIP park.

"The blond bodyguard will appear first, then the senator, Mrs. Glover and the other bodyguard."

The hatch opened, the stairs cascaded. The blond bodyguard adjusted his suit as he looked down at the people waiting in the rain, and he reached for a red umbrella. He folded it out, and there was no room on the stairs for both the bodyguard and the senator.

"Put that damned thing away, son. These people been waiting in the rain to see me and they'll damn well see me. So you give me some space. Can't even take a piss alone these days."

A minute later, the security detail did not have to lip read to know what was being said.

The umbrella quickly closed. John Glover stood on the second stair of the Lear jet and he lifted his hand to wave at the people, milling below. He stood there for fifteen seconds longer than he should have, and fuelled by relief that he'd made it thus far, his greetings to the crowd seemed more relaxed. Happier. It was as if he knew he would live after all.

Via the scope, Kelly followed Glover down the stairs and onto the tarmac. He tracked as the VIP shook hands with the American ambassador and the ambassador's wife. He embraced Carl Lindberg, Lakenheath's Wing Commander, but he touched Carl's wife's hand politely and moved on. He embraced Pete Hamill and Kelly was ready, but Rebecca's vision of a point blank shooting did not occur. Glover ignored Sheila. Kelly kept her in sights, waiting. But again, nothing happened. Glover then fulfilled his role as a security nightmare.

He kept walking. Where the hell is he going? Kelly looked away from the scope. The senator was making his way to the approaching ambulance, flagging it down. And from his earpiece, Kelly heard Rebecca's voice: He's only doing this because his wife said he shouldn't. He's going to ask the pilot how many hours he's flown. He's deliberately prolonging this. He's testing everybody. He's taking no prisoners. He's thinking that if he's going to die, he wants to go out with the whole world watching. He wants to show the world that if he can care about the welfare of one pilot, he can care about millions of them. If people get wet waiting to see him, then he'll get wet saying hello to them. He's saying, if the boy's under five-fifty hours, someone's ass is in a sling. Whatever that means. What's that mean?

The ambulance stopped and the man who would be President climbed into the back, accompanied by Carl Lindberg. The TV is loving this. It shows heart. It shows compassion. But the cameras aren't allowed into the ambulance.

"How old are you, son?"

The young pilot looked no older than the kid who delivered the senator's newspapers on his bicycle.

"Twenty-three, sir."

"Think you're some kind of top gun, do you?"

"Sir?"

"Drive a car like you fly a plane, son?"

"Sir?"

"How many hours you got?"

"Seven hundred and sixty one, sir. Almost."

John Glover turned to Carl Lindberg and said, "Sleeps up there, too, does he?"

"Senator, your car's waiting."

"Good. It can wait a few minutes more."

The ambulance drove away and the senator had a train of humanity following him now. At least the rain had stopped. People shook water from umbrellas and hoped he'd come closer to say a few words to them, touch a few hands, take the flowers.

"He's going to walk into the crowd," Rebecca said. "And I have no idea what is going to happen."

But neither did anybody else, except, perhaps, Kelly.

He tracked Glover. He could not see Sheila Hamill. Doubts rose. Who is it? Who is it? Come on, make a move. It's the last chance you got before the election, you got him if you want him, so show me your face... Beware the one bearing flowers, came Emmanuel's voice into his head.

Opposite, Nick Mancuso, with a perfect view of the crowd, had specific orders of his own.

The senator pushed the barricade aside and children swarmed. He was searching the crowd and Rebecca knew who he was looking for.

He was taking bouquets from the children and handing them in turn to his two bodyguards, who handed them down the line. The line ended with Pete. Beware the one bearing flowers. Roses. Carnations. Lilies. The kind of lilies that were present at funerals.

"It's Pete," Rebecca said. "It's your CO."

And at that moment, Pete saw Rebecca. She was not in uniform. Stafford was very close, as were four others. He looked up and about. Two. Three, he could see. What the hell was Nolan doing? This wasn't in the plan.

A few of the men in the crowd he recognized, but he couldn't see Kelly. Sheila had also disappeared. He looked back at the RAF vehicle and sighed with relief. She'd been ignored by John, so she'd gone back to the car. Elizabeth was standing by the limo, waiting and nervous, Carl's wife beside her.

It started to rain again as Glover was making his way towards the Australian. The TV cameras were closing in.

"Hi, darlin'. Good to see you again."

"Senator."

He took her in a warm embrace and Kelly heard the call: She's got a gun!

Flowers, umbrellas flying through the air. People were panicking. Stampeding.

Four seconds lasted an eternity.

John saw the .45, saw whose hand it was in and who it was aimed for. He tucked the girl behind him.

And then someone appeared beside Rebecca. Macpherson. With a strength she didn't know she possessed, she pushed hard against the senator's back. Her feet slipped on the wet tarmac—or was she pushed? Mitch Stafford dived, tackling the senator to the ground.

There were three shots for three targets.

Kelly fired the moment he saw Pete draw. The bullet hit Pete between the eyes.

Mancuso couldn't get what he wanted. She'd slipped. Both targets had dropped the instant he took the shots. The blond bodyguard caught the bullets instead.

Chaos.

Sheila was out of the car, running towards Pete and screaming obscenities as the remaining bodyguard dragged the senator away. Wearing her husband's blood like a shroud, Sheila picked up Pete's .45. She was on her feet, screaming, aiming at the senator. Kelly took the first shot, the remaining bodyguard an unnecessary second.

Glover was yelling something incomprehensible, trying to go back and he wasn't able. Elizabeth gave the final push to get him into the limo, and it sped away.

The threat was now over.

Kelly retreated.

Mancuso did not.

Rebecca sat on the wet tarmac, shaking, but not from the cold. By her feet, carnations. The smell of cloves was strong. Someone jumped over her, she didn't know who, she didn't care. There were people everywhere. A TV camera, a microphone in her face. Someone asked her name. How did she know the senator? Did she know him well? What did they talk about? There were also voices she knew, male voices. She was surrounded by Nighthawks.

And still, Mancuso could not get a shot. She wore armor, he needed a head shot.

A trail of crushed carnations and roses led to the blond bodyguard who lay dying. There wasn't anything Mitch could do except apply pressure and wait for the ambulance. While it screamed its way to the tarmac, the bodyguard died and Rebecca watched his spirit rise away. It hovered for a moment, and then it was gone.

Between the stampeding feet she could see Pete. His eyes were still open. Sheila's skirt was still billowing. She'd lost a shoe.

Then there was a hand she knew. She recognized the touch. She looked up. Kelly. He had that sniper rifle in one hand and he pulled her to her feet with the other. His hand was on the back of her head. She felt the uniform against her face. "It's over. It's over."

No. It's not over. Mac was pointing towards Nick Mancuso's roof.

Kelly pushed Rebecca away so hard that she skidded across the wet asphalt and rolled, twice. Two more shots. More screaming. She looked back. A black uniformed soldier was falling from a roof, and Kelly was on the ground.

"No!"

She crawled to where he lay sprawled on his back. He was making noises and his mouth was full of blood. There was a big hole in his uniform, right where her head had been a second ago. She didn't know what to do.

"Kelly, don't die. You can't die. You can't."

He opened one eye and tried to talk.

Hands on her. Pulling her away. Medics were there now but they were strangers, they didn't know her. Didn't know what she could do. "Please, let me touch him!"

Her pleas were ignored.

She clawed to get back to Kelly, but whoever was holding her wouldn't let her go, until a voice boomed from the chaos:

"Release that civilian immediately!"

In a heartbeat she was on the ground beside Kelly, ready to touch, to heal, but he seized her hand before she touched. Despite the searing pain from a fractured sternum, he managed, "No, girl. I need to feel this. My karma, remember?"

And then they took him away.

"He's not gonna die. He's one tough son of a bitch."

Rebecca looked up.

John Glover.

Why had he come back?

He offered his hand and heaved her to her feet, then he took her in his arms and held her tight, and over the top of her head, he surveyed the carnage. He didn't care that TV cameras were still rolling. No one could get close enough to them anyway: the psychic and the senator were surrounded by a wall of Nighthawks.

Chapter 17

SHE HAD A CHOICE. SHE could stay in England a month longer than anticipated, and live in the cottage until the new CO and 2IC were appointed, or she could go home.

Home was with Kelly so she waited until he had recovered, physically, before making any decision; not that the decision, in the end, was hers to make.

He was offered a training position in Pensacola, Florida.

But he kept his promise. She was going to be a tourist.

Rebecca was seasick on the ferry to Ireland and spent three and a half hours stretched across a seat with her head adhered to Kelly's lap. He related stories of the sea to her, and exaggerated most of them: especially the one where he was in a leaking dinghy with a guy who'd had his knee shot off, shark infested waters, fifteen foot waves, waiting for a submarine pick up. "Yeah, a likely story," she'd mumbled. He'd laughed at her for being seasick and it wasn't even a rough crossing, so she'd pinched his inner thigh. He should never have shown her those six hundred places on the human body. For some things, she had a photographic memory and would file information away for future reference—usually when he wasn't expecting it.

Rebecca froze on the Cliffs of Moher while he sat there, sketching, and they both posed with Charlie Chaplin at Waterville.

Long days and longer nights were spent in London. Museums, parks, galleries. Shows. She complained about the rubbish on the streets until Kelly told her why there were few garbage cans and described in graphic detail, as only he could, some of the horrendous injuries he'd seen from suicide bombers.

On the way to Australia, they spent three days in Singapore. Of course, he'd been there before. There was hardly a dot on a map of the world he hadn't already been. Champagne on the flights. Seats you could sleep in. Constant attendance and pampering. It was part of the lifestyle he was accustomed to, but it hadn't always been that way. He'd said he remembered having nothing except his heritage and a strong sense of self. And Rebecca knew it was because of that sense of self that Kelly could find a niche anywhere at any time.

He finally appeared from the non-Australian queue at passport control in Brisbane International Airport, looked at her and smiled. Rebecca's heart skipped all over again. Once, she'd wondered if the magic would end but she knew now it would not. It was in his smile, in the way he looked at her. In the way he never had to speak.

After they collected their luggage and passed through customs, she told him to brace himself. Yes, he could handle any situation and perhaps it was true that nothing could surprise or shock him, and yes, he may have been a Navy SEAL who could leap tall buildings with a single bound of his own ego, but, "You haven't met Annie yet," was all she said.

"That's okay," he said. "My sister's waiting for us in Vegas. She likes taking the odd pale-face's scalp."

Rebecca hadn't told Annie she wasn't traveling alone. She wanted Kelly to be a surprise. How could she have explained him anyway? She'd had weeks to think of a way, but nothing had come.

As they walked out into the spacious, airy arrivals hall, Kelly saw a child dart from the crowd and wrap his arms around Rebecca's legs.

Michael, he thought. And there was her friend, the one who could talk under wet cement. Annie had orange spiky hair. Her eyebrows, nose, and bottom lip were pierced. She had a weight problem. She was addicted to chocolate because it substituted for the sex she never got. She wore an orange top that had stains on it and was about three sizes too small because it barely accommodated her massive breasts; denim shorts, and pink flowered sandals that defied description on her otherwise bare feet. She's looking for love in the wrong places, Kelly thought as he lingered in the background, patiently.

"Who's the tall, dark and handsome?" Annie asked.

"Annie, meet Kelly. I found myself a live one."

"You're not wrong. Gidday, Kelly." Annie extended her hand and Kelly took it. It was sticky.

"Annie," Kelly said. "Nice to meet you."

"Sorry about the residue. It's not toxic. At least I don't think it is. Michael tipped his bottle of OJ all over me. I'm trying to wean the little shit. It's impossible. He's such a bloody male. Are you American?"

"North Carolina."

"Have you got some Indian in you?"

"Cherokee, yes."

"Wow," she said. "You ever been to a full moon tee-pee pow-pow thing?"

Kelly fought back amusement. "Maybe one or two."

"F… far out. Man! Beck, where'd you find this guy?"

"He found me and that's all I can say about it."

"You look different, and it's not just the hair thing," Annie noticed as she fished her car keys from her bag and then yelled at her son who had adhered himself to Rebecca's leg and was being dragged along the floor as she walked. The child took no notice of his mother, so Kelly picked him up, held him mid air, looked into his eyes for ten seconds, and set him down again. The boy behaved immediately. "How'd you do that?" Annie asked.

"We have an understanding, hey, buddy."

The child stared.

"Can I rent him, Beck? Can I? Huh? Can I?"

Rebecca didn't get a chance to say much on the drive from the airport—she'd been away for twelve weeks and was forced to listen to Annie's day-by-day recounting of virtually everything that had taken place in her absence.

Kelly didn't listen. He looked from the window instead. The toddler from hell was very quiet as he sat in his car seat with the Navy SEAL beside him, but occasionally he'd reach out to touch. Kelly would look at him and receive an evil smile. He knew this terrorist was planning some kind of offensive maneuver.

"Is Michael all right back there? He's too quiet." Annie met Kelly's gaze in the rear vision mirror. "He's never this quiet. What'd you do to him?"

"Like I said, we have an understanding."

"Car," the toddler said and pointed. "Fer-wow-az. Howse. Dog. Fuck!" he yelled, pointing to the oncoming traffic. A truck sped by and the kid was still pointing, this time out the back window.

"Oops," Annie said. "Sorry about that, he means truck. He has trouble with Rs and Ls too. It's an experience taking him anywhere. Little old ladies drop like flies, mate. Went up to Caloundra once in a bus and there was an army convoy coming the other way. I thought we'd be arrested. How long you staying in Oz, Kelly?"

"Two weeks," he said.

"So what is it? A holiday?"

"Annie, can we talk about this later?" Rebecca asked.

"What's going on, Rebecca? Something's going on here. I can feel the vibes. Out with it."

"I'm going to live in the States. Kelly and I are getting married at a place called Snowbird, in a traditional ceremony next month, and I've got two weeks to finalize my life here."

Annie said nothing else, not even a murmur, until she finally parked in the underground car park of the apartment block where Rebecca lived.

"Beck, you've got four hundred and thirty one missed calls. There are people here who need you. I've booked you from next week right up until August. You can't just up and leave."

"I can, Annie, and I will. I have to."

"But this is your life, here. With us."

"I'll be living in Pensacola, Florida."

"Where the fuck is that?" Annie almost screamed. "Sorry about this Kelly, I don't want to offend you, but Jesus Christ, Rebecca, how long have you known this guy? You know anything about him?"

"Stop this right now. Stop it!"

There was an everlasting moment in which Annie couldn't even think properly. "Why didn't you tell me? You were away for too long when it should have been three weeks. I didn't know if you were dead or alive or what was going on. I get two phone calls and you come home with some stray American you found, God only knows where, and you hit me with this, I'm going to live in fucking Florida, and you expect me to be happy about it? How'd you meet him?"

"I can't tell you. I wish I could but I can't. Oh, Annie. Don't. Don't."

Annie got out of the car. She was upset and slammed the door so hard the car shook. Kelly sighed, got out of the car, too, walked to Annie and raised his hand. Annie stopped what she was doing: heaving suitcases from the back of her old station wagon.

"Kelly Nolan, Commander, US Navy SEAL, and formerly second in command of Nighthawks, 32nd Special Operations Unit based in Wiltshire, England. Now, I'm not supposed to say this and you've heard nothing, is this understood?"

Annie's mouth dropped.

"An assassination attempt on a United States presidential candidate was averted at RAF Lakenheath in England recently. Did you see it on the news?"

Annie was struck dumb for a moment but at least her mouth was closed now.

"I asked, did you see it on the news?"

"No. I don't watch the news. It's too depressing." Annie paused for thought. "It wasn't that senator guy whose wife came to see Rebecca in Sydney, was it?"

"It seems we have an understanding."

"Fuck me," Annie said. "Really? What Beck said on the phone that day. It was true?"

"So how about we take the bags up, we have a coffee and nobody asks any more questions that can't be answered. How's that sound to you, Ann Maree?"

"Fine," she squeaked. "Sounds fine." How'd he know my second name, she wondered. Even Rebecca didn't know her second name.

Kelly had somehow intimidated Annie into a quiet submission of the like Rebecca had never experienced before. "What did you say to her?" she asked.

"Nothing much," he said, noting this time that the terrorist had regrouped and was clinging to his leg instead of Rebecca's.

She's never going to leave, Kelly thought. He sat on the apartment balcony, drinking a cold beer and looking at the Brisbane skyline, at the reflection of city lights in the river, the constant traffic on the bridges. She had a nice place here. Small, but it was nice. The girls were talking business in there. What they'd do. He looked back in. The boy was asleep in Rebecca's arms.

"I suppose I'd better go. Leave you guys alone and get horror-head here home to bed."

Rebecca had always replied, No. Don't go yet. Tonight, she looked at Annie and nodded. "I'm so sorry, Annie."

"Ah, it's all right," Annie said quietly. "You're in love, and I'm just being selfish. If it was me, I'd do the same. I'd grab him and run, too. If you want me to help you pack, just give me a call." Annie glanced at Kelly, out there on the balcony, listening to every word. She knew that Rebecca would never call again. That's life, she thought. "I'm happy for you. I'm not really crying. Not really."

With tears in eyes, Annie gathered up her sleeping son and walked to where Kelly sat. Gazes met. "I don't care who you are or what you do but I swear to God if you hurt Rebecca, I'll find you and what I'll do to you won't be pretty."

Kelly said nothing.

"Apart from that, it's been nice meeting you. Weird but nice. I'm glad she's happy. I'm jealous as hell, but I'm also glad." Annie tried to smile as she looked at both Kelly and Rebecca, and she knew she wasn't needed any more.

When the door closed, Kelly moved. He sat beside Rebecca on a huge white sofa and put his arm around her. Her head came against his chest, then she decided to stretch out, her head on his lap, looking up at him.

"Are you sure about this?" he asked.

"Yes. Nothing's the same. This place doesn't even feel like home any more. I don't have to pretend Annie's family is also mine. Michael's a monster. I didn't realize how awful he was until now. How could he have changed so much in three months?"

"Maybe he didn't. Maybe you did. You see things clearer from a distance sometimes." Kelly reached for the remote to kill the TV but the late news came on. John Glover had declared victory.

"Do you think he'll survive his first year?"

"I don't know. Will we?" Kelly turned the TV off. He didn't want to hear his old friend up there, telling lies to the world. Kelly had better things to do.

www.ingramcontent.com/pod-product-compliance
Lightning Source LLC
Chambersburg PA
CBHW052037240626

47153CB00006B/2119